**Also available from Kathleen Donnelly
and Carina Press**

National Forest K-9 Series

Chasing Justice
Hunting the Truth

T0014943

KILLER
SECRETS

——

KATHLEEN DONNELLY

carina
press

carina
press®

Recycling programs
for this product may
not exist in your area.

ISBN-13: 978-1-335-54792-3

Killer Secrets

Copyright © 2024 by Kathleen Donnelly

For questions and comments about the quality of this book,
please contact us at CustomerService@Harlequin.com.

® is a trademark of Harlequin Enterprises ULC.

Carina Press
22 Adelaide St. West, 41st Floor
Toronto, Ontario M5H 4E3, Canada
www.CarinaPress.com

Printed in U.S.A.

For Jeff, love you always

And for all the K-9s and their handlers
who work hard to keep us safe.

Chapter One

Trey Hansley stared down the slope and its perfect powder. He loved snowboarding in the backcountry mountains. He'd just discovered this awesome area in the Pino Grande National Forest and couldn't wait to test it out.

His brother, Chase, stood next to him. Trey put a hand on his shoulder. "This is going to be mind-blowing."

"Are you sure it's safe?" Chase asked.

"Seriously? You're still worrying about that, little bro? Look where we are. We're in the mountains with no other boarders. We have this slope to ourselves. It's rad. The sun is out and we have clear blue skies. It doesn't get any better than this."

Chase shrugged in acknowledgment, but Trey could tell he was still nervous. Chase loved shredding slopes and had spent time at ski resorts doing just that. But Trey had convinced him that there were even better places to go where you didn't have to purchase a lift ticket and you had peace and serenity. Just you and the mountain. But his younger brother wasn't fully convinced.

"You've got your gear, right?" Trey asked.

"I do."

"Then let's test your beacon and make sure everything is set. Just in case. That's why we have all that stuff. That way we can get out here, have fun and not worry about avalanches and shit like that."

"Yeah, okay," Chase said.

Trey went through a full equipment check and made sure their beacons were on. They also each had shovels, probes and an Avalung. The Avalung supplied oxygen if you were caught in an avalanche. People often died in avalanches because while they were buried, they re-breathed their own carbon dioxide. The Avalung helped that problem by allowing them to breathe through a tube, taking the carbon dioxide away from their faces. With that equipment, Trey had full confidence that even if something did happen, they would be fine.

"You go first," Trey said.

"Really? Don't you want to go?"

"This is your first time in the backcountry. I want you to enjoy it. I'll go first the next time we do this."

"All right," Chase said, a smile spreading across his face.

"It'll be a freakin' blast. I promise. Have fun shredding some pow and I'll see you down at the bottom."

Chase pulled his goggles down and turned his board, starting down the hill. Trey watched his brother as powder billowed around him. It was a great run and Trey was itching to get going himself, but he waited until he thought Chase was far enough down the slope. Often it was a skiing or boarding partner that kicked off an avalanche. Trey shoved those thoughts aside and started down on his board, feeling the rush as he picked up speed.

A few feet down, he could already tell something wasn't quite right. It was like the snow was disappearing underneath him. Then the slab let loose. More snow released and started sucking and pulling Trey with it.

Panic welled up inside him, but he fought against it. His brother. He couldn't help Chase if the avalanche buried him.

Adrenaline mixed with fear fueled him. Trey battled to stay on top of the snow, but the mountain became a monster and felt like it was eating him alive. His whole body trembled in terror.

He used his legs to try to turn his board. Trey's thighs burned from trying to get his board out of the snow that seemed to come alive and suck him in like quicksand. He saw a tree coming and flung himself toward the branches, grasping and clinging for his life, praying that the bough wouldn't break. He managed to hang on and the limb held. Other trees and boulders were caught in the large slide and being toppled and sucked under as if the mountain were alive.

Someone was screaming.

Was the screaming Chase?

Trey realized that the sound he heard was himself. He was yelling his brother's name at the top of his lungs as he saw the snow slide catch Chase and then suck him under. The noise of trees snapping filled the air, the snow creating a sound like a spring thunderstorm.

Then it stopped.

Silence.

Chase. Where the hell was Chase? Trey cautiously let go of the tree branch and tested the snow around him. It seemed to hold. He started down the slope, being careful to dodge debris and hoping another round of snow wouldn't release. Maybe after this one, the mountain would be a little more stable. He knew he was only trying to convince himself as he headed to the base of the slope.

After activating the beacon signal, he found the area with Chase's signal. Hopefully he wasn't too late. He would never forgive himself if something happened to his brother. Shoving his feelings aside for the moment, Trey pulled his probe out of his pack and started sticking it into the snow.

Desperation set in as the end of the probe sank into the powder without hitting anything solid. What if Chase was buried so deep that the probe couldn't help Trey find him? Why had he insisted that they come to this area today? Yes, it was the best slope, but he'd known with the recent storms and high winds that the snow was unstable. Not to mention that, while this area at the base of the mountain was not a major hike from the road, they were far enough away that getting help would take too long.

Most avalanche victims had about fifteen minutes before they died, unless Chase was using the Avalung. Avalanches could also crush their victims and sometimes people died from those injuries too. Trey pushed that thought away as he kept stabbing, double-checking the beacon. Chase had to be somewhere in this area.

"Chase!" Trey yelled out.

No answer.

He kept searching and just when he thought he would have to give up and try to find more help, his probe struck something other than soft snow. Leaving the probe, Trey pulled the shovel out of his pack and started digging. Even though it was cold, he had sweat pouring down his face and body. He stopped for a split second to take his jacket off and then kept digging.

"Chase!" Trey yelled over and over.

After what felt like an eternity, Trey spotted a sliver of blue. Chase's jacket.

"Please be alive. Please be alive," Trey chanted. Not only would he never forgive himself, but his parents would never forgive him either. He dug carefully so that he didn't hit Chase, but also quickly, until he managed to uncover Chase's torso and his face.

"Chase? Chase," Trey said.

His brother's eyes fluttered and then opened. He had managed to get the Avalung to his mouth and was using it to breathe.

"Holy shit, you're alive," Trey said, as he started sobbing.

Chase reached up and grabbed Trey's arm. "I think I broke my legs. I'm in pain and can't move."

"Okay, I'll get you out of here. I'll get you help, but the big thing is that you're okay. I'm so sorry, little bro."

Trey continued to dig, thinking through if it was better to try to move Chase or get him stabilized, make sure he was warm enough and go get help. As he debated both options, Trey's shovel suddenly hit something hard. But not hard like a rock or a tree. Whatever it was, it was draped over Chase's legs, making it hard to dig any farther.

"There's something blocking me from completely digging you out," Trey said.

Chase gave a thumbs-up but didn't answer. Trey kept working the shovel around, trying to dislodge whatever it was that had his brother pinned. As he dug closer to the object, a strange odor wafted out.

"What's that smell?" Chase asked. "It's disgusting."

"I don't know," Trey said, now carefully scooping more snow away.

Then he saw it. He screamed and flew back, landing on his butt and scrambling away from what he'd found. What the hell? That couldn't be…? Was it? No freakin' way.

"What?" Chase said. "What's wrong?"

Trey braved getting back up and going back over to where he had been digging. He took another look at the gruesome sight. That, along with the smell, made him run as far away as he could and puke.

"What the hell?" Chase asked. "What's wrong with you?"

Trey wiped his mouth. He had to be seeing things, but he glanced again and was certain he wasn't.

"Bro," Trey said, "the thing that's got you trapped under the snow is a freakin' dead body."

Chapter Two

Maya Thompson could see her breath swirling around in the cold air as Velvet, the little mare she was riding, picked her way through the snow. January in the mountains was not the best time to be out for a ride, but today the weather had improved and the temperature high would reach close to thirty degrees—a heat wave for a Colorado winter.

Maya had been helping her grandfather, Wayne Thompson, who she fondly called Pops, train the young mare he had foaled out and raised. Today was about as good as it was going to get temperature-wise to ride. The sorrel mare had her ears pricked forward, interested in her surroundings. Velvet hadn't been ridden or worked with consistently, so she could be a little frisky.

Luckily, there were several feet of snow they were forging through. If Velvet decided to spook or get excited, she would tire a little quicker in the snow. Not to mention, Maya would have a soft landing if they parted ways. Or so she told herself. She rubbed the little mare's neck and encouraged her into an easy jog. Velvet responded beautifully, making a nice transition and picking her hooves up a little higher, almost prancing through the snow. Maya loved the feel of the little mare and the fun of connecting with another living creature.

In the distance, she heard barking coming from her U.S. Forest Service patrol vehicle. Her K-9, Juniper, was in her heated compartment and indignant about the fact that Maya'd had the nerve to stop out at Pops's place and spend time with a horse. In Juniper's opinion, they should have been at work hours ago and patrolling the forest to keep things safe. Relaxing and hanging out was not one of Juniper's hobbies. Maya knew Juniper would be jealous and chew or rip something up to show her displeasure.

Maya sank a little deeper in the saddle and asked Velvet to come back to a walk; she didn't want to overdo the work since Velvet hadn't been ridden much. She glanced at her watch and realized she needed to start heading back to the barn where Pops was waiting. He was happy that she was able to get some training in on Velvet as he was still recovering from a leg injury from the past summer and didn't know if he was up for schooling a young horse.

He had asked Maya for her help and at first she'd hesitated, but after a while, she'd found the riding therapeutic and discovered it helped her relax. And she knew heading out on horseback for some patrols might be part of her job as a Forest Service law enforcement officer. Pops had already offered to let her borrow Velvet, so she figured she should spend some time with the mare and get to know her quirks.

As she shifted her weight in the saddle, the leather creaked and Velvet flipped an ear back toward the sound, but to Maya's relief, the mare didn't spook. Instead, she responded by following Maya's weight and turning toward home, picking up her pace as they headed back. Maya turned her in a few circles and worked on making sure Velvet didn't get in the bad habit of racing back to the barn.

Maya leaned slightly forward and rubbed the mare's neck again. Velvet had worked up a slight sweat, making her coat appear darker as steam rose off her and the sweet smell of horse wafted through the air. When Maya shifted back, she could feel the crinkle of a letter she'd stuffed into her coat pocket the day before.

Her little secret. At least for now.

The letter had arrived at the local Forest Service office where Maya was headquartered. It was from a federal prison, and as soon as Maya saw it in the mail pile, she'd known who it was from—Abigail Harper.

Abigail was a corrupt former detective from Montana in prison for killing Maya's mother, Zoey, and grandmother, along with other crimes and murders. Abigail's trial was still about six months away and Maya had worked hard to forget her, although it was hard not to think about Abigail. When Maya had reopened her mother's case, Abigail had burned down her cabin and tried to kill her and Juniper.

During that time, a man named Eric Torres had contacted Maya. Eric was a cop who'd been in the same department as Abigail. He'd known and had even arrested Zoey when she had run away to Montana. She'd become involved in prostitution and was found in possession of narcotics. But, when Maya was born, Zoey had become sober and decided to change her life for the better by moving back to Pinecone Junction. Maya had a childhood memory of Eric showing up at their house to warn and try to save her, but Abigail had killed Zoey before Eric could stop her.

When Abigail targeted Maya, Eric had helped save her life. He'd said that he had promised her mother before she died that he would keep Maya safe. He'd kept his promise, but Maya never fully knew his true motivations. Did he want something from her? Why save her when he too was guilty of so many crimes in his past? He had crossed a line by doing things like taking bribes and changing his testimony at trials. Was he simply trying to make up for those crimes? However, he maintained that Abigail had framed him for murder. Maya believed his claim based on some evidence Zoey had hidden that implicated both Eric and Abigail.

Rather than face justice for the less serious crimes he'd committed, Eric had managed to escape custody on his way to jail. He'd been on the run ever since and the U.S. Marshals continued to look for him. Last Maya had heard there were no leads.

But for some reason, Abigail had decided to reach out and give her a possible tip and perhaps more insight into why Eric had promised Maya's mother he would protect her. The letter claimed Eric Torres was Maya's biological father. To say Abigail was a liar and devious would be an understatement. Cunning was another word that described her, and Maya didn't know what to do about the letter. Dismiss it as Abigail messing with her? Throw it away? Or see if Maya could submit DNA and find out if Eric really was her father?

Was that something she wanted to know or not?

Maya still grieved the loss of her mother and grandmother. She supposed she always would to some degree. But to find out she might have a biological parent still alive was a shock. Then there was the fact that he was a criminal. On the flip side, he had also saved her life last fall and helped put Abigail behind bars. Did that give him some sort of pass? Maya had debated that question and couldn't make up her mind.

There were other questions too, including: Why had Abigail told her this now? Did she think Maya would go after Eric and find him? Abigail was probably using her. No, she was definitely using her. There was always an endgame with the former detective. Maya needed to process all of this before she talked it over with Pops or Josh Colten—the chief deputy sheriff and second-in-command to Pops, and the man she'd fallen in love with and had been living with since her cabin burned down.

Maya had sworn to herself she wouldn't keep things from Josh, but somehow, she hadn't been ready to talk to him about this letter. Maybe tonight, after dinner, she'd tell Josh more about what was going on.

As thoughts swirled through Maya's head, Velvet suddenly tucked her hindquarters and tensed up her back. A strange whooshing sound that escalated into sounding like a train coming down the tracks bounced off the mountainsides in the distance. Maya snapped back to the moment and gently turned Velvet's neck so she would step her hindquarters over and settle down. Adrenaline coursed through Maya's body. Even though she had told herself that a snowy landing would be soft, she didn't feel like being sore the rest of the day.

The little mare settled down and, after a moment, relaxed her back. Maya was relieved to feel like she wasn't going to be launched and turned into a lawn dart. Or in this case, a snow dart. Once the mare took a deep breath, Maya glanced over her shoulder to see what had startled

Velvet. The remnants of an avalanche were evident off
in the distance. Snow billowed and blew in a cloud as
the large slide settled.

Even though the avalanche was a fair distance away
on some of the steep slopes, the sound had carried down
the valley. Avalanches often took debris like trees and
rocks with them and this one appeared to have done
just that. This winter had been volatile, with a mix of
heavy snowstorms, warmer weather, and then wind with
more snow. Many of the research scientists felt climate
change was increasing the risk of avalanches.

Maya didn't know if that was true. All she knew was
this winter had been the perfect recipe for avalanche
danger and several people had already lost their lives.
Even those properly prepared had been caught off guard.
Hopefully the slide that just happened hadn't caught and
buried anyone in the backcountry.

Once Velvet relaxed, she and Maya continued their
way toward Pops, who had been standing ready to try
to help when Velvet was spooked. Maya's heart rate
started to settle down and she heard Juniper still barking and throwing a temper tantrum in the patrol vehicle.

She found a good spot to dismount and led Velvet
toward Pops and the barn, wondering if her workday
was going to include a search and rescue operation.

Chapter Three

"Thought she was going to start bucking there for a moment," Pops said, as Maya started to untack Velvet. "I was hoping she wouldn't get you off."

"I thought the same thing," Maya said. "Glad she has a good one-rein stop and I was able to get her settled back down."

She carried the saddle into the tack room and placed it on the rack, glancing at her watch. She had to keep moving if she was going to be at work on time. Pops had already started brushing Velvet and putting a blanket over her so she could cool off but not get chilled.

Maya stepped out of the tack room. "Velvet was really good today, though. I'm happy with how well she did considering we haven't been able to work consistently with the weather."

"I agree," Pops said.

Then there was silence between them as they worked to get Velvet ready to go back to her stall. Maya thought about the subject they were both avoiding—an investigation into Pops for a law enforcement ethics violation. Pops had committed the violation when Maya's best friend and Forest Service field training officer Doug Leyton had admitted to Pops that he was part of a drug-trafficking operation in the forest. Pops had not immediately arrested Doug and had been put on paid leave for a short time. The sheriff's committee finally relented and let him go back to work until it was determined through the investigation if there would be a trial. If there was a trial and Pops was found guilty, he not only would lose his job, but he could also serve prison time. Maya didn't want to think about how heartbroken and lost she'd be if that happened. Not to mention how Pops probably felt.

But he was strong and continued to say he had faith that it would all work out. Maya wished she had faith like that. She didn't know how she'd handle the possibility of losing another important person in her life. Not only had Josh supported her through this tough time, but his father, a prominent lawyer, was coming from Chicago to represent Pops. Josh said his dad was lethal in the courtroom and he was certain he would get Pops cleared of all the charges in the investigation. After all, law enforcement often witnessed people breaking the law while doing surveillance or investigating. Depending on the case, those suspects weren't always arrested. Josh thought it was a good defense. Maybe there wouldn't even be a trial.

Maya only wished she could have Josh's confidence.

Adding to the stress was that not only was Josh's father coming into town to start the trial, but his whole family had decided to visit. Maya was both excited and nervous to meet them. Somehow it made her relationship with Josh seem more official. The stress had also triggered some of her PTSD and she'd been on edge, finding it hard to relax. The ride on Velvet today had helped ease some of her anxiety.

She continued brushing the mare and didn't say anything about the upcoming investigation. Instead, feeling the note crinkle in her pocket again, she decided to ask another question that had been on her mind. She'd asked it before and Pops always told her that he didn't have the answer, but she knew that sometimes he liked to keep things from her, thinking he was protecting her. It wouldn't hurt to ask one more time.

Maya untied Velvet and as she led the mare to her stall where fresh straw and hay were waiting, she asked, "Did my mother ever give you any clues as to who my father was?"

Pops gave her a surprised look and crossed his arms. Just when Maya thought he wasn't going to answer, he said, "I'm so sorry. I really wish she had, but she didn't. If she told anyone, it would have been your grandmother."

Taking off Velvet's halter and closing the stall door behind her, Maya nodded.

"Why?" asked Pops.

She shrugged. "I just wonder sometimes, you know? Anyway, it's no big deal. I should get to work. It's good to see you, Pops."

She gave him a hug and headed out to her patrol vehicle, where Juniper was still barking. Hopefully the interior of the vehicle had survived. The last time Juniper was mad, some of the heavy-duty mats lining the special carrier for K-9s had received the brunt of her anger. Maya's boss hadn't been thrilled about the repair bills. But such was life with a young Malinois—especially one trained as a dual-purpose patrol dog. To say they were high-maintenance was an understatement.

And yet, as Maya climbed into the driver's seat,

opened the door between Juniper's compartment and the
cab, and received several slurps to her face, she couldn't
imagine life without her dog.

Maya pulled up to her parking spot in front of the Forest Service office in the small mountain town of Pinecone Junction. Snow piles lined the main street waiting
for spring to come and melt them. Then it would be mud
season. She wasn't certain which season seemed longer—
snow or mud.

She was ready to let Juniper out when she noticed a
woman standing in front of the Forest Service office.
Maya didn't want Juniper to scare her, so she left her in
the vehicle and went over to see if she could help. She
thought the lady looked familiar, but Maya didn't know
everyone in town like she used to. She had joined the
Marines and deployed to Afghanistan for six months
before coming back stateside and finishing out her time.
When she returned home to the mountains, her small
town had grown and changed, which made her sad. She
had hoped to heal from her PTSD and find peace in the
mountains, but instead, she had discovered that with
the town growing, there was more crime that she and
the sheriff's office had to deal with. "Growing pains"
was what Pops had called it.

The lady had on a heavy jacket and stood in the
sun with her hands in her pockets. Long gray hair in
two braids came down over her shoulders. With a cap
and sunglasses on, it made it harder for Maya to tell
if it was someone she knew. The lady bounced on the
balls of her feet, probably trying to stay warm, making Maya wonder how long she had been waiting and
what she wanted. In the summertime it wasn't unusual

for tourists to show up to get maps and other national forest information since Maya's office doubled as the visitor's center. Occasionally in the winter there were folks wanting to get snowmobiling, backcountry skiing or snowboarding information. This lady struck her as wanting something else.

"Can I help you?" Maya asked.

"Are you Officer Thompson?"

"Yes."

"Can I have a moment of your time?"

Maya hesitated. Hopefully this wasn't someone who wanted to complain about trails not being shoveled or something along those lines. Some tourists didn't understand the Forest Service or the mountains.

"Sure," she finally answered. "Do you mind dogs? My patrol dog, Juniper, will be upset if I leave her in the vehicle and it's a bit chilly to chat out here. I have a crate for her in my office if you're okay with that."

"I love dogs. No problem. And my apologies, I didn't introduce myself. I'm Kayleigh Anderson, but just call me Kay." The lady held out her hand and Maya shook it.

"Nice to meet you. Let me get Juniper. Here, head into the office and start warming up," Maya said, pulling out her keys and unlocking the door.

She went back to her patrol vehicle and made Juniper wait before snapping on her leash and allowing her out. A fur missile flew by Maya. Juniper landed on her feet, shook her whole body and then sat and glared at her.

"What?" Maya said. "You can hang out while I do other things."

Juniper grunted and headed toward the office. The dog peered back at her as if to say *hurry up*. A grin spread on Maya's face. She would have to make this

up to Juniper somehow. Especially once Juniper realized she would have to go into her crate since they
had a guest.

Maya opened the crate, and when she asked Juniper
to go inside, the dog's pointy ears drooped. Yes, at some
point today, the Mal would probably make her pay for
all this time doing nothing. Maya held firm on the dog
listening to her command. Juniper sighed, walked in,
curled up and turned away so her back was facing them.

"Can I get you some coffee?" Maya asked as she
pointed toward a chair on the opposite side of her desk.
"And you can have a seat here if you'd like."

"Thank you, coffee would be great."

Maya poured them each a cup, handing one to Kay,
and then sat down at her desk. She heard another heavy
groan from Juniper's crate. "What can I help you with?"

Kay gripped her mug until her knuckles turned
white. "My son is missing."

"I'm sorry to hear that. Tell me more. When did he
go missing? I haven't heard anything about a local missing person," Maya said, wondering how this pertained
to the Forest Service.

"He's been gone for over a month now. He'd moved
to Antler Valley at the start of this school year to go
to the community college. I thought it was perfect. He
was close enough to home to come visit, but far enough
away to start learning to be an adult.

"He didn't call one weekend and I was worried, but
I tried to give him some space." Kay set her mug down
on Maya's desk and leaned in closer, clasping her hands
together. "I drove over to Antler Valley and he wasn't
in his dorm room. His roommate hadn't seen him for
almost a week. I contacted the police, and long story

short, we believe he attended a party in the national forest and wasn't seen after that. The police turned over the investigation to the sheriff's office. The sheriff acted like he was concerned, but to be blunt, the search and rescue operation was a joke.

"I met some other parents who said their college-age kids were also missing. Those kids also attended these bashes in the forest. I'll admit, I was shocked to hear that they were all missing and that the Forest Service wasn't doing anything about these parties."

Maya nodded but didn't say anything. She wanted the mother to keep talking rather than defend herself and the Forest Service. Between her and Juniper, they had to work and protect the entire national forest, which was about one and a half million acres. Stopping college parties was the least of her worries.

Kay continued, "They spent about five days running a search and rescue operation. To be honest, the sheriff in that county is kind of a jerk, sorry to call him that, but it's the truth. The chief of police seemed nice and tried to get me information, but once the search went to the sheriff's office, there wasn't much he could tell me. Operations have ceased and my son still hasn't been found. All I want is to bring my boy home…" Kay trailed off, tears rolling down her cheeks, and then between stifled sobs she added, "Hopefully alive, but if he's gone, then I just want that closure."

She placed a picture on Maya's desk. It was probably a senior portrait, of a handsome young man with tousled blond hair and sparkling blue eyes. He wore a necklace with a gold cross. "Please, he's all I have. The asshole sheriff won't even return my calls anymore. I don't know who else to turn to. Can you help me and find out more?"

Maya hesitated. There were so many things running through her mind, including the fact that search and rescue operations on national forest land were headed by the local sheriff's office. She and Juniper might be called in to help and share what she knew about different areas of the forest, but this was not her case. Not to mention the weather limited where they could search. Unfortunately, often cases like this resumed in the summer and it was only to find remains. At this point, the likelihood of Kay's son still being alive if he was out in the forest was slim.

But staring at the desperate woman sitting across from her, Maya couldn't bring herself to say all that. She always wondered how, as a Marine, they were able to recover remains in a war zone and yet here at home, people could go hiking and never be found again.

"I can contact the sheriff's office and see what I can find out," Maya said, pausing again, trying to find the right words, and knowing there was nothing she could say that would help Kay's pain. "If you have any other information about the party or anything else you can think of, you can tell me that too. I'll see what I can find out, but I can't guarantee anything."

"Thank you," Kay said, her eyes tearing up. "What can I tell you?"

"Let's start with your son's name." Maya pulled out a notepad.

"Oh, of course. Avery. Avery Anderson."

Maya jotted down the name. "Can you email me a picture of him? Maybe a digital copy of that photo?

Does he have a history of running away or leaving without telling you?"

"I can send you a photo. And no, he's never run away or left without telling me where he was going. He even told me about his spring break plans to go to Florida this year. I was trying to still be there for him, but give him enough space to let him grow up and experience the world. I feel so guilty now that I didn't follow up with him. Maybe if I'd done something sooner…"

"You can't blame yourself," Maya said, knowing again that her words wouldn't help this lady's grief. How often had Maya herself thought that if she'd come home sooner from the military, her grandmother might still be alive?

"I've talked with other parents of students in the area. Quite a few of them have disappeared."

Maya raised an eyebrow. "How many kids are we talking about?"

"Last I heard, there were at least four other missing students."

Leaning back in her chair, Maya mulled that over. That many missing kids was unusual. She thought about the avalanche that morning that had cascaded down the mountainside. Had these kids attended the forest parties and gone missing from them? Or was this year's winter more extreme than she'd realized and they'd possibly perished from natural hazards? It wasn't like there was a ranger or someone in charge of any of these areas. Anyone who went into the forests was doing so at their own risk. "Do you know if they were all at these parties? Or did they recreate in the backcountry? Like skiing or snowboarding?"

"I don't know for sure. Some of the parents have

shared that they also think there's something going on at the parties like heavy drug use. Not just drinking around a bonfire."

"Do you have a list of names for the other missing kids? And their parents' contact info?"

"I do."

"Can you email me that information along with your son's photo?" Maya handed Kay a business card.

"I'll do that."

Maya stood. "Thanks for stopping by today. I'll make some calls and see what I can find out. I have to head out on patrol right now, but I promise I'll be in touch in a couple days."

"Thank you," Kay said, standing and shaking Maya's hand. "Thank you for listening, for your kindness and for being willing to look into this."

"You're welcome," Maya said, showing Kay to the door. As she watched the woman leave, she had to wonder, would she actually be able to find answers? Was Avery Anderson a victim of a crime or simply another victim of the rugged mountains and Mother Nature?

Chapter Four

After Kay left, Maya made some phone calls over to the Antler Valley Sheriff's Office. She'd been put on hold, listened to annoying elevator music and then been given the run-around, being told the sheriff wasn't able to take her call and she could try again later.

Maya called and left messages for Pops and her patrol captain, Todd Davis, to see what they knew. The thought of a mother not knowing what had happened to her son haunted Maya. She thought of her own family and the losses she'd experienced. She continued to grieve, but at least she had answers.

Juniper was happy to finally be on patrol. Being allowed to stick her head through the door into the cab area placated her. Maya wanted to go check out an area homeless were moving into in the national forest. This had become a problem over the past few years since cities were creating new laws and ordinances that simply moved the homeless out of their area.

Not knowing where to go next, many had found their way to the mountains and set up campsites. The problem was that there was trash, drug use and paraphernalia, and damage to ecosystems, not to mention harsh and hazardous weather conditions that threatened lives.

Maya had been working with several organizations to try to help the homeless who literally had nowhere else to go. It had become a passion for her as she recognized that many of the homeless were veterans. They dealt with their PTSD by self-medicating, not seeking help, and were unable to keep a job.

Maya had self-medicated herself with alcohol. Then she had met Josh, who helped her go to AA and work on becoming sober. She felt that if that hadn't happened, she too could have lost her job and found herself in a tough position. She had worked on reaching out to different programs and finding options to get the people the help they needed, whether it was veteran benefits, finding a shelter for a few nights, or contacting families to see if they could help.

Maya wanted to make going back into the area a priority today because there was a large winter storm forecast to move into Colorado, with upslope conditions and low temperatures by the end of the week. An upslope meant that they could get a couple feet of snow and someone could freeze to death.

Before she drove back into the area she needed to check out, Maya figured she better get Juniper out to run and stretch her legs. She came upon a meadow covered in snow that wasn't too deep. The wind had probably blown through there and evaporated the moisture.

Maya pulled over and let Juniper out of her compartment. She put on her snow booties and Doggles, eye gear to help with the UV rays reflecting off the snow and keep out blowing debris. Then Maya pulled out Juniper's favorite Kong toy and threw it as far as she could out into the meadow.

Juniper joyfully bounded through the snow until she

found her Kong. She brought it back and they played like that for about fifteen minutes. Maya hoped that would not only get some energy out but make Juniper happy too. Once Juniper started slowing down, Maya took all the gear back off, loaded Juniper up in her compartment and headed onward to their destination.

The area that had attracted the most homeless was back in a remote location. Maya had no idea how they'd found their way there, but they had. Last week there were several tents and campers. Today there was only one vehicle—a beat-up truck with an old camper on the back.

Maya pulled up behind the truck and radioed in to dispatch. She was glad that she had signal out here. Last year more repeaters had been installed in the area and that helped maintain radio signal in remote areas. Not like backup could get there quickly, but at least Maya could radio in her location and a license plate. She waited a minute until dispatch gave her the information for the owner of the vehicle. She learned his name, last known address and that he had been arrested a couple times for possession of narcotics.

No one stirred as Maya exited her vehicle. She had to be careful as she didn't know if there was someone in the truck or the camper or both. She let Juniper out and put her on leash. This far out in the wilderness, Juniper was her backup and would let her know if there was anyone in the vehicle, camper or even out in the woods watching and waiting to ambush them.

They walked up behind the vehicle and checked that no one was immediately at the camper door. Then Maya touched the back of the truck to leave her fingerprints and DNA. That way if anything happened, she would have evidence linking her to the vehicle.

The cab was empty and she didn't see any weapons lying out on the seat or anything else that would cause her concern. Juniper put her nose up in the air and took in the scent from the breeze. Her body language changed, her shoulders raising up and her body tensing; Maya knew that her dog had caught a human scent in the camper.

They stepped back around to the camper and knocked on the door. Maya stayed off to the side and did her best not to be in the line of sight where someone could shoot at her.

No response.

She knocked again and this time she thought she could hear someone inside. The door cracked open. A man's face with a scruffy beard and long unkempt hair peeked out. The odor of fermented vinegar wafted through the air. Only Maya knew it wasn't vinegar, it was heroin. Juniper sat and stared at the camper—her indication for smelling narcotics. Maya made a mental note to be careful, as heroin often had fentanyl in it now and could cause anyone who inhaled the powder to overdose. She carried Narcan with her for both herself and Juniper, and she hoped she'd never have to use it.

"Hello?" the man said tentatively.

"Hello, sir," Maya said. "I'm Officer Thompson with Forest Service law enforcement. I'm making a routine pass through this area to let you know that you will need to find another place to stay."

"But this is my home now."

"I understand, but I'm sorry, this is national forest land and you can't camp here long-term. There's also a big storm moving in at the end of this week. It could be dangerous for you to stay here. Do you have any friends or family that you can call? I'd be happy to help you connect with them."

The man opened the door more and stared at Maya.

"Will you come out of your camper? Let's talk out here." She didn't add that she wanted to know if he had any weapons and that out in the open, she'd have a better idea of what he might have in his hands or pockets.

Just when she thought he wouldn't comply, he opened the door and stepped down. She took a good look and didn't see him holding anything obvious like a knife, but she maintained some space between them so she'd have time to react if he tried anything. Juniper stayed between the man and Maya.

"What's your name?" she asked, trying to get him talking.

"Clarence."

"Okay, Clarence. It's nice to meet you. Like I mentioned earlier, I'm sorry, but you can't stay here. I'd be happy to help you get to a shelter. Or maybe there's someone you can stay with?"

Clarence stared down at the ground and kicked some snow around with his tennis shoes, which had holes and different-colored shoelaces. His jeans were dirty and he smelled like he hadn't had a shower in a while, along with the odor of the heroin.

"I'm not leaving," he said, looking back up at Maya and trying to stand his ground.

She didn't say anything for a few seconds. She had a choice—she could arrest him for possession of drugs and at least give him a warm place to stay in jail, or she could try to convince him to just come with her and she'd drop him off at the shelter. The problem was the truck and camper and what to do with them. If Maya arrested him, she might be able to find some family members who could at least come get them. She glanced at Juniper, who sat poised and ready to go.

"My K-9 is trained to find narcotics. Do you have any narcotics in your camper or vehicle?"

Clarence broke eye contact again and stared back down at the snow as if it would somehow solve his problems. "No, I don't have any drugs."

"Do you mind then if I let my dog check your vehicle?"

"Sure, she ain't gonna find anything."

"Okay, thank you for letting me do that. For both of our safety, I need to handcuff you and have you stay over by my vehicle while I let my dog sniff your truck."

Maya hoped he wouldn't argue. Clarence stared at some trees and then held out his hands.

"Thank you for cooperating," Maya said. "I need you to turn around and put your hands on the back of your head, interlacing your fingers."

Much to her relief, Clarence followed instructions. Most of the time, people she had to arrest were compliant. Once in a while, they decided to fight. That's when she was glad she had Juniper.

"I've got nothin' to hide," Clarence said as Maya put on the cuffs and patted him down.

"That's good. I'll let my K-9, Juniper, take a sniff of your vehicle and then we can talk further about how to keep you safe with the weather moving in."

Maya guided Clarence over near her vehicle and asked him to stay there, and then pulled out Juniper's collar for narcotics work. Juniper started turning in circles, yipping with joy. Maya waited for her to settle down, keeping an eye on Clarence as well. It was good that he was in handcuffs, but that didn't mean that he couldn't still try to come after her. Maya trusted her instinct, though. She didn't think Clarence was the type to do that. Of course, that's how officers got in trouble—they let their guard down.

When Juniper settled, Maya put on the collar and leash and then asked her to sit and settle for a moment. She needed the Malinois to focus and not get too excited about finding narcotics. That could lead to a false indication. Maya had Juniper check an area near the vehicle just to make sure she was listening and working the way Maya wanted. Once she was satisfied, she took Juniper over to the truck and camper.

Juniper immediately put her nose on the vehicle and started working her way around it. Maya pretty much stayed back and let Juniper work, except for directing her nose toward some areas that had good airflow from the vehicle, like the wheel wells and front grille. Most people thought that dogs couldn't smell through a vehicle, but cars had a lot of airflow and the scent was easy for dogs to work and find contraband.

Maya had worked a K-9 in Afghanistan. Zinger had been a dual-purpose bomb dog and running this vehicle brought back memories of working her dog in the military. She had to close her mind off to those memories as her military dog had lost his life because of handler error. No matter how much therapy she'd had, Maya still couldn't forgive herself.

Focusing back on Juniper, she noticed that as they came around to the cab of the truck, Juniper's body language changed. She tightened her muscles, her sniffing and breathing changed, and her tail went straight up in the air, indicating that she was in odor. The source of an odor, like drugs, would give off the scent in a plume. When Juniper's superior nose caught that scent, she would change her body language and be what handlers called "in odor." They had worked together for about six months now and Maya could read Juniper's body language better and better.

Give us another six months and we'll be a strong team. Juniper is amazing.

Juniper went past the passenger door and then whipped around, sticking her nose in the door crack, inhaling deeply. Then she sat and stared straight ahead at the door. Her tail sent snow flying as it wagged back and forth in excitement. Juniper didn't break her gaze and continued to stare straight ahead.

Maya praised her and then took her out of the alert. She put Juniper back in her compartment in the vehicle, making a mental note to hide something later for her. She couldn't reward Juniper with her toy until she searched the vehicle, and the thought of heroin with fentanyl scared Maya. Just like humans, Juniper could overdose from sniffing fentanyl.

After Maya put Juniper in her compartment, she approached Clarence. "K-9 Juniper alerted on your vehicle, which gives me probable cause to search your vehicle. I'll ask again, do you have anything in there?"

Clarence wouldn't look Maya in the eye.

"Clarence, believe it or not, I want to help you. But I can't do that if you don't start talking to me. Do you have anything in your vehicle?"

Clarence nodded and mumbled something in return.

"I'm sorry, I couldn't hear you," Maya said. "Can you speak up?"

"I said I've got some stuff under the passenger side."

"Okay, I'm going to find the drugs and then I'll take you to jail. You'll get a hot shower and a meal there and then you can have a public defender to help you with these charges. Do you understand?"

Clarence nodded.

"Good, then I'm going to put you in my vehicle while I search yours."

Clarence followed her guidance and went to the back, where she locked him in. She wasn't thrilled about the arrest as it meant more paperwork for her, but at least at the jail, his basic needs would be met. It would be nice to think this might change his life and he would want to get clean, but the chances of that happening were highly unlikely. Maya walked over to Clarence's vehicle and opened the passenger door where Juniper had alerted.

She put on gloves and carefully felt around under the seat. There were about ten dime bags under there, but as she pulled them out, she realized the powder in the baggies didn't look like normal heroin. The substance was a gray color, sort of like a light ash.

Maya was careful how she handled the bags. She didn't need any of the powder blowing into her face. She took extra care bagging them for evidence, finished her search of the vehicle and then closed the door.

She'd have to figure out how to have it towed before the storm moved in. Tow truck drivers weren't usually excited about coming this far back into the forest to get a vehicle.

Maya went back to her patrol SUV and stored the evidence bag with drugs in a safe location. Then she climbed in the driver's seat and turned around. She recited Clarence's Miranda rights so she could ask him some questions—she wanted to know more about the drugs she found.

"There were more drugs than I was expecting. Are you selling?"

"No. That was all mine."

Now Maya knew why he didn't want to leave. He'd probably just wanted to spend a few weeks here getting high.

"Who'd you get it from?"

"The devil. The devil sold it to me."

"The devil?"

"Yeah."

"Okay," Maya said, turning back around and starting up her vehicle. She'd have to check with Josh and Pops to see if there was anyone dealing in the area with the name Devil. Or the drugs could be distorting Clarence's mind. She would ask more as they headed back to town, but she might just receive convoluted information, making it a long drive to the jail. Even Juniper gave a heavy sigh and lay down.

Chapter Five

Maya delivered Clarence to the county jail and booked him. At least for now he was safe and she didn't have to worry about him freezing to death.

Maya wanted to know more about the substance she'd found in Clarence's truck, so she took it to the lab at the sheriff's office. Her friend Miranda was the lead tech and could help identify the drugs.

Before Maya went inside, she took out some of her training aids and hid some pseudo heroin for Juniper to find. She wanted to reward her dog for a job well done on a safe substance. Pseudo drugs were designed to smell like the real thing for training. At one time, she trained with real drugs released from evidence. Now she used pseudo drugs because they had a consistent scent and were not dangerous. Street drugs could have other toxins, from bleach to lighter fluid to fentanyl. These chemicals were added for an extra high and to increase the amount of the product.

Juniper knew what was happening and started yipping in excitement. Maya went and hid the heroin in a crevice in some decorative rocks at the front of the sheriff's office. She didn't want the pseudo drugs to get wet and possibly ruined by putting them down in snow. After putting on Juniper's narcotics collar, Maya waited for Juniper to settle down and worked on some obedience to give the scent time to set up.

After about ten minutes, Maya told Juniper to "Go find the dope."

Tail up and nose twitching, Juniper started checking different areas. Maya stayed out of her way, letting her dog work, only directing Juniper to check an area she had run by in excitement. All of a sudden, Juniper caught the odor and started working the scent cone. Scent cones were created when odor spread out from the hide in a cone shape. The dog would go back and forth, in and out of odor, until she pinpointed the source at the rocks. Juniper sat and stared at the location of her find.

Maya threw Juniper's Kong in front of her, rewarding her dog for a job well done. They played tug for a few minutes and she also threw the toy out into the snow. Juniper bounded around, thrilled to play. Maya grinned, feeling joy from her dog's happiness.

"Are you actually working today or just playing with your dog?"

The voice came from behind Maya, only making her smile bigger. Josh. Her heart still beat a little faster when she saw him.

Josh had moved to Pinecone Junction from Chicago. He and Maya had started working together on a case the previous summer and despite how hard she'd tried to deny her feelings, she'd had to admit the handsome deputy with dark eyes and a dimple on his cheek had won her over. She went over to him and gave him a quick kiss, trying not to get lost in his touch as he tucked some loose strands of hair behind her ear.

"Who wants to work when you have the fun of play-ing with a Mal?" Maya asked.

"Good point," Josh said with a laugh that charmed Maya and made her heart rate increase again.

Get yourself together. It's not like you don't get to see him every day.

Maya stepped back and whistled for Juniper to come. Juniper responded, bounding over and sitting down in front of them. Juniper turned her head away, hoping that Maya wouldn't ask for her toy back. She managed to get Juniper to drop the Kong and then loaded her back up into her compartment, making sure she had water. Juniper took a drink and then turned in a couple circles and lay down.

Josh had followed her to her vehicle and said, "Great. Juniper will take a nap now and be ready to play again by the time we get home."

"Yep," Maya said, closing her vehicle. "Just remem-ber, though, you were the one who begged us to move in with you."

"And I wouldn't have it any other way," Josh said, coming closer and pinning Maya between her vehicle and him. He caressed her cheek and gave her another kiss. She responded as warmth spread throughout her body, then placed her hands on his chest.

"Maybe we should resume this when we get home tonight," she said.

"I think we should," Josh said, letting his hand trail down her thigh below her vest and duty belt.

"Okay, I'll think about it," Maya said in a teasing tone as she pulled Josh in closer and wrapped her arms around him. They stayed like that for a minute and then he stepped back. She could tell by the look in his eyes he was thinking about what he wanted to do when she arrived home.

"Try to stay focused on the job," Maya said, again in a teasing tone.

"You make that really difficult."

"So do you, but I better get back to work before someone complains about public displays of affection in the parking lot."

"You dropping something off with Miranda?" Josh asked.

"I am. Arrested a man who was camping on Forest Service land and Juniper found drugs in his vehicle. The smell from his camper was basically heroin, but this looks different. I thought I'd have Miranda test them and see what we're dealing with. Could be that we have a new type of drug in the area."

"Seems hard to keep up with all the different drugs," Josh said.

"It is. And I think sometimes it's a losing battle with the dealers. I better get these to Miranda and see if we can get at least a basic identification done in a safe setting. I didn't want to test it with a NIK test out in the field in case there was fentanyl."

"Good idea. Well, I look forward to seeing you at home tonight," Josh said with another sly grin.

Maya laughed and said, "I'm looking forward to it too."

They parted ways and Maya grabbed the evidence bag with the drugs. She glanced back over her shoulder at Josh walking away. How did she get so lucky?

A cold breeze picked up and she put on her jacket. The note Abigail had sent from prison about Eric Torres being her father was still in there. Maya didn't want to say anything to Josh about the note just yet. She felt a little guilty. Especially since she planned on discussing a secret DNA test with Miranda.

Josh watched Maya walk into the sheriff's office and then headed to his own patrol vehicle. He was fortunate and he knew it. He never thought he'd meet someone like Maya. She could make him laugh, she listened to him, she cared, and yes, she frustrated the hell out of him sometimes too, but she'd become not only his lover, but his best friend. He couldn't imagine life without her. Or Juniper.

Josh climbed into his squad car, but waited to radio in for duty. His family would soon be coming to Pinecone Junction and with them came Josh's past, which he had desperately worked to escape. He wasn't proud of who he'd been when he lived and worked in Chicago. He had spiraled out of control after losing his partner and good friend. His family never seemed to understand.

When he became sober, Josh moved to Pinecone Junction knowing that the only reason the sheriff, Maya's grandfather, had even offered him a job was because they were a small department and didn't have many applications. The sheriff, or Pops, as Josh had started thinking of him as after being around Maya, had become like another father. He'd given Josh a second chance—and his blessing to date Maya. How much better could life get? Josh had learned to appreciate things more when he became sober.

But his family was another story, except for his sister, Bianca. They had remained close. He loved his parents, but they were triggers for him. Josh hadn't told Maya this, but he hadn't been fully honest with his parents about his relationship with Maya. Not because of her, but because of them. He'd told them she was just a friend because he didn't want to deal with all the questions and expectations that would come when he told them he was in love like never before.

Bianca thought his parents would understand, but Josh had experienced the pressure they liked to place on him in regards to his personal life and his job. Maya was nervous about meeting his parents and he wanted to support her. Knowing how overbearing and pushy they could be didn't help him sound convincing when he told Maya there was nothing to worry about.

Josh put the squad car in Drive and radioed in to dispatch that he was on duty. Then he took a deep breath before pulling out of the parking lot. He had to tell his parents about Maya before they arrived. That way they could have twenty-four hours to chill out. He had to admit he was nervous to tell them as his mother had always wanted him with someone who was high up in Chicago social circles.

Josh didn't care about any of that. He only cared about Maya and would make sure they knew that before they arrived. Going out on patrol and dealing with the public would be easier than talking to his parents.

Maya arrived at the lab and placed the narcotics into an evidence locker for chain of custody protocol. Then she went to see when Miranda might test the drugs. She knew that Miranda had Narcan on hand in the crime lab—another change since illegal fentanyl became so popular—and thought maybe she should stick around while Miranda tested the substance just in case she ended up needing Narcan.

Knocking on the door, Maya entered Miranda's office. It was empty, but she could see through to the test center where Miranda was working on processing evidence.

"Hey there," Maya said, going into the lab. "How's it going?"

Miranda stopped what she was doing. Her dark hair was pulled back in a ponytail, her makeup applied perfectly to highlight her blue eyes, as usual. She grinned and answered, "Going well today. Thanks. How have you been? It's good to see you."

"I've been good," Maya answered.

"What's up?"

"I just logged some drugs into evidence. I didn't know when you might have time to test them, but I'd like to know more about what type of substance this guy had. I was also worried that you might want someone with you in case you needed Narcan."

"I'm actually at a good stopping point here and I can run some tests on the drugs now," Miranda said, putting away the evidence she was working on and taking off her gloves. "Let me go grab it."

Miranda went to the lockers and pulled out the evidence bag, peering inside. "What do you think this is?"

"The whiff I got from the camper definitely smelled like heroin, but I think there could be other substances too."

"I agree. It could be Gray Death, but I'll run some more tests."

"Now that you mention it, it does look like that."

Now Maya was happy she hadn't tested the drugs in the field. Gray Death was a combo of synthetic drugs with heroin. It usually contained fentanyl, carfentanil—

a tranquilizer for large animals like elephants—and U-47700, or "Pinky," another synthetic opioid. If these drugs were Gray Death, then Clarence was lucky to be alive. And if it was coming into their area, Maya needed to warn Pops and surrounding law enforcement and first responders to have extra Narcan on hand. They could have an epidemic of overdoses.

Miranda carefully handled the drugs and started her tests. She set them up and then said, "It'll take a few minutes to get preliminary results. So, while we're waiting, how's Josh doing?"

Maya noticed the twinkle in Miranda's eyes and knew her friend still liked to give her a hard time about her relationship since she had dragged her feet at admitting that Josh was special.

"He's good," Maya answered. "In fact, it seems like he's perfect. That still drives me nuts about him. I mean, can he do anything wrong? He's like a Boy Scout."

Miranda laughed. "So, what you're saying is that he's the best-looking guy in town, he's nice and a gentleman and he's totally in love with you, but you're not sure about him because he's like a Boy Scout."

"Yeah." Maya shrugged. "Something like that, but enough about my relationship. How's Lucas doing?"

Miranda's face suddenly flushed red. Lucas was a good friend of Maya's from the military. He worked for the Colorado Bureau of Investigation and had helped Maya solve the murders of her mother and grandmother. That's how he had met Miranda, and Maya had noticed that his SUV was at her house on his days off. She didn't want to embarrass Miranda, but it was fun to give her a hard time back after all the ribbing Maya took about Josh.

"Uh, Lucas is good."

"I've known Lucas a long time. He's a good guy. I'm happy for you both," Maya said. "Any chance he'll be around tonight? I don't know his work schedule right now."

Miranda shook her head. "I should have known that I couldn't sneak anything past you. And yes, Lucas is coming up tonight."

"I don't want to interrupt your evening, but do you mind if I swing by your house on my way home and talk to him? I have a favor to ask him."

"No, that's fine," Miranda said. "If you don't mind me asking, what's the favor?"

"I want him to run a DNA test using a profile he already has on file."

"A new case?"

"Not really. It's my DNA. I want to find out if Eric Torres is my biological father."

Miranda stared at Maya. "Why do you think he would be?"

"I received this letter from Abigail Harper claiming he is." Maya pulled the letter out of her pocket and handed it to Miranda, who read it and then gave it back. "If Eric is my father, then I don't know what I'll do, but if he isn't then I can ignore Abigail and get on with my life."

"I'll let Lucas know you'll be stopping by and I'll let you fill him in on all this," Miranda said as the machine she was using to identify the drugs chimed that it had results. "Looks like we do have a formula with all the components of Gray Death. Not good that it's coming into this area."

"No," Maya agreed. "Not good at all."

"I'll do more in-depth tests to try to figure out how

much of the really nasty killer drugs are mixed into this, but I'd definitely spread the word to be careful. I'll send out notifications to other crime labs too."

"Thanks again for running this now. I appreciate it," Maya said. "And thanks for letting me swing in tonight."

"No problem. Although, no offense, don't stay too long," Miranda said with a wink.

"No offense taken."

Maya headed back out to her vehicle thinking about the substance they'd just found. Dangerous and fatal—not something she wanted to deal with.

Chapter Six

Maya and Juniper finished up their patrol for the day. The rest of the day was quiet and she texted Josh to let him know she'd be heading home soon. She left out telling him about the stop at Miranda's house.

Pulling into Miranda's driveway, she parked behind another SUV with Colorado government plates—Lucas's vehicle. She felt a little bad about interrupting their evening, but she also felt like Lucas was the only one who could help her. He had access to Eric's DNA. She picked up the cheek swab that she had done on herself and went up to the front door and rang the bell. Miranda answered and invited Maya inside.

"Is that my favorite Tree Cop?" Lucas called out as he walked into the living room where Maya and Miranda were.

Maya laughed at Lucas's use of *Tree Cop*. He liked to give her a hard time about patrolling the forests. "The one and only," she answered.

"Good to see you," Lucas said, giving her a hug. "Miranda said that you had a favor to ask me."

"I do." Maya paused and handed Lucas the tube with the cheek swab. "This is my DNA. I'm hoping your lab would be up for comparing it to the samples you have for Eric Torres. You're one of the main investigators on the case, so I thought you might be willing to contact the lab and see if they can run this and find out if it's a match."

Lucas raised an eyebrow. "You want to tell me more?"

Maya sighed, pulling the letter out of her pocket and handing it to Lucas. "This arrived at my office the other day."

Lucas opened the letter and read it. He had helped put Abigail Harper in prison and had interrogated her many times. He knew her well. "You think this is for real?" he asked.

"I don't know. At first, I was going to throw it away and ignore it, but then I started to wonder if it could be true. I thought about how much Eric Torres protected and helped me. If it hadn't been for him, Abigail might have killed me. I barely remember my mother and I only have Pops, so I guess I wouldn't mind knowing if Torres is my father. Not like he's in the running for father of the year or that I think I'll be spending the holidays with him, but I'd like to know."

"What are you going to do if he is your father?" Miranda asked.

"I honestly don't know. He's a wanted felon. The Marshals are looking for him. I should stay out of the way, but it's bugging me that Abigail decided to send this. It makes me wonder what she wants and I'm curious."

"Curiosity killed the cat, as the saying goes," Lucas said.

"I know, but I think I at least want to know the truth. Once I know for sure, I'll decide what to do."

Lucas handed the letter back to Maya. "If our lab

has enough DNA evidence to do a cross exam, I'm sure they will. I'll take it to them and find out when I go back down to Denver. If they can run the tests, I'll let you know the results as soon as possible. As usual, they're really backed up, but I'll see if I can put a rush on this since it pertains to the Abigail Harper case and we're preparing for her trial. If she's telling the truth and Eric is a match, maybe we can figure out what she wants and use it against her."

"There's one other thing," Maya said. "I haven't told Josh about this yet. I don't want him to worry. He has enough stress with everything going on with Pops and with his family coming into town tomorrow. That has him on edge too. I don't need to add to his worries. Although I know I need to tell him soon."

"Your secret is safe," Lucas said. "Although as your friend, my advice is to tell him. He's still involved with the case since it happened here, not to mention you and Josh are dating and living together, so I think he'd want to know. But that's up to you."

"I know. You're right. I'll tell him in the next day or so. Thank you," Maya said. "I owe you."

"No, Tree Cop. You and your K-9 saved my life in Afghanistan. I'll always owe you."

"Semper Fi," Maya said.

"Oorah, Tree Cop," Lucas said with a smile.

Maya shook her head and grinned. "Keep calling me Tree Cop and I'll send Juniper after you," she said, zipping her jacket and stepping out into the winter evening. Closing the door behind her, she stuck her hands in her pockets. The wind gusted and blew snow into her face. Maya would be glad to be out of the bitter cold night and home by the warm fire with Juniper and Josh.

* * *

Snow crunched under the tires of Maya's patrol vehicle
as she pulled into the driveway and put the SUV in Park.
The letter sat on the passenger seat and she grabbed it,
shoving it into her pocket again. She did need to tell
Josh for many reasons. For so long she didn't tell anyone anything. It was easier to hide things than to face
emotions.

Maya had started really hiding things and trying to
tell everyone she was fine when she came home from
Afghanistan. She'd been going to a veterans' support
group and working on the PTSD. Therapy had helped
her sleep better and lessened her anxiety, but she still
had a hard time being honest—especially with those
she loved. In some ways she had convinced herself if
she didn't share with those she loved, then she couldn't
hurt them and they couldn't hurt her. But deep down
she knew that wasn't the truth.

Maya saw the front porch light flip on as Josh peered
out the door. She'd better get inside with Juniper before
he wondered what she was doing. She stepped out and
let Juniper out of her compartment, then they walked
to the front door and went inside.

"Hey there…" Maya said, her voice trailing as she
saw Josh holding what appeared to have been one of his
sheriff's uniform shirts. At least it used to be. The shirt
was in tatters and looked like someone had taken a bad
pair of scissors to it. "Is that one of your work shirts?"

"It was."

"What happened to it?" she asked, noticing Juniper
had slunk behind her and was peering around Maya's
legs at Josh. Her usual perky triangular ears were droop-
ing. Maya figured between Juniper's reaction and the

evidence Josh was holding, she knew what had happened. "Oh, Juniper. I'm so sorry, Josh. I'll buy you another one."

He went over to the trash can and threw it away. "It's okay. I guess we need to be more careful where we throw our work shirts when we're ripping clothing off each other."

Maya tried to stifle a laugh, but she remembered the previous night when she'd put Juniper in her crate because she and Josh could barely make it through the door before undressing and heading to the bedroom. She couldn't contain the laughter anymore and burst out giggling.

"Sorry, but I guess she gets jealous. I really will get you another shirt."

Josh seemed to be trying to stay mad, but even he cracked a grin and started laughing. "I don't quite know what I'm going to tell your grandfather. 'Juniper ripped up my shirt when I was in the throes of passion with your granddaughter'?"

"Yeah, I wouldn't go there," Maya said. "I'll just tell him Juniper got a hold of the laundry pile and I need to get you another one. I don't think a little white lie will hurt."

Juniper grunted and left her hiding spot behind Maya, heading to the back door. Maya let her out and then went back over to Josh, giving him a kiss and holding him in a hug.

"There's something else I need to talk to you about," she said, getting ready to pull the letter out of her pocket.

"You think it could wait?" Josh asked, drawing Maya closer. His fingers trailed down her back.

"Mmm… I think it could," Maya said.

Heading toward the bedroom, Josh had started un-
buttoning Maya's shirt, exposing her bra. His lips trailed
down her throat and lower. She moaned in pleasure.
There was something about him that got to her. She'd
never felt like this with anyone else.

Maya started to unzip Josh's pants when the door-
bell rang.

"What the…?" Josh said.

"We could ignore it," Maya said.

Then it rang again. The moment gone, Josh zipped
his pants back up and headed to the front door. Maya
heard him mutter some expletives and then open the
door. She decided she'd better get herself dressed again
too and buttoned her shirt back up, then tucked it in.
Maya heard several voices she didn't recognize.

As she came out of the bedroom, pulling her curly
auburn hair back into a ponytail, the voices stopped.
Maya froze. Staring at her was Josh's family. She hadn't
met them in person, but she'd seen pictures. Even Josh's
sister had come along to visit. Standing with the family was a tall blonde Maya didn't recognize from any
pictures. Josh's face was flushed red.

He managed to get out, "Maya, this is my family and
uh, Amber." He gestured toward the blonde. "Everyone,
this is Maya Thompson."

Josh's mother raised an eyebrow and Maya knew she
hadn't missed that Maya had stepped out of Josh's bedroom and was looking a little disheveled.

"Nice to meet you all," Maya said, hesitantly. She
had been under the impression Josh's family was showing up the next day.

Bianca, Josh's sister, rushed over and wrapped her

up in a hug. "I'm so excited to finally meet you. Josh has told me so much about you."

Maya awkwardly returned the hug. "Nice to meet you too."

When Bianca let go and stepped back, Maya didn't know what to say.

Josh broke the silence first. "I didn't think you all were coming until tomorrow night and I didn't know that Amber was joining you."

"We've missed you," Josh's mother, Natalia, said. "You haven't come home once since you moved here. I wanted an extra day with my son. Is that a crime?"

"No," Josh said, running a hand through his hair and then taking a deep sigh. "No, it's not. Here. Come on in. Let me take your jackets. We don't have much here for dinner, but maybe we can go to the Black Bear Café and get something."

Natalia turned her cheek toward Josh and he gave it a quick peck. Maya realized Juniper was still outside in the cold. She needed to go get her. She pointed to the yard and Josh nodded, understanding that Juniper needed to come back in. Maya grabbed a leash and found Juniper at the back door looking chilly and put out.

"Sorry, girly," Maya said, snapping on the leash and bringing her inside. "I'm also sorry because you're going to have to go to your crate."

Juniper's ears drooped again.

"You're getting good at that pathetic look, but it's not going to work tonight."

They headed to the living room, where Juniper's large crate sat in the corner. As they entered, the blonde stepped toward Josh and gave him a friendly kiss on the cheek that lingered too long. Josh pulled away and pushed her back. Juniper, seeing someone enter Josh's space, started barking and growling.

Natalia screamed and leaped back toward Josh's father. Amber turned and glared at Maya and Juniper.

"Pfui," Maya said, giving her dog a reprimand and hoping she wouldn't try to apprehend Amber. Although Maya had to admit that after seeing Amber make a move on Josh, she wouldn't mind letting her dog bite her. Juniper probably sensed that too, so Maya hustled her over to the crate and locked her up.

"Maybe you need better control over your dog," Amber said.

"Maybe you need to be careful what you do around a patrol dog that's trained to bite," Maya snapped back.

"Okay, okay," Josh said. "Let's all leave Juniper alone and let her settle. We can go to the sunroom and sit down and catch up."

Josh herded the family members out of the living room. When they were gone, he stopped by Maya and said, "I'm so sorry. This is a shock to me too."

"Who's Amber?" Maya whispered.

"An old friend."

"Seems like a good friend."

"Yeah, there's more to it, but I'll tell you later. I can't believe my mother invited her. Actually, I take that back, I can. Right now, let me deal with my family and get them out of here and to their Airbnb tonight."

"Okay," Maya said, touching Josh's arm. "It's okay. I'm here for you."

"Thanks," Josh said, giving Maya a quick kiss and then heading to the sunroom area.

Maya could see Natalia and Amber were sitting where they could watch the exchange between her and

Josh. Good, she thought. Maybe they needed to see that she and Josh cared for each other, since from what she gathered, Natalia was up to some games. Maya took a deep breath, ready to join everyone when her phone rang.

It was her patrol captain and boss, Todd Davis.

Not a good sign this late at night.

Chapter Seven

"Hello, sir," Maya answered, stepping into the bedroom for some privacy.

"Hey there, Thompson. Sorry to interrupt your evening, but I just received a call from the Antler Valley Sheriff's Office. Apparently, some backcountry snowboarders triggered an avalanche. Luckily, they were prepared and managed to make it out alive, although the one snowboarder who got caught in the avalanche broke both legs due to the debris that hit him. But the problem is that when his brother dug him out, they found a deceased person. Since then, the sheriff's office has found a couple more victims, making this most likely a homicide investigation. We need an officer there on scene to help our new criminal investigator for the region, Ben Easton. Do you think you can get there tomorrow morning? Early?"

"Yes, sir," Maya said. "I can leave early and get there probably by nine. Will that work?"

"Perfect. I'll let Easton know you're coming and that you have Juniper for tracking and evidence searches and whatever else she may be needed for."

"Did you receive my message about the missing persons in that area?" she asked.

"I did. Who knows, maybe these victims are the missing persons. But talk to Easton, maybe together you two can find out more when you're there. Not sure there's much any of us can do with the weather. It unfortunately might be a case of looking for remains this summer. But that's not our jurisdiction. I get families feeling desperate, though. Do what you can, but the remains that were found are your top priority."

"Understood," Maya said.

"And Thompson?"

"Yeah?"

"Try to stay out of trouble over there," Todd said, with a hint of teasing in his voice.

Maya laughed. Her boss had backed her on several occasions when she had pushed some boundaries. She had vowed that she would try not to put him in that position again, although somehow, things like that always seemed to happen. "I'll do my best, sir."

"Thanks. Keep me posted. You'll like Easton. He's a good criminal investigator."

Maya hung up from the call and headed back out to the sunroom to join Josh and his family. As she entered, she heard Natalia talking passionately.

"So, what you're saying is you're living in sin?" Natalia said.

"For Christ's sake, Mom," Josh said.

"Don't take that tone or use that kind of language with me."

"I'm an adult. I can do what I want."

Maya slid to a stop, trying to plan an exit again. Bianca was standing near the couch and came over to whisper, "Don't worry. Once Mom chills out, it'll all be good."

"What are they fighting about?" Maya whispered back.

"Josh just told them that you two are living together. Like, you know, *living together*."

"They didn't know?"

"Josh just told them you were staying in the guest bedroom since your cabin burned down. He hadn't mentioned to them that you'd moved out of the guest bedroom. He'd told me, but we learned a long time ago it's best not to let Mom know. She still thinks we're kids."

Maya nodded as hurt and anger built inside her. Had Josh been ashamed of their relationship? At what point had he been going to let his family know? Maya hadn't grown up in a normal family, though. Maybe this was how things worked.

She stared at Josh standing in the middle of the sunroom, his face still flushed, hands on his hips as he faced his parents. He caught Maya looking at him and their eyes connected.

"Maya is the best thing that's ever happened to me. I love her. If you can't deal with that right now, then I think it's best you all leave. We can talk more in the morning."

"It'll all work out," Bianca said, giving her another hug. "Once Mom cools off, she'll get to know you and love you. Until then, I'm glad I got to meet you."

"Same here, glad I finally met you," Maya said.

Josh's family stood up and headed to the door, shuffling out. Bianca was the only one to say goodbye to Maya. Josh shut the door behind them and leaned forward, resting his forehead against the wall. "I'm so sorry, Maya."

He turned around. Maya hugged her arms to her chest. "You hadn't told them about me? About us? We've been together for several months. You've talked about how serious our relationship is."

"I know. I wanted to tell them, but they're impossible."

"Or maybe our relationship isn't what I thought," Maya said.

"No, Maya. Please."

"Who's Amber?"

Josh took a deep sigh. "She's just a family friend."

"One who obviously has feelings for you."

"I know. We were engaged."

"What?" Maya stared at Josh, anger burning deep. "You never thought to mention that?"

"It was in the past. I didn't think it was important."

"Until she showed up here throwing herself at you."

"It's not like that," Josh said. "I promise. It's over. I have no feelings for her. I love you."

Maya shook her head. "I need some space. Todd called. I'm being sent to work on a case in Antler Valley and leaving early tomorrow morning. I think some time apart might be good. I'm tired. I'm going to bed."

She turned and left for the bedroom. Part of her wanted to go and hold Josh, tell him it was all okay. She still had her secrets too, like running a DNA test to see if a wanted felon was her father. That would only endear her to Josh's mother even more. But the other part of her was hurt and angry. And scared.

Maybe their relationship wasn't as strong as Maya thought.

Chapter Eight

Standing at the edge of the grove of trees where the national forest land officially started, the man observed the party starting in front of him. There were good festivities. Singing. Dancing. A bonfire. But what bothered him was how these parties had become out of control. No respect for the forest or the wilderness. No respect for each other. And no respect for their own bodies.

It was disgusting.

He'd heard about the parties through the grapevine. Mostly it was college kids, but some of the ski resort workers also participated. He was tired of how the environment was being treated. Climate change was happening and no one cared. But he was watching his beloved forests change with less snowfall, drier summers, pine beetle kill, forest fires, the list went on and on. Water supplies were dwindling and it all started here. The next generation polluting the forest to have fun.

Screw them. Someone had to teach them a lesson. He was the perfect guy for the job.

And parties like this provided great opportunities for his passion.

He hated how people not only trashed the environment, but themselves as well. He had a job to do and it was important. Who would pay for their sins tonight? Who would do the double whammy of hurting themselves and killing nature? Parties like this contributed to trash on the ground the next day and people who were just like his father—they thought they could do anything.

He'd become angry after the last party. The victim had cried and pleaded with him, and for a moment, he'd thought about letting him go. But then he'd killed the young man with his own poison—drugs. A good overdose didn't seem like a bad way to go and now there was one less person to pollute nature.

It felt good, releasing his anger.

After he'd disposed of the body, he'd ventured back to the scene of the crime where the party had taken place and cleaned up the trash. His lovely victim would rot and decompose in the woods, providing fertilizer for the trees and other vegetation, but these parties killed the forests with people trampling the ground until it became just dirt. Cups and bottles littered the whole area. Disgusting. Someone had to pay. Who would be next?

Observing the party, he could feel the rage building again. There was only one way to release it: find another person who would suffer for everyone's sins. No, killing one person at a time from the area wouldn't totally solve the problem, but if he picked the worst person out, he could at least feel like he was doing his part.

Sort of like the people who recycled. They always told themselves that they were saving the environment. Made themselves feel better sorting through plastics, paper and cans. But at the end of the day, they were all hypocrites. They still drove their fancy gas-guzzling cars and drank their bottled water. Unlike them, he was not a hypocrite. He was making a difference. Changing the world. And he loved the power it gave him.

Even more ironic was how nobody ever looked at him. They all seemed to look through him or past him. No one gave him the time of day. No one cared or noticed that every time he showed up to a party, one of their friends went missing. He sauntered around taking in all the different faces, watching some people make out, but they weren't who he was hunting.

He fingered the needle and syringe in his pocket. He'd had the good luck of connecting with a local dealer who had something new. Something special. Potent and perfect for what he wanted. He wanted to make someone endure the pain. He wanted to have the power of killing them and bringing them back to life.

The Gray Death he'd bought was perfect for that. Give someone the right dose and watch them start fading away, the light inside them dying. Give them some Narcan and they'd snap back. Sometimes it took several doses. Occasionally he didn't figure the dose out correctly and he'd kill someone quicker than he wanted. But most of the time he had the power of life and death and he loved that.

He continued to saunter around the edge of the trees that lined the open area where a bonfire was already raging in the firepit. Some people sat on rocks, holding out sticks with marshmallows. Others stood in groups chatting and drinking beer. He needed to find just the right person. Who would it be?

Then he spotted him. The man was over in the trees, off by himself. He was shooting up, and when he finished, he dropped the needle and syringe on the ground.

Poison to the forest. Poison to the animals that might come along later and be exposed.

The perfect victim.

He walked over and pretended to say hello. The man was already getting a little woozy from what he'd shot himself up with. He'd have to be careful he didn't OD him.

"You want some better stuff?" he asked.

The young man stared at him, eyes glazing over. "Yeah, man. What do you have?"

"Hold out your arm, I'll show you."

The man complied. He took out the needle and syringe and administered a dose of Gray Death.

"Thanks," the young man said.

"You're welcome. You're very welcome."

He waited for the young man to start getting sleepy and then he put his arm around his shoulder, taking him down the short path toward his car. A few people in the beer-drinking groups glanced in their direction, but no one said anything. They were all so dumb and naive. Here he was kidnapping someone right under their nose and they didn't notice a thing. The snow crunched under his feet as they neared the parking area. Smoke filled the air from the bonfire, but the noise of the music and people chatting diminished as they approached his vehicle. There were no clouds and the stars dotted the sky. The moonlight shimmered off the snow, lighting a path to his car. A perfect night to hunt and how easy it had been.

Hunting was about power and the ability to manipulate. He had to admit, that was also what made this fun. He helped the young man into the back seat, checking his vital signs. He was okay, but would need to be monitored. It would be a shame if he died on the way back to his special spot. His lair, as he'd started calling it.

He'd done his good deed for the night. The forest would have one less person trashing it.

And he would get to have some fun.

Chapter Nine

The next morning, Maya sat in the sunroom, gripping her mug of coffee and watching Juniper out in the yard. In the past, Juniper had been known to dig holes and destroy trees by jumping up and hanging on branches until they broke off. At least with the winter weather, she went out, took care of business, rolled around in the snow for a couple minutes and then wanted to come back in. The Malinois's destruction probably wouldn't start until the snow was gone and the weather warmed up.

As she watched Juniper, thoughts of the previous night played through her head. She hadn't slept well and finally got up early. She was on her third cup of coffee and would need to pack soon to leave for Antler Valley. She hadn't been this relieved to leave town in a long time. She also realized she hadn't been gone overnight since she returned home from the military. Maybe some of what she was feeling was restlessness.

Juniper rushed up to the door, smudging it with her nose, staring at Maya and demanding to be let in. Maya kind of enjoyed the nose art that Juniper created on the glass. It was somehow endearing.

She opened the door, and as Juniper came in from

outside, Josh walked into the room. Juniper saw him and gave him a dirty look. Usually she liked going and greeting Josh, but this morning, Juniper walked past him, grabbed her worn out teddy bear and went over to her bed where she lay down and turned her back to both of them.

"What's her deal?" Josh asked.

"I think she's upset that some blonde chick tried to make out with you last night."

"Seriously? That might be why you're upset. But would Juniper be mad about that?"

"She feeds off me. We're partners. So yeah, that might be what's bugging her," Maya said, crossing her arms. "I made coffee. Should still be hot."

"Thanks." Josh went to the cabinet and pulled down a mug, pouring in some coffee. "I know you're upset and I understand why. You want to talk about it?"

Maya shrugged and stared into her mug as if the coffee were tea leaves that would tell her the future. "Why didn't you tell me about Amber?"

"I don't know. I guess I didn't think it was important."

"That's such a guy thing to say."

"Well, it's true. I broke it off with her after I lost my partner and started having my addiction issues."

Maya nodded. Josh had told her about the night his partner was shot and how it sent him into a downward spiral of drinking and using drugs. He'd been sober longer than she had and had moved out to Colorado for a fresh start. Pops was desperate for deputies in their small town. Not many people wanted to move up to the remote mountain town and work the long shifts that came with a small department, but he was willing to because it was his only opportunity if he still wanted to be in law enforcement. Pops had served with Josh's grandfather in the military. When Josh's grandfather asked for a favor, giving Josh a job, Pops gave him his second and only chance. If Josh screwed up here, his career would be over.

"I just need time to process this. That's all. It didn't help that you didn't tell your family we're living together," Maya said, after a moment of silence.

"I know. I'm sorry. They know now and I meant every word I told them. I love *you*, Maya. There's no one else for me. I will make sure my family knows and understands that. I'm sure my mother was hoping I would see Amber and want to move back home. This is why my family is a trigger. Chicago is a trigger, and I don't want to be anywhere you aren't. I want to be here with you."

She took another sip of coffee and then set her mug down on the counter. "I want to believe all that. I really do. But right now, I need to get ready to go. Let's continue this conversation when I get home."

"Okay," Josh answered.

Maya could see the hurt on his face, but she needed space right now. This was how she was—a lone wolf. She'd liked having her space at her cabin in the woods. She really missed it right now. It would be summertime before rebuilding could be done, but she wanted nothing more than to escape. Going to Antler Valley with Juniper would do just that.

Now would be a good time to tell Josh about the letter, but Maya didn't want to start another argument. She would tell him when she returned home. Who knew how long it would take to match the DNA anyway. Lucas had said he'd try to put a rush on it, but finding out if Eric was her father wouldn't really help the investigation in any way.

Unless he contacted her, which he hadn't. Only Abigail had reached out and Maya didn't know why. She'd fill Josh in when she actually had some results and not just a letter from an inmate in federal prison.

Maya headed to their bedroom to pack. As she was pulling out extra uniforms, there was a knock at the door. *Crap, I hope that's not his family coming for breakfast. I better pack quickly.*

Maya had just pulled out her suitcase when she heard Pops greeting Josh. She stopped what she was doing and went back to the kitchen to say hi. Juniper had decided to leave her dog bed and also greet Pops. Pops rubbed her head and then asked her to go lie back down. Juniper complied, but made sure she took her time walking back over to her spot. She turned her back on everyone again.

"What's up with her?" Pops asked.

"Long story," Maya said. "Let's just say she's feeling emotional right now."

"Oh. All right." Pops looked back and forth between her and Josh. Maya could feel his scrutiny. He'd been in law enforcement long enough to know when there was tension. "Everything okay with you two?"

"Yeah," Maya said. "Texted you earlier about heading out to Antler Valley."

"That's why I'm here," Pops said. "Do you usually text at five in the morning?"

"Sorry, wasn't thinking about that. I'd been up for a while. Thinking about this case and all," Maya added, trying to deflect from why she'd really been awake.

Josh stayed quiet and Maya watched Pops stare at him. Pops finally spoke up. "Heard from your father.

Sounds like your whole family is in town. I look forward to meeting them. I'm glad your father was willing to come help."

"He's a great attorney," Josh said. "Ruthless."

"So I've heard. And it's nice he's worked both as a prosecutor and defense attorney. He knows what to expect from each side." Pops put his hands in his pockets. "I just came over to wish you well in Antler Valley, Maya, and also to give you a heads-up."

"About what?" Maya asked.

"I'm friends with the chief of police over there. Good guy. I've had the privilege of getting to know him at some of the law enforcement conferences. He called me not too long ago. His daughter Aurora—or I guess she goes by Rory—has wanted nothing more than to follow in her father's footsteps and become a police officer. She did just that, graduated from the academy and landed a job with the sheriff's office. But what she's telling her father is that there's a lot of issues, mainly with the sheriff, Logan Jackson. She says he's cocky and it's bordered on harassment, especially with the female deputies. She's putting in for jobs elsewhere, including here. Her father wanted to put in a good word for her and was hoping I'd consider hiring her so she could get out of that area. I told him to send her application over.

"Anyway, I guess I just wanted to warn you. The chief isn't the only one who's mentioned issues there with the sheriff. Stay alert and keep Juniper by your side as much as you can. You're a hell of a shot too, so keep your gun close."

"You think he's that bad?" Maya asked. "I mean, it's one thing to stay alert and have someone harass you.

It's another to think about having your gun with you and shooting someone."

"I guess I could be exaggerating, but I felt better telling you this. Just listen to your gut instincts and Juniper. She can read people better than any of us."

At the mention of her name, Juniper lifted her head and gave a quiet woof. She stood and turned around, lying back down to face everyone.

"Okay, Pops. I'll be careful and I'll keep Juniper close. Thanks for the warning. I know you wouldn't say anything without a good reason."

"Thank you," Pops said. "It'll make me feel better. Well, I best get on my way. I need to meet Josh's father soon and start preparing for the investigation."

"I'm so sorry I won't be here to support you," Maya said.

"Don't worry about it. Josh will keep you posted and it'll be fine. I'll let you two finish your coffee and talk about whatever you need to talk about before you leave. Love you, Maya Bear. Josh."

Maya shook her head. Pops always knew how to get to the point when he needed to. "Love you too, Pops."

Pops headed out and she shut the door behind him. "I need to go pack," she said. "But I do want to talk more. Maybe just not now."

"That's fine," Josh answered. "Just know that I don't know what I'd do without you."

Maya didn't know how to answer. The truth was, she couldn't imagine life without Josh.

And that scared her.

Josh watched Maya walk down the hallway to go back to packing. He found his cup of coffee and headed out to the sunroom. He figured he'd give her some space to get ready to go.

The sun illuminated the snowy peaks, making them various shades of pink. He loved the mountains and living in Colorado. He loved Maya and Juniper. His house would feel empty without them. Coming here to start over had been the right move.

And right now, he was totally screwing all that up.

He could blame his family, but after attending AA and NA to stay clean, he had to admit his mistakes. Not telling Maya about Amber was a big one. Maya had trusted him with information about her past serious relationship. He should have been honest with her about his past with Amber.

Why hadn't he confided in Maya about Amber? Maybe it was because that was a time in his life when he had many regrets. He wanted his past to go away, but he knew that never happened. He should know better. As a law enforcement officer, he dealt with people whose pasts caught up with them all the time. He had to somehow make this right.

While he would miss Maya and Juniper, maybe it was a good time for them to leave. That way he could sit his family down and have a serious talk with them. Lay the ground rules, including not bringing ex-girlfriends to his house.

Amber. He needed to deal with her too.

He could tell by the way she'd kissed him that she was hoping there was still a flame. Josh took another sip of coffee. He'd hoped Maya hadn't noticed that the kiss from Amber had lingered too long, but she was right—that was a guy thing to think and say. Of course

Maya would notice. She was intuitive and that was one of the many things he loved about her.

He had to make things right. And then hope Maya would forgive him.

Chapter Ten

Maya finished packing for Juniper and herself, thinking about what Josh had told her. As she carried her bags to her patrol vehicle, she realized she would miss him. She'd never felt this way and was glad to have time alone to sort through her feelings. She didn't want to depend on anyone. Every time she had depended on someone, something had happened to them. Dealing with her PTSD and her addiction had been at the top of her priority list, not falling in love. And yet, it had happened.

Maya loaded up Juniper and Josh came out to say goodbye. He came over to Maya and gave her a tender kiss.

"I love you," Josh said.

"I love you too."

"We'll figure this out. Together. Call me when you get a chance. I'm sure when you get there, you'll have to get to work, but let me know how you're doing."

"I will," Maya promised.

She climbed into her vehicle and headed to her office, still thinking about where this relationship was headed. How serious were they? Had she been impulsive moving in with him? Maybe she should back off and take their relationship down a notch.

Maya made a quick stop into her office to grab a few things, including maps of the forest in the Antler Valley area; she hadn't spent a ton of time on that side of the forest. As she came back out of her office, she saw Kay waiting by her vehicle. Maya shut and locked the office door behind her and made sure the *Closed Until Further Notice* sign was on display. Then she approached Kay.

"Hi," Maya said. "How are you doing today?"

Kay turned toward her and Maya could see her eyes were red and puffy from crying.

"Not great," Kay said.

"Did you get news on your son?" Maya asked.

"No. I was hoping you might have heard something. I heard about the bodies that were found near Antler Valley. Do you know who they are yet?"

Maya took a deep breath. "No, I'm so sorry. I'm headed over there to help with the case. I was also going to look into your son's case more. So far, I haven't been able to get answers. I can keep you updated when the remains are identified."

"I feel like one of them is him. You know? Mother's intuition or some crazy thing like that. Do you have kids?"

"No, I don't, so I can only imagine your pain. I lost my mother, though, when I was young, and my grandmother not too long ago. I know that the pain and grief run deep and can hit you when you least expect it. But you don't know yet that your son is one of the deceased. I promise I'll keep you posted."

Maya felt guilty keeping any hope alive for Kay. Even if her son wasn't one of the victims, if he was lost in the forest, then there was a good chance he wasn't coming back. The mountains had a way of keeping and revealing their secrets when they wanted, including the missing. And the missing were rarely found alive.

"If you have kids one day, I hope you never have to go through this. I think the not knowing is the hardest part."

Maya didn't know what possessed her—she wasn't the type of person to hug someone, but she did anyway. Then she stepped back. "I promise I'll keep you posted."

"I'm driving over there too," Kay said. "I'm not leaving until I know what happened to Avery."

"Okay, I'll see you there. Drive safe and you have my phone number if you need anything," Maya said.

"Thank you," Kay said.

"For what?"

"For caring."

Maya nodded, again uncertain how to answer. She had shoved down and run away from her emotions for so long, it seemed strange that someone would see her as caring. But it felt good to help someone. She just hoped she didn't have to be the one to tell Kay if her son was one of the victims.

Two hours later, Maya drove into Antler Valley. She was struck by how the town had grown and changed as the ski resort expanded. When she was a little girl, she'd come here with Nana and Pops. At that time, Antler Valley had been a small Western town like Pinecone Junction. Then people with money started buying up the ranches and developing the ski slopes. Now Antler Valley was trying to compete with areas like Vail, Steamboat Springs and even Aspen. *But with change comes growing pains, and this town seems like it's experiencing some of those.*

Maya passed some of the turnoffs to the ski resorts. The town had worked hard to make the slopes a training area for Olympic athletes. Not just for downhill skiers, but also for ski jumping and even bobsledding. The track for the bobsleds stood out against the mountain, and down the road was the training center with the looming ski jumps nearby.

"You're all nuts to jump off of that," she muttered to herself. She certainly wasn't brave enough to give it a try.

Maya decided to find the Saddle Rock Falls Inn, named for the famous waterfalls that brought in ice climbers in the winter from all over the world. The ice-climbing area was just down the road from the inn. She wanted to visit the ice falls while she was there. But first, she decided to check in at the motel before she headed to the sheriff's office. She knew that with Juniper she wouldn't be staying at the Hilton or the Ritz. Okay, it wasn't fair to blame Juniper. There was also the government budget thing.

She put the motel into her GPS and found it on the other side of town. The inn looked like it had seen better days, with an outdated building where the rooms were side by side, but at least everything was painted and kept as neat and tidy as it could be with snow covering everything. Maya didn't care as long as it was clean and had a comfortable bed.

Who was she kidding? After being in Afghanistan, anything in the United States was great. Maybe she was getting picky and going soft being stateside and back in civilian life. She checked in at the front desk, threw her belongings into the room and then found her way to the sheriff's office.

Parking, she took a deep breath. Time to see what this sheriff was really like. She let Juniper stick her head through the compartment and gave her some love, getting a slurp in return. Juniper also seemed happy to get out of town, but she wasn't going to be thrilled at being left behind in the vehicle.

"Sorry, girly," Maya said, gently pushing Juniper's head back in and closing the door behind her. She made sure the climate control settings for Juniper's compartment were set correctly. "I'll try not to make you wait too long."

She heard a whine and grunt in return.

Maya stepped out of her vehicle as another Forest Service vehicle pulled up and parked next to her. She waited, figuring this was the criminal investigator, Ben Easton. She was glad that their old investigator had retired. He and Maya hadn't seen eye to eye when it came to the case involving her friend and Juniper's first handler. The old investigator thought she was involved along with Doug in taking bribes to look the other way for a drug-trafficking operation in the forest.

Easton stepped out of his vehicle and came over to say hello. He was a little taller than Maya, with sharp eyes that took in his surroundings. He had a strong presence and reminded her of a drill sergeant she'd had in the military. She found herself standing a little taller and ready to snap a salute. Juniper peered out her window and decided that Easton was too close to the vehicle. She started barking and snarling.

Maya tried not to laugh as Easton jumped. It wasn't good to laugh at your boss's boss. She suppressed her grin and instead held out her hand and said, "I'm Officer Thompson and sorry about Juniper scaring you. She tends to be protective of the vehicle."

"Nice to meet you, Thompson. I'm Ben Easton and I have no problem with your K-9 protecting one of our vehicles. I worked K-9s with a police department before I started working for the Forest Service. I've heard your dog is top-notch."

Easton shook Maya's hand and his grip was firm. She liked that. Pops had always taught her to have a strong handshake.

"She's pretty amazing, thank you. And I'm looking forward to working with you," Maya said.

"The feeling's mutual. Your reputation precedes you."

"Hopefully it's not too bad."

"No, and I've heard you're passionate about your job. That's good. Let's go inside and meet the sheriff. I'd like to get filled in on the case and then get out to the actual crime scene."

"Works for me, sir," Maya said, reminding herself to thank Todd for calling her passionate about her job and not headstrong or impulsive.

"That's right, you were a Marine."

"Yes, sir, although, no offense, I still am a Marine."

"I tend to forget, once a Marine, always a Marine."

"Yes, sir. Something like that," Maya said.

"Well, this isn't the Marines. Just call me Easton or Ben or even just say 'hey you.' No need to call me sir."

"Yes…uh, got it, Ben."

"Perfect. Let's get inside."

Ben held the door open for Maya and she went in ahead of him. She could still hear Juniper barking in the vehicle. She hoped that Juniper was needed to investigate; otherwise the hotel room might not survive.

They headed to the front desk and checked in with the deputy there, who told them Sheriff Jackson was already at the crime scene. The deputy called another officer down to meet with Maya and Ben.

As they were waiting, Maya decided to bring up Avery Anderson's case with Ben. She filled him in. "Do you happen to know anything about this case or what happened?"

"No, haven't heard about it, but maybe we can convince Sheriff Jackson to share his information. But that'll have to come later."

"I know," Maya said. "I can look into it after hours too. I just feel for his mother. She's come to my office twice now looking for answers."

"Did you tell her that county sheriff runs the search and rescue operations?"

"I did, but no one in the sheriff's office is responding to her."

"We'll see if we can find out more," Ben said.

"Thanks," Maya said. "I appreciate it."

She took in her surroundings. Unlike the Western River Sheriff's Office in Pinecone Junction, this sheriff's office showed that there was money in the community. It was a new building with high ceilings and two stories. There were large prints of mountain paintings and photographs from famous Colorado photographers. The feeling was different from home, but Maya realized she liked the simple home feel better.

She glanced at her watch, wondering if the sheriff would leave them sitting there instead of including them in the investigation. She pulled out her phone and sent Josh a quick text that she had arrived and missed him, then checked her email and voice mails on the off chance that Lucas had called or messaged her with results, although she knew better than to think a DNA test would be back this soon. It would probably take a few days.

Maya put her phone back in her pocket, focusing on work. A deputy finally came through some doors that led back to a cubicle area. He walked over to them and held out his hand. "Sorry for the wait. I'm Deputy Porter Glen. It's nice to meet you both."

Maya and Ben shook his hand. After introductions, Deputy Glen said, "I'm supposed to have you two follow me out to the crime scene. The sheriff is already there. He wanted to get an early start."

"Thank you," Ben said. "And quick question for you, Deputy Glen."

"Yes?"

"Officer Thompson has been trying to get some information and follow up with a missing persons case here in Antler Valley. We'd like to learn more about the case. How do we make that happen? We're just trying to find out more details."

Maya shot a grateful look toward Ben. She liked him already.

"That would be up to the sheriff," Deputy Glen answered. "And I'll tell you both a little secret right now, he doesn't like sharing information with anyone. He tends to keep things close."

"What about your city police department? He doesn't share things with them?" Ben asked.

"No, very little. He believes we have county jurisdiction and therefore, we are in charge. If we need information, we'll get it, but we don't share it. Don't shoot the messenger. You can always ask him."

Maya found this odd. Most agencies tried to share

information. Criminals didn't stick to one jurisdiction. A crime in the forest could have started at someone's house in the city. They all needed to work together. She thought about Pops's warning and took note that Sheriff Jackson was already proving everyone right—he seemed like an arrogant pain in the butt.

"Okay, good to know," Ben said. "Let's get going to the crime scene. Since that's on Forest Service land, the good sheriff is going to have to share this one with us."

"Right," Deputy Glen said, glancing back and forth between Maya and Ben.

They headed outside to their vehicles and Juniper was still barking and carrying on.

"What kind of dog?" Deputy Glen asked Maya.

"A Malinois. Two years old and full of energy."

"I love Mals. I have extensive experience as a K-9 backup officer. If you need to work her and need someone to cover you, let me know. I'd be happy to do it. It would be fun to work with a dog-handler team again."

"I'll keep that in mind, thanks," Maya said. She climbed into her vehicle and started it up, waiting to follow the others. She didn't usually like working with a backup officer she hadn't trained with, but in this case, she might have to if Juniper was needed.

Back home, Josh was her backup officer. This made her miss him even more. Although missing him didn't mean she wasn't still mad at him.

Chapter Eleven

Maya followed Deputy Porter to the parking area closest to the crime scene. Luckily, even though the location was in the backcountry, it wasn't too far from the trailhead parking. That made sense, though, assuming these were homicides and not something strange like a mass suicide. Dragging a dead body took strength and effort. The killer wouldn't want to or even be able to go very far with someone who was deceased.

Unless they made their victims walk to their final resting place.

Maya parked and got out of her vehicle. She let Juniper out for a quick break and to stretch her legs and then put her back in her compartment. She rubbed and scratched around Juniper's ears.

"I promise if you can help in some way, I'll come get you," Maya said.

Juniper gave her a half-hearted lick of the face. Maya closed the door and headed in the direction that Ben, Deputy Glen and other law enforcement personnel were headed. The crime scene should only be a short hike away.

She put on her sunglasses to block the light reflecting off the snow and then her gloves and hat. A mild breeze blew, and for January, the temperatures weren't too bad, but she could still see her breath. She made the trek through the snow to where the yellow crime scene tape billowed in the wind. She spotted Ben and headed over in his direction.

She took in the scene around her. The terrain didn't have too much slope until you arrived where the avalanche had deposited a large snow slide filled with debris. This avalanche had been large and fast—Maya had heard that they could go sixty to eighty miles per hour. The path of this particular slide had taken out trees and even dislodged large boulders to the point that once the snow melted, the entire landscape in this area would look barren and different.

"It's amazing that those snowboarders survived this," Maya said to Ben.

"It really is. Let's go find the sheriff and introduce ourselves."

Maya followed Ben over to where a short, stocky man stood talking to some crime scene techs and investigators. He had a high and tight buzz cut like she hadn't seen since she left the Marines. He chomped viciously on a piece of gum and was bellowing directions, but not listening. The deputies and crime scene techs seemed used to his demeanor as they nodded in agreement but didn't speak back. Ben waited for the techs to leave and then approached the sheriff.

"Sheriff Logan Jackson?" Ben asked, holding out his hand. "Forest Service Criminal Investigator Ben Easton and Officer Maya Thompson. We're here to help assist with the investigation."

Sheriff Jackson looked them up and down, his face displaying a hint of displeasure. "Yeah, I heard you were coming," he said, shrugging. "You can do your thing, whatever that is. Just stay out of our way."

Looks like what Pops warned me about was correct. Maya decided she'd let Ben handle it. She might end up saying something she regretted and Ben far outranked her.

"Well, we'll do what we do, but keep in mind, these bodies may have been found in your county, but they're on federal Forest Service land. We will be involved and it would be easier if we could all get along," Ben answered.

"We'll all get along if you let me do my job," the sheriff said.

"We're only here to assist," Ben said.

"Good. Just remember that and don't overstep your bounds."

Ben raised an eyebrow. Maya had to look away so that she kept her mouth shut. To say this guy wasn't a team player would be an understatement. Most agencies worked well together and welcomed the help of others since they were often short-staffed. But there was always someone who didn't play well with others. She peered off at the white snow-covered peaks in the distance and took a deep breath.

"We need you to fill us in more on the crime scene," Ben said.

The sheriff examined a piece of paper he was holding as if it was the most important thing on the planet. Ben crossed his arms and waited. Maya put her hands on her duty belt. She'd learned to keep her hands free so placing them where she did was her way of crossing her arms too. When the sheriff finally realized that they weren't leaving, he let out a deep sigh.

"Fine. Don't know much yet. We have the victim the

idiot snowboarders found, but between the avalanche and rescue workers coming to get those dumbass kids, the crime scene is pretty much destroyed. Not much evidence. The rescue workers happened to spot what they thought were more remains. They were correct. So right now, we've got three bodies and no evidence. We may not be able to find any evidence until all this damn snow melts, and by then, anything worthwhile will be destroyed. So that's where we're at. Got it?"

Ben nodded. "Thank you. I appreciate the update."

Maya had stayed quiet, but she had an idea. It was a long shot, but this was why she had Juniper. "What if I get my K-9 and see if she can find any evidence? She may also find some more remains. Sometimes patrol dogs find human remains even though they're not trained to. I've heard of that happening."

"What? Do you have a freaking wonder dog or something? Don't you think the evidence would have lost the scent by now?" the sheriff said.

"Like I said, it's a long shot, but I also think Juniper *is* a wonder dog. If any dog can do it, it's her. If we were working in town, the scent off of evidence would probably disappear in a couple days, but out here in the wilderness the odor might hang around for about a month. Plus, avalanches tear up the ground underneath them. Who knows what has now been exposed under the snow? You'd be better off getting an HRD dog here to work if you believe there are more victims, but I can try this with my dog first."

"HRD?" the sheriff asked.

Maya was surprised he didn't know the acronym. "Human remains detection dog, or cadaver dog."

"I might know of one that could come. Why don't

you try your wonder dog first and if she can't find anything, I can call the guy I know."

"Works for me," she said. "I'll go get Juniper now."

Maya headed back toward her vehicle and was surprised to find Ben following her.

"Good job, Thompson," he said. "I'm going to find our avalanche expert while you get Juniper. I don't want to track back into an area that triggers another slide."

"Good idea. And if the snow gets too deep, I may have to stop tracking anyway."

"All right. Meet you back at the crime scene."

Chapter Twelve

Juniper tried to be patient while Maya put all her gear on her, though she made it clear she didn't love her snow booties. Every time those were put on, Juniper would pick up her paws and shake them, even nibbling at the boots, but eventually she got used to them. She didn't seem to mind the Doggles, though. Maya swore that Juniper thought she looked cool when she had them on.

After snapping on the long leash, the pair headed back to the crime scene. While they were trudging through the snow, Maya let the leather tracking lead out and Juniper ran around, sniffing here and there and then bounding back onto the trail. Her dog's joy always made her smile. There was nothing better than a four-legged partner.

As they approached the crime scene, she called Juniper back to walk by her side on a shorter leash. Juniper complied and gave her gloves a couple licks. All seemed to be forgiven for making Juniper stay in the vehicle for as long as she had.

"What do you need for your dog to do its job?" the sheriff asked gruffly.

"Nothing. Right now, I'm going to hike up and see if I can find where the avalanche started. I'll work from there down. If you have another deputy available to help mark evidence if we do find something, that would be great."

"Hey, Deputy Glen. Get over here," the sheriff belted out.

Juniper, not liking his tone, changed her body language to a defensive stance and locked eyes with the sheriff. As much as Maya wouldn't mind seeing her dog hanging off the sheriff's arm, she settled Juniper and took her a little distance away before Juniper decided to turn into a Maligator.

As Maya was debating where to best start her hike up the avalanche slide, Ben and Deputy Glen came over. She asked Juniper to sit by her side and wait. Juniper's obedience was improving and she made Maya proud by doing what was asked.

"I talked to the avalanche expert and she said where the slope becomes steep, the snow is very unstable. We've had some high winds and there's some snow slabs that are waiting to let loose. Be careful going near the start of the slide, but I know you need to start there so that you're not backtracking with Juniper," Ben said.

"Okay," Maya said. "That gives us a fairly good area to search. Plus, I think if we go up much in elevation past the trigger point of the slide, the snow will get too deep for Juniper. The wind seems to have cleared the snow away from much of this area. This is a long shot, but we might as well try it."

"I agree," said Ben.

"I'll come with you and mark evidence. I know where to stay so I don't interfere with your dog's tracking," Deputy Glen said, adding, "She's a beauty, by the way."

"Thanks," Maya said proudly. "Her name's Juniper. If you're going to back us up, you better know that."

"Good point," Deputy Glen said.

"Okay, let's go," she said.

Juniper sprang to her feet and danced around, ready to work.

"All right, girly," Maya said. "Let's go see what you can find."

The trio hiked up the avalanche path. Maya stopped every so often, making sure that they were still in stable snow. They came close to where the slide started and she could see some areas that could be triggered if they weren't careful.

"Let's start here and see what Juniper does. Seek," Maya said. "Let's go find 'em."

She cast Juniper out and directed her to different locations. Usually when Maya started a track, she had an idea of where to send Juniper to try to find the scent. If they were tracking a suspect, then she could start with a vehicle or that last known location, but in this case, they were literally finding a needle in a haystack. Or snow slide, in this case. She didn't know if the remains started in this area or further down, but she let Juniper work the slope.

Maya continued to direct Juniper around, watching her body language to see if she came into odor. Juniper worked hard and cleared several spots without picking up a scent. Stopping Juniper for a minute, Maya praised her dog and then took in their surroundings. They had worked downhill and were almost back to their starting point. The sheriff stared in their direction, a smug look on his face. Maya was certain he was happy they weren't finding anything yet.

She ignored the sheriff and went back to analyzing the path of the avalanche and where the remains were

located. She decided to go around the crime scene tape
and try tracking on the other side. There was a small
gulley in the direction that part of the slide had gone
through. It could be a good spot for the killer to have
dumped their victims.

"Let's try the other side," Maya said to Deputy Glen
as she started around the crime scene tape. He didn't
say anything, but followed her and Juniper.

After they made the trek around to the other side
and back uphill to where the slide started in the gulley,
Maya cast Juniper out, telling her to go find 'em. She
still wasn't certain that Juniper would track the human
scent since she was used to sniffing a living person, or
if any evidence would have a fresh enough scent, but
she kept telling herself it was worth a try.

Juniper put her nose to the ground and started sweep-
ing back and forth. Maya noticed a slight change in
the tension of her body and her tail started to go up
a little higher. She tried not to get too excited, but it
seemed like Juniper was onto something and coming
into odor. Hopefully that something was to do with the
crime scene.

Maya continued to feed Juniper leash, but she didn't
say a whole lot, letting the dog work and process the
odor on her own. Juniper started working a scent cone
back and forth and suddenly, her body tensed. Her
breathing and sniffing changed. She was in odor.

"Atta girl," Maya muttered under her breath, not
wanting to distract her dog.

Deputy Glen sensed the change in Juniper too and
Maya was impressed as he made sure he stayed behind
her and out of the way of Juniper. Sucking in air, Juniper's sniffing seemed to be all Maya could hear. She

followed her dog as she bounded downhill through the gulley.

Maya was about ready to pull her up because they were starting to get into deep snow when Juniper stopped, turned back, went up the side of the gulley, and then sat near a large divot in the ground where a boulder had been.

Maya realized that as the avalanche slid down, some of the trees and debris had caught the boulder and rolled it. She could see another victim down in the divot. It appeared that the body had been buried under the boulder. Her only guess as to why someone would go to that trouble was that maybe they were trying to keep animals from scavenging the bodies. It seemed to have worked as the remains appeared intact.

"I think we just found one of the killer's dumping spots," she said to Deputy Glen.

"I'll get crime scene tape and notify the team," he answered.

Maya praised Juniper and rewarded her for a job well done by playing with the Kong away from the crime scene. She closed her eyes for a second and tried to rid the sight from her mind. Flashes of other remains that she'd seen in Afghanistan flooded back.

They'd been out on patrol and had found a mass grave. Maya could still remember what it'd been like. She didn't get sick easily, but that day she'd wanted to go throw up, though she managed to hold it together.

Maya took a deep breath and calmed herself, bringing herself back to the moment. In Afghanistan there'd been nothing they could do, but here, at home, she could bring a killer to justice.

Chapter Thirteen

He observed the action at the crime scene, fascinated but also frustrated. No one was supposed to find them. No one was supposed to know where they were. Except him. And yet the mountains had exposed his secret. His favorite hideaway.

Every now and then when he visited to see his trophies, he could tell an animal had managed to scavenge one, but he liked having the final power. He liked knowing that even in death his victims weren't at peace. He had the final say. Something he'd never had throughout his life with his father.

His father. What a joke. And his first kill.

He'd enjoyed every moment of it. Of finally being the one in charge. The one to say if someone lived or died. He'd never been able to re-create the feeling of power he'd had with his father. But he'd come close with his later victims.

Now he wouldn't be able to visit them anymore. That was okay. He could start fresh. Maybe it was time to move again. He liked doing that. Seeing different resort towns. Going out for a night on the town. Having a drink—only one, though, he wasn't like the victims who couldn't control themselves. No, he had control.

He could blend in anywhere and no one gave him a second thought.

Until he captured them and had his fun. Then all of a sudden, they were begging and pleading.

Yes, he had the power and he enjoyed every minute of it. Like all predators, he had evolved.

He watched the officer work her dog. He controlled his emotions as he watched the dog track back to where some more of his trophies—his lovelies, as he sometimes thought of them—still were. The dog sat and the officer rewarded the dog.

The lady officer was intriguing. Her dark red hair was pulled back in a tight bun and she appeared fit and strong. What would it be like to be with someone like her? Not to kill, but to actually be with. Most women didn't give him a second glance. He was average in every way—height, weight, looks. That's how he could be here now, watching everything without anyone noticing.

Maybe he should get to know her better. Or maybe that would be a mistake. He hadn't made a mistake yet over the past couple years. Sure, every now and then, some of his victims were discovered, but many of them were now cold cases. Never solved. The cops were all too dumb.

He had the upper hand here in Antler Valley due to a wild card. He'd taken on a partner, something he'd never done before. But this special someone wanted to learn the tricks of the trade and he was only too eager to share. In return, he had the opportunity to steer this investigation the way he wanted it to go.

The sheriff would receive a nice little package tomorrow.

* * *

As Maya praised Juniper, she could observe Deputy
Glen speaking with the sheriff, pointing in their direction. The sheriff seemed upset and pulled out another
piece of gum, putting it in and chewing hard.

She understood why he'd be upset at this crime scene.
Everything about it was unusual. What she didn't understand was why the sheriff didn't want help. A case
this big was going to take a lot of manpower. Maya not
only had Juniper, but she could help interview families,
gather evidence and generally serve as boots on the
ground. Most agencies would welcome that assistance.

There was something off about the sheriff.

Maya managed to convince Juniper that playtime was
over and that she needed to give up her Kong. Juniper
gazed at her, her golden eyes conveying her hope that
Maya would change her mind, but then realizing that
wasn't going to happen, she reluctantly spit out the toy.

Maya put the Kong away in her BDU pocket. As she
did that, she noticed Juniper air scenting again, taking
a few steps back toward the body.

"You already found it, girl. You don't need to do
that again."

Juniper turned away from Maya and pulled at her
leash. She decided to follow her dog and see where she
went. She needed to be careful about the crime scene,
but Juniper was in odor and Maya wanted to see what
she might be smelling.

Nose up in the air, Juniper went back over by the
body, but this time she went around the remains and
closer to the middle of the hole left of the boulder. She
sat and stared down in the area. Maya peered over and
saw an old jacket.

Juniper continued to stare.

Sitting and staring were Juniper's alert for narcotics.

Maya saw Deputy Glen coming back and she shouted, "Can you get a crime scene tech over here?"

The deputy gave her a thumbs-up and yelled at one of the techs to come with him. When they both came over, she filled them in on Juniper's alert. The tech put on gloves and went down to the jacket, marked it, photographed it and then started going through the pockets. There was a side pocket with a zipper and the tech opened it, pulling out a baggie with gray ashen powder.

"Be careful," Maya said, pulling Juniper back so she didn't get close to the powder. "That looks like something I just found during a recent arrest called Gray Death. It not only has fentanyl, it has carfentanil and some other synthetic opioids."

The tech carefully bagged and sealed the product. The coroner, Ben and Sheriff Jackson came over and joined them.

"What did you find?" the sheriff asked.

"I believe it could be Gray Death," Maya answered. "I arrested a man yesterday who had some. It's new to this area, or at least I've never seen it. I'm wondering if we should call the DEA and see if they're investigating anything like this?"

"I'm not having the damn Drug Enforcement Agency come in here and take over this investigation," said the sheriff. "Or any other alphabet soup agency."

Maya felt her face flush and knew it was turning red. Juniper, sensing her change in emotion, stepped in front of her, ready to help protect her handler. Maya was getting ready to snap a comment back, but caught Ben out of the corner of her eye. He shook his head no.

He was right—she needed to leave this alone right now. Sheriff Jackson was the type of person who would thrive on a fight and use it against her. She took a deep breath and worked to stay calm.

The coroner, who had stayed quiet, broke the silence. "I'll run tox screens on all the victims. Maybe these are all drug overdoses."

"Could be," Maya said, thinking of a group suicide again. "Except someone took the time to stash the bodies under a large boulder. They literally dug out a spot to shove the bodies back under there, making them hard for predators to get at. That's not an easy task, especially in the mountains. I think we're looking at something bigger than a bunch of ODs."

"I agree," Ben said, turning to the coroner. "When do you think you'll have COD?"

"Once I get the remains back to my lab, I should be able to work the rest of the night. I'll look for signs of homicide versus overdose and give you manner of death by tomorrow. I'll see if I can also find cause of death."

"Do you think you'll be able to identify them pretty fast?" Maya asked, thinking about Kay. Could Avery be one of these bodies?

"Depends. If there's something that I can use to quickly identify someone, like dental records or a surgical metal plate with a serial number."

"That makes sense," Maya said. A chill came over her, as if someone was watching, and she shook it off. A cold breeze picked up. That's probably all it was.

"I'll suggest this one more time," she said to the sheriff. "If you have someone with your SAR team that has an HRD dog, I'd give them a call. I think there could be more bodies. Juniper can find the evidence and drugs, but an HRD dog would be able to at least check this area and let us know if there are more victims."

The sheriff stared back at her and Maya thought he might step in close and challenge her, but then his gaze dropped to Juniper. She knew that he was rethinking getting in her personal space with Juniper right there. He'd end up getting a ton of stitches from a Malinois tearing up his arm.

"I have someone I can call. He's been working with our SAR team. I'll do it now," he said.

Maya muttered a response about it being a good idea, shocked he had listened.

Chapter Fourteen

After arriving at their patrol vehicle, Maya loved on Juniper and then took off her gear. Content from having worked, she did a couple circles and then lay down and curled up into a pooch ball, tucking her nose under her tail. She'd sleep well while Maya helped secure the crime scene.

Her phone rang. Lucas. "Hey there."

"Good news, Tree Cop," Lucas said.

"What's that?"

"The lab said they have enough samples to run the DNA. I have a buddy who said he'd move it up as a priority. I think I'll have results in a couple days."

"That's great news," Maya said. "Thank you."

"You're welcome. I'll be in touch."

They hung up and Maya put her phone away. She was relieved that there was enough DNA to test. Maybe she'd get some answers that she'd waited her whole life to find out. A little bit of guilt hit her that she hadn't told Josh, but it still made sense to only mention it if Eric really was her father. If he knew, that would only make him worry and she didn't need that. She started making the trek back to the crime scene when she was stopped by the sound of Juniper barking. She turned around. Why had Juniper woken back up?

Returning to the parking area, Maya saw what was upsetting Juniper—a yellow Lab and his handler were headed in their direction. Juniper didn't like the competition of other working dogs. She always thought *she* should be the only dog to work and seeing a yellow Lab walk by was a serious violation in Juniper's mind.

The Lab had on his orange search and rescue vest and, like most Labs, appeared happy about everything. Maya went back to greet them and apologize for all the ruckus that Juniper was making.

"Hi there. I'm Officer Maya Thompson." Maya held out a hand and discovered the man had a strong grip with a pleasant smile as he shook her hand back. "Sorry that my dog is making so much noise. She doesn't like other dogs coming to help her out."

"No problem. Finn here doesn't mind. Oh, and I'm Tanner Drake. The sheriff gave us a call. Sounds like there's quite the commotion going on here."

"That's one way to put it," Maya said as they started their trek toward the crime scene. "Glad you could come on such short notice."

"I was just at home hanging out for the day catching up on my to-do list. It's no problem. Glad we can help." Tanner reached down and petted Finn on the head. Finn responded with a tail wag. Maya enjoyed Labs. Their demeanor was less intense and very different from a dog like Juniper's. A Lab was likely to lick you to death or decide to be a lap dog. Although they did tend to chew up things *and* eat them. At least Juniper had never ingested anything she'd chewed up.

Maya pointed out where the sheriff was standing and

they headed in that direction. Maya figured she could be of help by being Tanner's backup officer to mark any evidence they found and, assuming they found more remains, run crime scene tape.

"Hello, Sheriff Jackson," Tanner said, holding out his hand.

The sheriff ignored Tanner and he dropped his hand back down. Tanner didn't seem fazed by the sheriff's rudeness.

"Just so you know, I didn't want you here," the sheriff said. Maya was shocked that was how the sheriff greeted Tanner. Pops would be thrilled to have the help of someone like Tanner and his K-9. The more help on a case, the better, and usually those were the cases that were eventually closed. Did Sheriff Jackson not understand that he had more resources than the average department?

"Understood," Tanner said. "I can head back home too. I'm just a volunteer so doesn't make a difference to me either way."

"No. Let's see if your dog can find anything. I'm just letting you know that I didn't want you here, but everyone else seems to think it's a good idea. No pressure, but don't mess up. You can go with her." The sheriff nodded toward Maya. "She knows the crime scene area and where you can and can't go."

"Sounds good. We'll do our best," Tanner said, adding, "Like we always do."

The sheriff nodded and dismissed Tanner. Maya was annoyed with the sheriff. Cocky and arrogant didn't even begin to describe him. But she was impressed with how Tanner handled the situation. He didn't get upset and professionally stood his ground.

"Let's go this way." Maya nodded toward the area where Juniper hadn't found any scent. "There's some spots I think we should check."

"I'll follow you," Tanner said. The trio headed back in the direction where Maya had started with Juniper. Hopefully another dog's scent in the area wouldn't throw off Finn, but so far, he seemed like a steady, easygoing dog.

They arrived at a location where the avalanche hadn't destroyed anything. Maya had noticed some rocky areas where there was less snow. Some small ravines were there, probably created from the spring runoff every year. They were deep enough to conceal a body back in the rocks, but not so deep that they couldn't go down in them, although they might sink into the snow that had settled at the bottom.

"I think this would be a good area to start. We're out of the crime scene area and still at a safe place in regard to avalanche danger. I'll stay back and let you and Finn do your thing."

"Okay," Tanner said. He took Finn off-leash and started talking to him. Finn responded by wagging his tail and bouncing up and down on his front paws. Tanner squeaked Finn's toy, a ball that would last about five seconds with Juniper, and then directed him out into the area.

Finn put his nose to the ground and started sucking in air. Tanner stepped back and let his dog work. At first, Finn worked the area well, but at times he would pause and look back at Tanner. This concerned Maya, but each dog was different and maybe Finn was still new to the job. If dogs became dependent on their handlers by looking at them, then they might give a

false indication. This was something Maya worked or
in daily training with Juniper. She noted, though, tha
Tanner would direct Finn back out when he did stop to
stare at Tanner. They continued to work the area in a
grid pattern.

They made their way along the ravine, eventually
finding a good path down into one of the rocky areas.
Maya followed at a distance, the snow getting deeper,
but not enough to be of concern yet. They were still a
decent distance from where the mountain slope became
steep, making the snowfall heavier and the avalanche
danger higher. She made a mental note of where they
should stop to stay out of danger.

"Go find it, boy. Go find it," Tanner said, snapping
her out of her thoughts.

He continued talking to Finn and encouraging him.
Maya was again worried that too much talking could
bring on a false indication, but it wasn't her job to train
Finn and Tanner. Maya did wonder if Finn would miss
something. Worrying about a dog missing a find wasn't
a good feeling.

She didn't know if Finn and Tanner had passed any
kind of certification. In Colorado, certification wasn't
a requirement, but most agencies did it anyway. Who
knew if Finn really could find human remains or not.
Hopefully this wasn't a waste of time.

Tanner kept talking to Finn and the yellow Lab continued to glance back at his handler. In Maya's opinion,
even if Tanner didn't elicit a false alert, he was creating
an issue with his dog staring back at him.

They worked their way up the ravine and she was
about ready to tell Tanner to stop and turn around. The
snow had become deeper and they were heading closer

to where the mountain slope angle drastically increased. Just as she opened her mouth to speak, Finn's body language changed. Exactly like Juniper's body language when she was in scent, Finn tensed his muscles and his tail went up higher. His breathing changed as he air scented. Tanner quieted down and followed his dog. Maya trailed behind.

Finn led them off to the other side of the ravine. Maya's legs burned as she climbed back up, slipping in the snow that was softer due to the sun exposure. Tanner also slid around, but then managed to keep up with his dog.

They came up to a rocky area where ledges and crevasses had formed over millions of years. It amazed Maya how fast the terrain could change. They literally had a wall in front of them made of granite, diorite and other types of rocks; she couldn't remember all their names. High school geology had been a while ago.

Finn had started taking Tanner back downhill until he came to an area with deep rock shelves. He sat and looked at Tanner.

"He's alerting somewhere in here," Tanner said.

Maya wanted to say that he needed to work on Finn's alert so that he knew exactly where his dog was finding an odor, but she kept those thoughts to herself.

"I'll take a look around," she said, coming over to the area where Finn had alerted. She tested her footing and found the rocks held and, in this area, they were almost like stairs. She climbed up a couple rocks and found herself peering back into a deep rock shelf. She sucked in her breath when she saw human remains.

She didn't know how long the remains had been there. The body still had clothing and appeared past the bloating stage, so Maya guessed that in this mountain environment, these remains had been there about a month. She didn't know for sure though and the cold weather would preserve the body too, slowing down decomp. Because of the way the body was stuffed back into the opening in the rocks, Maya couldn't tell for sure, but she thought the remains were a blond male. Was there any chance this was Avery Anderson? She both hoped it was and wasn't. If it was, then Kay would have closure. If the remains weren't him, then Kay still had some hope, but wouldn't know what'd happened to him.

"Something there?" Tanner asked.

"Yeah, unfortunately we have another victim," she said, stepping back down from the rock ledges. It didn't matter how many times Maya saw death in this job, she never quite got used to it.

"Reward your dog. He did a really good job tracking this scent."

Chapter Fifteen

Josh pulled up to the Black Bear Café for lunch. He'd contacted his mom and sister and asked them to join him. His father and Pops were back at the station working on the investigation. Putting his patrol vehicle in Park, he sat for a moment thinking about what he needed to convey to his family. Especially his mother.

He was different now. Not just from being sober, but from the aftermath of his partner's death. How could someone not change when trauma happened? Especially a law enforcement officer. He had heard through a police psychologist that the average person experienced five to eight serious traumas in their life. Law enforcement officers experienced around eight hundred traumas due to their jobs. It was hard for civilians to understand that and the repercussions.

Just another reason why Maya was so important to him. She dealt with her PTSD and understood that he had his own. She was the first person who really understood him and he wouldn't allow anything to get in the way—not even his family. He would tell his mother to either accept Maya or back off and leave them be.

Stepping out of his vehicle, Josh went inside the café and found his mother and sister already seated in the corner. There was a third menu waiting for him. Saying hello to several of the patrons that he'd come to know while living in Pinecone Junction, he made his way over to the table.

"Hi, Bianca, Mom." He pulled out the chair and sat.

"Hi, honey," his mom said, patting his hand.

"How's your day going?" Bianca asked. "Arrest anyone?"

Josh laughed. "No. No arrests today. It's a pretty quiet day, although now that I've used the Q word, I'll probably pay for it."

"I wish you had a more normal job," his mother piped up. "I mean really, dear, why do you want to run around after criminals all day?"

Josh sighed. *And so it begins. Mom always has a way of making my job seem insignificant.*

"I love my job. I help people and keep communities safe. It's what I like to do." Josh paused, trying to find the right words. "Look, I know you mean well, but my job is important to me. I'm proud of what I've accomplished and I'm happy. I think that's the most important thing."

"I agree," Bianca piped up. "You seem like you're doing really well and that's great. Right, Mom?"

Their mother shrugged and went back to studying the menu, which Josh knew was limited. She was probably trying to think of a way to keep on him about finding a new career.

"And Maya," Bianca said, "she's fantastic. I've never seen you this content with anyone else."

"Thanks," Josh said. "Speaking of Maya, Mom, we need to talk."

His mother set the menu back down and said, "What

about? I don't see your relationship going anywhere with that girl. She has issues, can't you see that?"

Josh took a deep breath, trying to keep calm. "Here's what you need to know: Maya is very, very special to me. I've never felt this way about anyone. Ever. You can either accept that and stay a part of my life, our life, or you can go back home and leave me alone."

"Are you going to marry this girl then?"

"I'd like to. Someday," Josh said, hesitating as he surprised even himself by admitting that out loud. But it was true. He couldn't imagine being with anyone else. Mom needed to understand that. "Maya and I both have our pasts to deal with, but we also have the future, and my future includes her. You need to get used to that and start keeping your thoughts to yourself. Got it?"

His mother raised an eyebrow and stared out the window, not answering. Bianca gave him a thumbs-up and mouthed, *Good job.* Josh had to smile at his sister. Thank God for her.

"There's something else we need to discuss too," Josh said.

"What's that?" his mother asked, looking back at him.

"Amber."

"What about her?"

"I don't want to see her again. It was wrong of you to invite her here. You should have asked me. Amber and I are over. Done. You need to get that through your head. Speaking of which, where is she?"

"She told me she'd dreamed of visiting the Colorado mountains. What was I to do? And she wanted to get her nails done. She said she'd join us for dinner."

"Why don't you tell her to stay away from Pinecone Junction? From me."

"What are we going to do then? She's here right now. I can't just send her back home," Mom said.

"Sure you can. You can take her to the airport, put her on a plane and get her back to where she belongs—Chicago."

"I won't do that."

"Fine," Josh said. "When you get together with her then, make sure I'm not around. I don't want to see her again."

"I can't control her."

"Yes," he said. "You can. It's your specialty. You brought her here. She's your problem."

"I can't guarantee anything, but I'll do my best," his mother said.

The server came over to take their orders. Josh's mother and sister ordered, but when it was his turn, he stood up and said, "I'm sorry, I'm not hungry anymore."

Josh glanced back as he left. Saying his mother was stubborn would be an understatement. He only hoped he'd gotten through to her.

Maya radioed the sheriff what they had found and their location. She taped off the crime scene and then joined Tanner and Finn to check the rest of the area. Other than trying to eat a pinecone that Tanner managed to grab out of his mouth before he swallowed it, Finn didn't have any further alerts and wasn't interested in anything else.

Maya needed to wait to keep the scene secure until the crime scene techs and coroner could get there. She figured it would be a while. Tanner offered to stay as well and she didn't turn down the company. Securing a crime scene sounded important, and it was, but it really meant standing out in the elements and waiting until the coroner and investigators showed up.

Maya checked to see if she had cell phone service. She was wondering about any news on Pops's investigation and if Lucas's friend had happened to run the DNA yet. She was also thinking of Josh and how much she was already missing him, but she was still upset over the way she'd learned about Amber. As she suspected, she didn't have service and she put her phone away. Tanner had given Finn another toy to play with.

"How long have you and Finn been working together?" Maya asked, making small talk to pass the time.

"I've had him about a year and a half. Started training a year ago and certified before the holidays," Tanner said proudly.

"He's a good working dog."

"Thanks. I was lucky to find him."

"Where'd he come from?"

"I actually found him at the local shelter," Tanner said. "He was probably a cute puppy that grew up and wasn't so cute anymore. He was destructive. I have to watch that he doesn't chew up things or eat anything. He ate a couple of my socks a while back. Luckily, he didn't need surgery."

Maya laughed. "Labs, they definitely eat everything."

"That's an understatement."

"Who have you been training with?" Maya asked.

"I've worked with some of the avalanche dog trainers and search and rescue trainers in the surrounding areas. He's Antler Valley's first cadaver dog. It's been hard to find consistent training. I just keep trying to learn and improve."

"I don't know how long I'll be here or what my schedule will be like, but I'm happy to give you some pointers if you want. Maybe do a training session together?"

"I would *love* that," Tanner said. "I'll take all the help I can get."

"It's a plan then. I'll see how this investigation goes and give you a call when I'm free."

"Thank you."

"Of course. My pleasure."

Maya rubbed her hands together. Even with her heavy gloves on, the cold was starting to seep in as the sun was blocked by the mountain peaks. It wouldn't get dark for a couple more hours, but it seemed like you lost light in the mountains quicker—especially in the wintertime. A shiver ran through her body and Maya wished she had Juniper with her too. It was as if she could feel the ghost of the person they'd found. At least the victim and their family could have some closure.

The coroner and a crime scene tech finally showed up as the sunlight dwindled more. Maya was glad to see them because otherwise someone would have to stay at the crime scene all night long and she wouldn't want it to be her. She showed the coroner where the body was located and then stepped back out of the way.

"If you don't need us anymore, I think I'll head out," Tanner said, gathering up Finn's leash.

"No, we shouldn't need you to check anything further, although it's really the sheriff you need to ask," Maya said, being careful not to cross any lines or step on any toes. She didn't feel like a confrontation with the sheriff. At this point she was cold and tired and might not have enough patience left to not say something she'd regret.

"I'll double-check," Tanner said. "I look forward to hearing from you about doing some training."

"I'll be in touch," Maya said. "It does depend on how the investigation goes, but if I get some free time, I'll let you know."

"Thanks."

Tanner and Finn headed out as the coroner and tech worked together to process the scene. Like the avalanche area, there wasn't much evidence to process. Or if there was, it might not be found until summertime. It wasn't like a house where you could vacuum the floors to find evidence, run DNA or dust for fingerprints. The forest was a difficult crime scene and the weather made it harder. The victim had been here long enough that there weren't even footprints in the snow to cast.

The coroner pulled out the body bag, and together, he and the tech carefully worked to dislodge the body and slide the remains into the bag. Maya glanced over despite trying to will herself not to look. It seemed like every crime like this took a piece of her with it. She sometimes questioned her career, but when she could catch the killer, put them in cuffs, take them to jail and watch them stand trial for their crimes, she knew she couldn't imagine doing anything else.

She sucked in a deep breath, her heart dropping as she noticed the remnants of blond hair and a necklace with a cross. Her initial thoughts were probably correct. There was a good chance this was Avery.

"I may have an idea of who this is," Maya said. "If it's who I think it is, his mother talked to me about his case."

"Do you have a name?" the coroner asked, pulling out a notebook.

"Avery Anderson. He grew up in Pinecone Junction."

"I'll contact the dentist there and see if I can get some records. Maybe we can make this one a fairly quick ID."

"Will you let me know?" Maya asked.

"I will," the coroner said.

Maya took another peek at the remains, sadness filling her. If this was Avery, his mother would be devastated. Was it better to know that this was Avery? Or easier to keep some hope by knowing he was still just missing? Closure was a strange beast and she admitted to herself that she'd never really dealt with the loss of her mother and grandmother. Josh had pointed that out to her one day. She'd blown him off, not wanting to hear it.

As the body bag was being zipped up, the breeze picked up and blew some pine needles that were stuck to the victim's clothing.

Pine needles.

"Stop," Maya said.

The coroner and tech paused, staring at Maya. She stepped closer and took in her surroundings. *Long pine needles.* They were at a higher elevation where trees like fir, spruce and lodgepole pine trees grew. Lodgepole pines had short needles. Not ponderosa pines. Their needles were about five to six inches long and grew at a lower elevation.

"What is it?" the coroner asked.

"Those needles stuck to the victim's shirt, I'm certain they're ponderosa pine needles. They're longer and very different from the trees around here."

The tech started nodding, understanding where Maya was going with her thought.

"That means the body was moved from another location from a different elevation. I know that doesn't narrow it down much, but at this point, it's better than nothing."

"Good catch," said the coroner. The tech was already handing him an evidence bag and some tweezers. The coroner took the needles and bagged them. They were finishing zipping up the body bag, and Maya was helping to secure the remains in a carry litter when a flash of light blinded her.

Chapter Sixteen

Maya blinked in surprise, dropped her corner of the body bag and reached for her Glock, unholstering it.

"Forest Service law enforcement! Come out with your hands up," she said. The coroner and crime scene tech were staying behind her. They didn't carry guns, so they were relying on Maya to keep them safe.

There was movement in the trees uphill, not the best advantage for her. She signaled to the coroner and tech to get down. They followed her instruction. Maya kept her gun pointed in the direction of the shadow that lurked in the tree line.

"I said, come out with your hands up. Now!"

"Don't shoot," said a male voice.

"Then come out of the trees, hands up, and stay where I can see you." She kept her gun steady, but her finger off the trigger. She wouldn't move it to the trigger unless she was going to commit to pulling it—something she didn't take lightly.

A young man in his early twenties stepped out from the trees. He had a camera hanging around his neck and one hand up. The other was holding something. Maya couldn't get a good visual on what it was, but she wasn't going to take any chances.

"Drop whatever you have in your hand and put both hands up in the air. Now."

"Okay, okay. Geez," said the young man. He dropped what he was holding and put his other hand up.

"Now turn around, keeping both hands up. Get down on your knees and stay where you are. I'm going to handcuff you, but I'm not arresting you. At least not yet. The cuffs are just for our safety."

The young man complied and Maya walked up to his location. She kept her gun out but pointed down. When she got closer, she said, "Interlace your fingers and put your hands behind your head."

He complied again, so Maya went ahead and holstered her gun. She pulled out her cuffs and, taking one hand at a time, put them on.

"You can stand back up," she said. She started patting him down, feeling for weapons or other contraband.

"I should write a story about police brutality. Although you're hot, so maybe I should just enjoy the moment."

"Excuse me? Are you trying to talk your way into going to jail? I can grant that wish for you," Maya said, annoyed but knowing she had to keep her patience. Having people be smart-asses was part of the job. She preferred to be less confrontational, but some citizens didn't want to have it that way. "What's your name?"

"Bryce Riley."

"What are you doing here, Bryce? This is an active crime scene."

"I'm a reporter."

"Seriously?" Maya blew out an exasperated breath. She didn't usually have to deal with reporters. That was more of a city cop's problem, although more and more journalists were starting to venture out for the big stories. If they could get the exclusive, it could mean a book deal, movie or television show, or other lucrative opportunities. She supposed it was something she was going to have to start thinking about more.

"This is an active crime scene. All the photos you took will be confiscated," she said.

"Does the sheriff know you're doing that?"

"Not yet."

"Then I'd be careful. He's the one who's been letting me know about things going on in the area. He sends me tips because he trusts me."

"Seriously?" Maya said, exasperated again. If Bryce was telling the truth, she needed to talk to Ben.

The sooner the better.

"Start walking," Maya said, pointing in the direction of the main crime scene. She escorted Bryce while the coroner, crime scene tech and several other deputies who had arrived on scene carried the litter with the body bag. They all arrived at where the sheriff stood barking orders at some deputies.

He turned around and saw Bryce in handcuffs. "What now?"

"I found this reporter taking pictures of the crime scene," Maya said. "I didn't know what you wanted to do with him."

"I'm not arresting a reporter. That would start a shit-storm I don't want."

Maya nodded, trying to contain her frustration. How could the sheriff blow off the reporter sneaking behind the crime scene tape? Something like that could affect a trial and set a killer free. She said the one word that she thought wouldn't get her into trouble: "Understood."

"Uncuff him and I'll escort him out of here."

Bryce peered back over his shoulder and smirked. Maya took out her key and loosened the cuffs, putting them back on her duty belt. The sheriff patted Bryce on the shoulder and then strolled with him toward the parking area.

They're sure chummy, Maya thought. *Go figure. Why would a sheriff trust such a brazen reporter?*

After a long day, Maya was happy to get back to the Saddle Rock Falls Inn. She didn't care anymore how uncomfortable the bed was as long as there was hot water when she showered. Even with the heater blasting in her patrol vehicle, her fingers and toes were still frozen. She couldn't wait to warm up and get some sleep. Juniper was quiet and lying down, tired from her work and barking at Finn. At least she had her heated compartment so that Maya didn't have to worry about her getting hypothermia.

She parked in front of the door to her room and let Juniper out, snapping on her leash. She took her over to a snowy area away from the road to let her stretch her legs. Maya still had on her heavy coat, hat and gloves, but it didn't matter—she had a chill down to the bone.

She let the leash out so Juniper could explore and stretch a little bit before they went into the room. Another vehicle pulled up and parked a few doors down. Maya glanced over her shoulder and saw Ben getting out of his patrol vehicle. She waved and he headed over.

"You frozen yet?" he asked.

"Totally. I can't wait for a hot shower."

"Me either. Good work today. I heard about your

catch with the ponderosa pine needle. Every little piece of evidence counts."

"Thanks," said Maya. "I didn't realize you were staying here too. Figured since you had a higher rank maybe you'd get a better place to stay."

Ben laughed. "Nope, a government budget is a government budget. Doesn't matter what rank you are. At least for our jobs. Maybe the chief of the Forest Service gets more money. Or who knows. Maybe not."

Maya grinned as Juniper continued to explore the area. As they strolled near some bushes, she gripped the leash tighter. She didn't need Juniper flushing out a skunk, raccoon or other critter tonight. Especially a skunk. That would stink, sort of like the sheriff in this town. She didn't like how the investigation was going or being run. These victims deserved more. Maya stopped Juniper and turned to Ben.

"Permission to speak freely?" she asked.

Ben shook his head. "I told you, this isn't the military. What's on your mind, Thompson?"

Maya stopped and turned and stared at Ben. "Sheriff Jackson and this investigation, sir…uh, oops, Ben."

"What about it?"

"I have some serious concerns that the sheriff can't handle this investigation. I saw quite a few red flags today, the final one being escorting a journalist out of the crime scene area. He claims he was tipped off by the sheriff himself." Maya filled Ben in more on the journalist surprising them at the final crime scene. "He had a lot of photos. If he hadn't screwed up a setting on his camera and the flash hadn't gone off, we might never have known he was there and the story could have been leaked, potentially ruining the investigation and a prosecutor's ability to convict someone for these crimes. I know I don't need to tell you that, but what if these victims don't get the justice they deserve and even worse, a dangerous predator is turned loose again all because of an incompetent sheriff?"

"I don't disagree, but what are you proposing?" Ben asked.

"We both know that these crimes ended up on national forest land. Federal land. What if we call the FBI?"

"They would have to take over the case then. They would have jurisdiction."

"Exactly," Maya said. "I kind of know the special agent for this area, Mark Kessler. He's good. He had some good experience in law enforcement before he went to Quantico and he's passionate about solving cases. I think it could be worth it to call him."

She declined to mention that she'd met Agent Kessler because he'd been interviewing her the previous summer about her friend and fellow Forest Service officer's crimes. Her opinion of Agent Kessler had been different then, but she knew he was good at his job, and if he'd interviewed her, a fellow law enforcement officer, about a crime, he wasn't afraid to do what was right for an investigation—including taking over.

"I agree the sheriff seems to be in over his head. At least his deputies, crime scene techs and coroner seemed competent," Ben said. "But we have to be very careful about how we handle this. If I call the FBI and they come in and take over, then there's a good chance that our favorite sheriff could become political and call his congressperson to complain. A phone call like that would be the best way to get us out of the way, which we know Sheriff Jackson would love. That's a headache neither of us want. Not to mention I just got this job and I know you're pretty new too. I don't think either of us want to be looking for new jobs at this point."

"Very true," Maya said. "That's why you earn the big bucks. You understand the politics better. I think I just know how to piss people off."

Ben laughed again. "You got that right, but don't lose your passion. Just channel it a little better. Look, I'll see if I can talk to the sheriff. Maybe we can convince him that letting the FBI in on all this wouldn't be a bad idea. This is a big investigation and if the manners of death are all homicide, we definitely have a serial killer in this area. That's more than any of us can handle."

"I can't imagine the manners of death being anything other than homicide. Most group suicides or weird things like that don't involve the victims burying each other. I'd bet you a hundred dollars that we have a serial killer here in Antler Valley."

"I'm not a betting man, but even if I was, I wouldn't agree to that wager. I agree this has all the marks of a serial killer, and one who's been quite busy. If it hadn't been for the avalanche, we might never have realized what was going on."

"What if we, or maybe better you, convince our favorite sheriff to take the evidence and put the case into ViCAP?" Maya asked, talking about the Violent Crime Apprehension Program, which was a database the FBI had put together to help different agencies share information about violent offenders. The database had helped catch notorious killers like the Highway Serial Killer. "Maybe our killer was traveling through or moved here from somewhere else. It could help solve the case. And if our killer has been active in other states, it only makes the case stronger that the FBI should run the investigation."

Ben shrugged. "Wouldn't hurt, I guess. I'll talk to him about it and if we do get a hit in ViCAP, you're right, it might help our case for bringing in the FBI."

"Exactly."

"I like the way you think, Thompson. All right, I'll work on that in the morning. Until then, it's freezing out here. You and Juniper have a good night."

"You too," Maya said, as she and Juniper headed back to their room.

As she was closing her door, she saw Ben get back into his patrol vehicle and leave again. He was probably getting food or something, but Maya wondered what he was up to.

Chapter Seventeen

He sat in a parking spot down the road near a gas station, just hanging out in his vehicle. It was a great vantage point to watch and surveil from. He prided himself on his ability to observe others. That's what made him so good at what he did.

She had gone into the motel room with her dog. Why was he so obsessed with her? She really wasn't his type, but there was something so captivating. Maya. Maya. That was a nice name. A good name. He'd looked up the meaning—"good mother" or "from God."

He'd like to think that God had brought her to him. She was perfection, the way she laughed and her eyes lit up—although much of the time she was serious, like she was haunted. That intrigued him and he wanted to find out more.

Yes, she was someone that he didn't feel compelled to sacrifice. And since she worked for the Forest Service, she must also believe in his cause of helping the environment. She was pure, unlike anyone he'd ever met.

He lusted after her like he never had before. Not even his first love. The girl his father had caught him with and humiliated him over. Anger surged through his body, but he took a deep breath and calmed down. He couldn't lose control thinking about his father and he reminded himself that he had ended up with the ultimate control over his father anyway. The old man had paid for his sins.

Taking a deep breath, he started up his vehicle. Maya was in her room for the night and she appeared tired. He was tired too, and he needed to get some rest and think anyway. His favorite hiding spot was gone. No more visiting his lovelies.

Now he had to come up with a new place to stash the bodies. He had to come up with something quickly because his latest victim had given up, and that was no fun. Once someone lost the will to live, he quit toying with them and ended things. He liked it when they had a good fighting spirit and he was able to break that.

He liked that very much.

It was time to go home, get some rest himself.

Even someone like him got tired after a while.

Josh crashed on his couch, exhaustion seeping through him. His afternoon patrol had been smooth. He'd written a couple tickets and a few warnings, but nothing major. Then he'd spent some time at the office doing paperwork and catching up on some administrative work. His workload had increased with Pops out of the office due to the interviews and everything else related to the investigation. Josh was doing both his job and filling in for Pops at the same time.

Rubbing his eyes, Josh grabbed his phone and was about ready to call Maya when there was a knock at the door. Now what? He dropped his phone onto the couch and went to the front door.

"Great," he muttered to himself as he peered through the window and saw his entire family standing outside.

Amber was with them. He shook his head in anger. Hadn't he made it clear to his mom that he didn't want to see Amber? He wanted to go back to the living room and pretend he wasn't home, but it was too late. They'd all seen him.

Mom held up a dish. Probably homemade, something Italian. Josh sighed and opened the door. "Hey there."

"Can we come in?" his father asked.

Josh hesitated. He supposed leaving family outside in the cold would be considered an asshole move. He stepped aside and gestured for them to come in.

"We won't stay long," Mom said.

"Good, because I'm tired."

"I figured you were so I brought you some dinner. My homemade tortellini. I thought we could all have a quick dinner and then we'll head back to our place."

His mom was about ready to follow the rest of the family, who had filed ahead into the kitchen. "Hey. Mom. I told you that I didn't want to see Amber."

"We couldn't leave her at the Airbnb."

"Sure you could. It's easy. You drive here without her in the car."

"Oh, stop it," his mother said. "Just come eat dinner and then we'll be out of here."

Josh didn't know what to say. He finally decided that the food did smell good. He could eat a quick dinner, maybe keep everyone happy and then send them on their way. He'd be glad when they all went back home and he could move on with his life with Maya in Pinecone Junction.

Maya took a hot shower, pulled on her favorite Marines sweatshirt and jogging pants and bumped the heat up in the room. She was missing the fireplace at home and snuggling up next to Josh. This room seemed cold, isolated and bare.

Juniper stood, stared at her dog bed and then back at Maya and then back at the dog bed, not moving. Maya sat down on the bed with her phone to call Josh and catch up with him, but she watched Juniper to see what her dog was up to. Juniper knew she should go lie on the bed Maya brought for her.

Juniper trotted down to the end of Maya's bed and peered up and over, resting her head on the covers and giving a pleading stare. Maya didn't say anything. She wanted to see how far her dog would take this. She also figured if Juniper ended up on the bed, it wouldn't be so bad. It was a motel room. Not home. They could break the rules here.

When Maya was stateside in the Marines, the dogs lived in kennels. But once they went to Afghanistan, the dogs were with them 24/7 and her military K-9 Zinger had slept with Maya, bringing comfort to each of them. Maya had to admit she missed those moments, but she'd worked hard to make sure she followed the working dog rules and Juniper never became a pet who didn't want to work. Although Maya couldn't imagine Juniper ever not working.

Juniper put a front paw up on the bed and hesitated.

"Oh, come on up."

With a happy tail wag, Juniper jumped up and settled herself next to Maya, curling up so that her back was pressing against her leg. Maya reached down and scratched Juniper's back. Juniper gave a contented sigh.

Maya dialed Josh. The phone rang and rang. She thought it was going to voice mail when Josh answered.

"Maya," he said, sounding out of breath.

There was noise in the background that sounded almost like a party. In all the time Maya had known Josh, he'd never had anyone over. They both liked their solitude. Or at least she thought they did. *What else don't I know about Josh?* She worked to shove her feelings down and not fight. Not tonight. She was too tired.

"Hey there," she said. "How are you?"

"I'm good."

Maya waited for him to say more, but when he didn't, she was hesitant for a moment. She could hear people in the background. "You having a party tonight?"

"I guess. Sort of. My family is over here and Mom made her signature tortellini."

"Oh," Maya said, hearing more laughter in the background. "How's it going with Pops's investigation?"

"My dad feels it's going well, although he still thinks there could be a trial. Who knows, though, we'll see."

Maya could hear someone calling Josh in the background. A female voice telling him to get off the phone and come back over.

"Is that Amber?" Maya asked.

"Uh. Yeah. It's her."

"What's she doing there?" Anger started to build inside Maya. What wasn't Josh telling her? She had shared with him that she'd been in a serious relationship in the military only to find out that the guy'd had a wife. Maya had broken it off, of course, because she'd been horrified, but she'd sworn she'd never again be involved with someone who hid things from her. She'd always thought Josh had been honest with her, but now she was starting to feel angry and hurt.

"My mom brought her along. I had to let her join us. She's staying with my family," Josh answered.

Maya gripped her phone harder, as if squeezing it to death would fix the situation. "You didn't have to have her over. You could have said no."

"There was no arguing with my mom. In a couple days they'll all be gone anyway."

"Stand up to her. What happens when your mom decides you should move back to Chicago or something like that? You need to put a stop to this now."

"You don't have a mother, you don't understand what it's like," Josh said.

As soon as he said the words, Maya felt like a knife had been stabbed into her gut. How dare he throw that at her when he knew that her mother had been brutally murdered when Maya was a little girl? That was why Pops and Nana had raised her. And Nana had been taken away from Maya by the same killer as her mother.

Tears threatened to fall, but Maya held them in. Her hand shook and she didn't say anything.

"Shit. Maya, I'm so sorry. I didn't mean that the way it—"

"Have a good night," she said, interrupting Josh. "Have fun with your family and enjoy your ex-fiancée. If that's what she still is."

Maya hit the end button and pulled her knees up to her chest, hugging them tightly. She hadn't felt hurt like this in a long time. She also hadn't felt the urge that overwhelmed her now. She wanted nothing more than to go buy alcohol and drink until she passed out and forgot everything that'd just happened.

She stood up and grabbed her keys, still holding back tears along with the urge to scream.

Juniper lifted her head up and tilted it slightly, peering straight at her, questioning if they were going back out. Maya set her keys back down. She couldn't do this. She'd been sober for six months. Her job was solid. She had Juniper to think of. If she lost her job, she lost Juniper. Getting drunk tonight might lead to that.

Instead, Maya grabbed her phone and called her sponsor, holding back sobs.

Josh heard the call click off. He gripped his phone. How could he have just said that to Maya? Maya of all people? She didn't deserve that. How would he ever apologize for that? Yes, his mother was pushing her boundaries and being impossible, but he shouldn't have taken his frustration and anger out on Maya. He would have to figure out how to apologize later.

Stomping back into the kitchen, he stopped at the doorway and stared at his family. "You all need to leave. Now."

"Josh, honey," his mother began.

"No, don't 'Josh, honey' me. I need you all to go. Now." Everyone stared at him. "I mean it. Please leave."

One by one they all stood up and filed out. Amber went to give him a kiss on the cheek, but Josh held his hand up. "No. Please. Don't."

Her lips became pouty and then she turned and left. Bianca gave him a quick hug.

"It'll be okay," she said.

"I don't know," Josh said. "I just said something to Maya that I'll regret the rest of my life."

"Apologize and mean it. Maya will forgive you."

"I hope so," Josh said.

As his sister shut the door behind her and the silence

of the house surrounded him, he dialed Maya's number and listened to the phone ring and then go to voice mail. Hanging up, he tried her one more time with the same result. Not that he blamed her. He left a voice mail apologizing and then hung up. He knew he deserved this. If he had to, he'd drive to Antler Valley and beg her forgiveness.

Josh sent Maya a couple text messages apologizing. Nothing. No answer. Maybe she was out walking Juniper. Hopefully that was the case and she wasn't ignoring him. Or even worse, what if he had triggered her into drinking? He'd never forgive himself. She'd worked so hard for her sobriety. He sent one last text telling her what a jerk he was and apologizing. It was late, so for now he'd try to get some sleep and see if he could reach Maya in the morning.

Chapter Eighteen

The next morning Maya was up early, having not slept well. She needed coffee and lots of it.

After pulling her tangled hair back into a ponytail, and putting on her sweatshirt and jeans, Maya headed to the front office where she got a cup of coffee and a complimentary pastry. She saw Ben out in the parking lot, already in uniform, talking on the phone. She'd better get ready to go quickly. It didn't look good to have your boss beat you to work.

Maya grabbed a second cup of coffee, feeling the strain of the previous night. Josh had called her back a couple times leaving voice mails with apologies. Then he'd switched to texting, but Maya couldn't bring herself to talk to him or answer.

Not yet.

The pain was still too sharp, although talking to her sponsor had helped. Maya trusted Josh, but this had hit a nerve for her, what with her previous relationship in the military. She would never be the other woman again.

Juniper was snoring on the bed when she returned to the room. How her dog could go from a hundred miles an hour to sound asleep was beyond her. One golden eye flicked open and an ear twitched.

"Rise and shine, sunshine," Maya said to her. "And don't get too used to sleeping on the bed."

Juniper groaned and stretched, splaying out her toes, and then thumped the bed a couple times with her tail. Maya gave her head a quick rub while she gulped down some coffee. She quickly showered and dressed, pulling her hair back into a tight bun. Juniper didn't stir until Maya put on her duty belt and poured Juniper's breakfast into a bowl. Then she slithered off the bed, did a full-body shake and appeared ready to go.

Juniper ate her breakfast while Maya gulped the other cup of coffee, hoping the sheriff's station might have more. They rushed out the door and were ready to go by the time Ben was off the phone. Maya wasn't sure who he was talking to, but he didn't look happy.

"We need to head to the sheriff's office first," Ben said.

"Got it. See you there," Maya said as her phone rang. Josh. She hit Reject and sent the call to voice mail. She needed to focus on work—she'd deal with Josh later. It was better to wait and sort through her feelings anyway.

Arriving at the sheriff's office, Maya decided to send Josh a quick text that she'd call later. It wasn't fair to give him the silent treatment, but she needed to calm down before she called back. She made sure Juniper's compartment was set to a good temperature since it was another bitterly cold January morning. The nasty winter storm was still scheduled to arrive tomorrow afternoon. Maya would be okay without a big winter storm, but when you lived in the Colorado mountains, you had to roll with the weather. It was unpredictable. *If you don't like the weather in Colorado, then wait five minutes* was the famous saying.

But this storm was estimated to bring twelve to twenty-four inches of snow. Skiers were rejoicing, but for Maya, that would mean holing up in the motel room until the storm cleared out. Right now, sitting in a motel room where all she had to do was think about Amber being at their house didn't make her excited about the storm.

Ben and Maya walked inside the front entrance. The sheriff was waiting for them, arms crossed, chomping his gum. *Some things never change.* Maya didn't know if she could handle his bullshit today. She needed to put last night behind her though and remain professional. She'd learned how to compartmentalize in the military. She could do it now.

"Let's go to my office," the sheriff said. "This way."

They followed him up the stairs and into a large office with views of the ski slopes to the west. A few people were already out on the hills for the day. He gestured for Maya and Ben to take a seat.

"I wanted to let you know that the coroner has determined that the manner of death for the first few victims is definitely homicide," the sheriff said. "Even though I don't feel like I need you two helping with this case, I have decided to keep you filled in…and I might need more manpower than I have. If you two really want to be involved in this, then congratulations, you're in the loop."

Maya wondered where the sudden change of heart was coming from, but she didn't want to question it. Maybe it was a full moon. Of course, what Ben and Maya didn't say was that they had some jurisdiction in this case whether the sheriff liked it or not. It still struck Maya odd that he was so against the help. Why would he want to control the investigation to this extent? What was in it for him?

Ben cleared his throat. "Officer Thompson and I both believe we have a serial killer here. It's hard to tell if he's killing his victims in the forest or if he's just dumping them there. Either way, we are glad to help. I'd also like you to consider putting this case into ViCAP. Maybe he's killed in other towns or states. ViCAP could help with that."

The sheriff sat back and put one foot on his knee. He formed a steeple with his fingers and stared back at Maya and Ben. "I'll consider it."

"Thank you," Ben said. "We know the field agent for this area. He's very good and could provide some good support."

"If I call the FBI, they'll take over jurisdiction."

"Not necessarily," Ben said. "They might be able to offer assistance and resources that none of us have access to. They could send the case info to their behavioral analysis unit and probably get some good ideas of what type of offender we're looking for."

"Isn't every serial killer a white male, my age, with a bad childhood? Hell, maybe I should tell the FBI to look into me," the sheriff said sarcastically.

"Actually, that's not true," Maya spoke up. "About the serial killer profile, that is. Serial killers can be any race, and while the majority are male, some are female. Not every serial killer had a bad childhood, although most of them probably did."

The sheriff stared at Maya. She figured he was going to say something smart-ass when he finally spoke up. "Fine. Call your FBI friend, but they need to understand, this is my jurisdiction and my case."

"I'm sure they will," Ben said.

A knock on the door interrupted them. A young deputy stood there, appearing awkward and unsure of whether she should be cutting in on their meeting. Despite this, she held her ground, holding herself tall even though she was on the petite side. Dark hair in a ponytail accentuated intense dark brown eyes. Maya was pretty certain this was Rory Lopez, who was putting in for a job at Pops's office and maybe someone who could give Maya some more insight into the sheriff.

"Sorry, sir," Rory said, staying right at the door to the office. "I don't mean to barge in, but we have another missing person report. I thought with this case going on, you might want the information right away. This missing person disappeared about two days ago. His family officially filed a report this morning when he didn't come home."

Maya's heart dropped. Another victim. Another family wanting answers. She hoped they could find this missing person before it was too late.

Chapter Nineteen

Rory remained outside the sheriff's door, an uncertain look on her face. The sheriff didn't answer her. Instead, he motioned with his fingers that she could step into his office. Rory nodded to Maya and Ben as she handed the sheriff a file. He opened it up and flipped through the papers, not saying a word.

He eventually looked up and said, "Anything else?"

"Yes, sir. This also came for you." Rory handed him a large manila envelope.

The sheriff peered inside the envelope, his face turning a dark shade of red. "Where did this come from?"

"Someone dropped it off at the front desk."

"I want you to go find out who dropped it off. Now. Got it?"

"Yes, sir," Rory said, turning to leave.

Maya jumped to her feet. "You know what? I drank too much coffee this morning and need to find a restroom. I'll let you two finish talking and then, Ben, I'll meet you downstairs."

Ben gave her a perplexed look but shrugged in agreement. Maya followed the young deputy out and, after closing the door behind her, said, "Are you Rory Lopez?"

"I am. You must be Officer Thompson. My dad men-

tioned that you would be over here working. Guess he
met your grandfather at a law enforcement conference
for chiefs and sheriffs. It's nice to meet you."

"Nice to meet you too," Maya said. "You mind if I
walk with you and ask you some questions?"

"Works for me," Rory said. "I'll just be trying to figure
out who dropped off this envelope. Probably means I'll
be sorting through video footage of the front desk for the
next few hours."

"Not a fun job, but I'm happy to keep you company
while you go through the video," Maya said.

"Sure, let's go this way."

They headed into an office with computers where
Rory could pull up the security footage. She shut the
door behind them, taking a seat. Maya followed suit as
Rory pulled up video.

"My dad said I should talk to you too while you're
here," Rory said. "I'd like to be a K-9 handler at some
point. My dad was a handler when I was a little kid.
I loved our dog and want to follow in his footsteps."

"I'm happy to answer any questions you have," Maya
said. "And after you work K-9, get other experience in
different areas. Then you can follow in his footsteps
and be a chief of police or sheriff."

Rory gave her a shy smile. "That would be awesome.
First, I have to survive my rookie year here, though."

"Tell me about Sheriff Jackson," Maya said.

"What do you want to know?"

"Is there any kind of mic in this room?"

Rory shook her head. "No."

"Then how do you feel about how he's running this
department?"

"He's okay. I guess you have to be tough to be a

sheriff, and I'm a rookie, so really, I don't know how he compares to anyone else," Rory said.

"True, but I'm not going to say anything to anyone. I promise. I'm trying to figure out how to best work this investigation so that we bring justice to these victims. Why doesn't the sheriff want to cooperate with other agencies on an investigation this big?"

"He's like that all the time," Rory answered. "He's kind of sharp with his words, but he runs a tight department, if you know what I mean. No one messes around here."

"My grandfather mentioned you'd put in an application for his sheriff's office. He said your dad thought there was some harassment going on. Is Sheriff Jackson harassing you in any way?"

Rory shrugged and started watching video. "He hasn't harassed me at all. Some of the other female deputies have complained. I've never had an issue, though. I think it's because of who my dad is. But I'm also ready to leave where I grew up. It's tough being a deputy here when you know people and you're arresting someone you went to high school with. I mean, that guy who just went missing, the case I just told the sheriff about, I've known him since elementary school. It's just weird. I'm ready to move away, but not be too far from home. I still want to be able to visit my parents and get some of my mom's good home cooking."

Maya smiled. "I understand what it's like to work in the town you grew up in. What do you know about our latest missing person? Is he someone who's disappeared before?"

"No. He was always a party guy. He loved skiing and boarding and anything else outside, but he was never one to run away from home or anything like that. I have heard that he's been going to some of the parties on the weekends."

Maya's interest was piqued, and she thought back to what Kay Anderson had told her about her son. He'd supposedly been at a party too. Maybe that's where the killer was finding some of his victims. "Tell me more about these parties."

"It's sort of like a club from what I've heard. They have them at different locations out in the forest. You have to be on the 'in,' if you know what I mean. I don't know a ton, because being a deputy doesn't put you high on the list to invite to a party where people are drinking and using drugs. But I have some friends who go and they've filled me in on some of the things that have happened. Sounds a little crazy to me."

"Not to mention a little illegal," Maya said. "Have you heard what types of drugs are being used there?"

"I think for the most part it's been marijuana, but one of my friends told me a week or so ago that some harder stuff was starting to come in. She was thinking of not going anymore because of that."

"What kind of hard stuff?"

"I don't know," Rory said. "But whatever it was made her nervous. She said there's another party happening late this afternoon."

"Do you think you could find out where it's going to be held? If these parties are happening on Forest Service land, maybe I need to stop by and make sure everything is on the up-and-up. I wouldn't want to slack on my job and let illegal activities happen out in the forest. Plus, if this is how our latest victim went missing, maybe the attendees at the party saw something."

"I can see if I can find out," Rory said. "I can text you details."

"That would be great," Maya said. "If you get that info, are you interested in going with me to back me up? I'll run it by the sheriff."

"I'd love that," Rory said. "That would be awesome. I'd love to get the experience."

"Okay, let's stay in touch." Maya gave Rory her card with her phone number. "I'm happy to help you get more time in with new situations. I remember what it's like being a rookie. No one wants to talk with you and it takes a while to get comfortable with the job."

"I feel like every time I'm out on patrol something new happens. My field training was great, but I don't always feel confident."

"Give it time. Rookies make rookie mistakes. Heck, experienced officers make mistakes. We're human. I started as an MP in the Marines. It took a while to get comfortable with the work."

She was about ready to stand up when Rory stopped the video feed and pointed to the screen. "There's the guy with the manila envelope."

"Interesting," Maya said, taking a glimpse of the grainy footage. "It seems like he knew where your cameras were and managed to stay where he needed to to make sure there wasn't a good shot of him."

"And he wore a hat," Rory said. "That helped completely block his face. He also managed to leave the envelope while the front desk deputy was distracted. I'll ask that deputy if he remembers him, but he did a good job making sure we couldn't ID him."

"Wonder what was in the envelope," Maya said.

"Yeah, the sheriff was not happy. And he's really going to be unhappy now. Guess I better go tell him."

"Good luck with that," Maya said, getting to her feet. "And good luck with your application to the Western River County Sheriff's Office. They'd be lucky to have you."

"Thanks," Rory said. "I'll be in touch soon about the party."

"Text me with the information."

Maya headed out of the room. This case seemed overwhelming, what with the number of victims, a sheriff who was barely competent and no answers yet. Hopefully they could bust this party and learn something that would help find the killer.

Chapter Twenty

Maya glanced at her watch. There wasn't enough time to go out on a full patrol and she wanted to work later in the afternoon anyway to find the party that Rory had heard about. Maybe they'd get lucky and the killer would show up. She decided that when they crashed the party, she would get the attendees' IDs and run background checks. Maybe she'd get lucky and find the killer that way.

She had some spare time, so she contacted Tanner about doing a training session. She received a quick response that he could meet up and he also sent his address.

About fifteen minutes later, Maya arrived at Tanner's place on the outskirts of town. His homestead had a nice feel to it, with a large log cabin, outbuilding and a split rail fence around the property. The log cabin had large windows facing the southwest peaks and a deck that she imagined was nice to sit out on in the summer. While the place was tasteful and modest, she knew Tanner must have some money. Places like this had high price tags in the Colorado mountains where, despite the millions of acres, private property was at a premium.

As she parked in the drive, she saw Tanner come

out of the outbuilding and wave to her. Finn was by his side, wagging his tail. Juniper growled.

"It's okay, girly. You don't need to be jealous. In fact, you might like him if you gave him a chance."

Maya hadn't had Juniper with other dogs because she was a working dog. Working dogs didn't do things like go to dog parks—especially not one trained to apprehend. While Juniper was sweet, if she detected a threat, she could possibly attack another dog. Maya had been careful in training sessions with other dog-handler teams as Juniper could quickly get upset and become aggressive with another dog.

Stepping out of her vehicle, Maya greeted Tanner. "Glad this worked out today," she said. "Finn did a great job searching the area. What I noticed he needed work on was going to source for what he's trained to find. Why don't you show me what you've been doing for training the actual odor?"

"This way," Tanner said, turning and heading toward the outbuilding. Finn followed and Tanner put him in a pen with a heated doghouse before going into the shop. When they entered, Maya saw that Tanner had about six scent boxes set up in a row. "I've been using these to work on Finn learning the different odors."

"That's good," Maya said. "And you're keeping one set aside that consistently has the odor so that there's no residue in the others?"

"That's correct," said Tanner, pointing at one near the middle. "It's that one right there."

"Do you have anything in there yet?"

"No."

"Let's get a hide in there," Maya said. "We'll give it about ten minutes to set up and then run Finn and see how he does. I noticed he likes to look at you while working, so we're going to start with his toy in the box with the hide. That should help him get an immediate reward."

"Okay, sounds good. Let me go and get some training stuff."

He walked over to a freezer in the corner specially marked as having biological materials. It had a giant padlock and he pulled out the key to open it up. Maya knew that HRD handlers had the real deal to train on, meaning body parts, blood, tissues in different stages of decomposition and other biological materials. Sometimes women even donated placentas after birth, but some HRD handlers worried about the hormones teaching the dog an incorrect scent and wouldn't train off those. The sheriff probably had to sign off on the paperwork. There was of course a lot of red tape, so to speak, when it came to HRD training materials. If Tanner was doing things right, he should have the origin of the materials listed in a file somewhere. Maya was happy to have a dog that found narcotics.

"If there's any scent he's struggling with, grab that," she said, "it'll help to have him find the toy with that scent."

"Okay," Tanner said, putting on gloves to keep his scent off the training aids and grabbing a jar out of the freezer.

Maya didn't even want to know what it was. Most likely Tanner had tissue samples, although if he had an in with the right hospital it was possible he could have a finger or something along those lines. She fought to push back a flashback of being in Afghanistan and seeing Marines lose fingers and worse from IEDs or other casualties of battle. She tried to look away as he put the jar in the scent box. Some of Finn's toys sat on a bench and Maya grabbed one, handing it to Tanner.

"Just put it either next to or on top of the jar," Maya said.

Tanner did as instructed and Maya took a look at her watch.

"We'll wait about ten minutes," she said. "Then I'll have you get Finn and we'll run the scent boxes and see how he does. Since we have a little time to pass, you mind if I ask you some questions?"

"I don't mind," Tanner said.

"How well do you know the sheriff?" Maya figured any and all information she could get would be helpful. The more she knew about the sheriff the better.

"I don't know him well personally or anything, just through working with the sheriff's office for search and rescue stuff. Finn and I were only recently certified, so I haven't done much with them yet, but I've been out on a few ops."

Maya nodded. "Is Sheriff Jackson always this difficult?"

"No. Usually he's worse. I think he's actually on better behavior with you and your boss around."

"Really?"

"Really. I mean, I have no issues with him. I just do my job. I'm not a deputy, I'm a volunteer, so he's usually fine with me. I've just observed him with his deputies and I'm amazed they don't look for jobs elsewhere. He's rough on them, in my opinion. On the other hand, you don't hear about deputies getting into trouble around here, so maybe that's good."

Maya nodded. She'd learned from Pops that a well-run department started at the top. You couldn't give too much leeway because that's when things happened that could tarnish a department's reputation. That's why Pops was in the position he was in right now, being under investigation. But there was leadership and then there was someone who managed out of fear and intimidation. "You hear anything else about him?"

"You know, there's rumors here and there. Antler Valley isn't totally a small town, but there's a core group of people who live here year-round unlike the tourists who travel in and out or the seasonal folks who own second homes. There's some talk."

"About what?" Maya asked.

"His personal life mostly. Rumor has it the sheriff likes to sleep around."

"Is he married?"

"Yes. And his wife is expecting their first child in a few months."

Maya took that information in. Things like that could lead to blackmail and other issues. Maybe that's what the manila envelope was about. "Anything else I should know?"

"He's up for reelection this November. His opponent has many years of law enforcement experience and has a good chance of winning the race. I've heard it's already heated. That's really all I know. If I hear of anything else or think of anything else, I'll let you know."

"That would be great," Maya said, thinking again about blackmail. "Thanks. So where do you get your training aids for Finn? Do you have to deal with the sheriff for that?"

"Only in that I let him know what I have. My family has donated money to the local hospital for years.

When I decided to get Finn and start this project, I asked if they could save things. You know, like amputations, bloody gauze. Anything with human remains. I keep a log of what I've been given and have permission for all parts, so to speak. I've been able to collect quite a good amount of training aids."

Maya nodded, once again glad that she didn't have to do that. "What made you decide to work an HRD dog?"

"I wanted to do something with dogs to help others. It seemed like live scent SAR dogs were abundant in this county, but there were no HRD dogs. I'm not bothered by stuff like body parts. I'm not squeamish at all, actually. I thought having an HRD dog would be an asset to the SAR team and the sheriff's office. They've been happy to have us and I look forward to doing more work. I'm lucky in that my family gave me a trust fund, so I have the freedom to do something important. Something to give back. And I can volunteer, which is even better."

"That's fantastic," Maya said. "If you don't mind, I'll let my grandfather know about you and Finn. It would be nice to think we won't need you, but unfortunately things come up and we don't have an HRD dog team in our county."

"I would be glad to come help anytime."

"Great. All right, go get Finn and let's see how he does running these boxes."

Tanner disappeared outside to get Finn out of his kennel. Maya knew he was coming when she heard more barking from Juniper. They came around the corner and she had them run the boxes like they normally would. Finn wanted to watch Tanner too much, so she had Tanner take his dog off-leash and send him out on his own. Finn stood frozen in place.

"Use your command for him and direct him out. Then step back and see if he'll work it."

"Okay. Finn, go find it. Let's go."

At first Finn was a little hesitant, but then he realized it was up to him to find the odor. He trotted down the line of scent boxes, passing the one with the hide. Tanner was going to redirect him back, but Maya stopped him.

"Let your dog work it out. Watch his body language. He's in odor, he just needs to work the scent cone. He'll come back and forth until he pinpoints the source."

"It's hard not to stop him," Tanner said.

"I know what you mean, but out on a live search, you need to trust him and let him do his job. You won't know if he's gone by a scent. You just have to listen to him and go with him."

"That's true," Tanner said as Finn suddenly whipped around and came back to the box with the hide. The dog sat and looked at Tanner.

"Go open the box, let him realize that the toy is there and that he did a great job. Really praise him up," Maya said.

Tanner followed his instructions and Finn pulled his toy out of the box and started squeaking the ball. Maya heard Juniper outside start barking and whining again.

"Good. We'll repeat that again and this time, I'll throw the ball when Finn alerts on the correct box. Go outside. I'm going to put the boxes in a different location and I don't want you to know this time where the hide is."

"Sounds good," Tanner said.

Maya moved the boxes around and Tanner and Finn came back in and worked the area. Finn had more confidence this time and located the odor. She threw the toy for him. They continued doing some more exercises and then she had Tanner put Finn away to give him a rest.

She hid some narcotics for Juniper and did some of the same exercises. It didn't hurt to go back to the basics. Juniper worked well and Maya's phone buzzed. She had several text messages. One from Josh about talking later. One from Lucas saying they were still waiting on DNA results, but his friend was going to get to it soon. The final text was from Rory. She had a time and location for that night's party.

"We'll have to wrap up," Maya said. "I need to go back out on patrol soon."

"Thanks for your help," Tanner said. "I'll practice hard with those exercises."

"Finn is a great dog. He'll get this figured out quickly."

With that, Maya said her goodbyes and headed back into town. She had a party to crash. As she drove up Tanner's drive, her phone buzzed again.

It was Ben and the text read, Come to the sheriff's office ASAP.

Chapter Twenty-One

Maya parked at the sheriff's office. Even after her training session, Juniper was ready to go out and work. She danced with her front paws. As her paws hit the mat in her compartment, it sounded like little drums.

"You may get to work tonight," Maya said. "Save some energy."

Although she really wasn't worried about Juniper not having enough energy. Juniper always seemed to have plenty. Maya had rarely seen her tired.

Ben came walking out of the front entrance, spotted Maya and came over to her.

"What's up?" she asked, getting out of her vehicle.

"The coroner was able to identify some of the remains today. You were right, the body that the HRD dog found was Avery Anderson."

Her heart dropped and her stomach churned. She had been hoping she was wrong. Thinking about his mother, anxiety started taking over. "Does his mother know?"

"That's the reason I called you. The sheriff and I were hoping you'd do the death notification."

A headache started spreading across Maya's temple. She massaged her forehead with her fingers, willing herself to take a deep breath. She'd done death notifications before. It was the worst part of the job. She'd also made the mistake of visiting a family of one of the Marines who she'd served with who had been killed in action. She'd thought it would help her feel better and bring the family some peace. In the end, they'd kicked her out and she had gone to a bar and drank until someone put her in a cab and she'd stumbled back home. She'd come a long way since then, with the veterans' support group and joining AA, but this was going to be a trigger. Kay's entire world would change in an instant and Maya would always be the one tied to that.

"If this is too much, then let me know," Ben said.

"No, it'll be fine. It's just never easy and I was just thinking about the past. But I'll do it," Maya said. "I feel like I owe her that."

"Okay, she's in a visitor's room this way."

Maya followed Ben, thinking about how she needed to find an AA meeting tonight. Something. What she really wanted to do was call Josh and talk to him. He'd understand all of it—the difficulty of a death notification and the urge to drown her feelings in alcohol. But right now, Josh only added to her triggers. There was Pops too, but he was probably knee deep in the investigation into him and working with Josh's dad to keep his case from going to trial. Maya would either call her sponsor or find a meeting.

And Juniper. She had Juniper now, and she was so often what kept Maya going.

As they walked to the visitor's room, Ben said to her, "I also meant to tell you that the drugs Juniper found out at the crime scene were Gray Death like you thought. The coroner is running a tox screen on all the victims.

We should hopefully get results soon. We think that maybe the killer was subduing his victims with the drug, or picking out people who were using it. Right now, there's nothing else connecting the victims. They're male and female, ages are similar, but still a range, and they come from diverse backgrounds. Drugs may be the common denominator."

"Maybe he thinks he's justified in killing by murdering someone with a drug addiction," Maya said.

"Could be. There's another thing, which is the bodies are missing some parts, for lack of a better way to say it. The coroner said it could be from scavengers, although he found marks on one victim that indicated they might have been partially dismembered. The sheriff has agreed to put this case into ViCAP, so I'm helping with the paperwork, and if we can get enough details, maybe there'll be a match to another case."

"I hope we can catch this guy soon," Maya said.

"Me too," Ben said as they rounded a corner and headed into a room where Kay sat.

Maya took a deep breath. "Hello."

Wringing her hands together, Kay peered up, tears already falling. At least she was sitting down. Maya knew that everyone reacted to bad news differently, sometimes even passing out, so she always made sure a victim's family members were sitting down. She pulled up a chair and sat across from Kay.

"I'm so sorry," she started out. Kay started sobbing and Maya paused. Taking another deep breath, she handed Kay some Kleenex and continued. "Yesterday we found some more victims in the avalanche area that you knew about. Today the coroner did identify one of the bodies as your son, Avery."

Kay continued sobbing, taking in large gulps of air. Maya gave her a moment. When Kay's breathing seemed to be closer to normal, Maya said, "Right now, because Avery is part of this investigation, his belongings and remains can't be released, but I will let you know when that changes."

Nodding, Kay took several more gulps. "How did he die?"

"That's still under investigation," Maya said. "I can't tell you much at the moment. But we'd like to ask you some more questions. Are you up for that right now?"

Kay blew her nose, wadded up a tissue and threw it away. "I don't know. I don't think so. Can we do this another time?"

Maya hesitated. This was the best time to get information out of a family member. Family often knew more than they realized or wanted to admit. She also knew that she couldn't push too hard either. Not with the news Kay had just received. "Sure. I'll check in with you tomorrow. And you have my phone number in case you think of something. I know this is hard, but do understand that I'm asking these questions so we can do our best to find justice for your son."

"I know," Kay said, blowing her nose again. "I just need to process this first."

"Do you have anyone I can call to stay with you?"

"I called my sister. She's on the way here to pick me up. Should be here any minute."

"That's good," Maya said. "If you want, I'll walk you outside and wait with you."

"I would very much appreciate it." They stood up, and as they headed out of the room, Kay stopped Maya again. "Officer Thompson?"

"Yes?"

"Thank you again."

"For what?" Maya asked.

"For not giving up and finding my son."

Chapter Twenty-Two

The hallway seemed longer walking to the front entrance of the sheriff's office. They walked in silence, the only sound Kay blowing her nose once in a while. Maya wanted to do something to console her, but she didn't know what. She had learned to compartmentalize her feelings, stuffing them down when she was in Afghanistan. It was the only way she could survive. But part of the reason she'd wanted to go into law enforcement was to help people. Growing up she had witnessed Pops helping others through some of their toughest times, like losing a loved one. Maya wanted to do the same. She'd have to talk about this more in her veterans' support group.

They arrived at the front entrance. Sunlight spilled in through the doors and windows. Deputy Glen, who had helped Maya out at the crime scene, was near the doors, talking with someone. Because of the sunlight, the person was silhouetted and she couldn't make out who it was. Kay was heading out the door when she too caught sight of the person Deputy Glen was talking to.

Kay balled up her fists, her gaze locking on to the person by Deputy Glen: Bryce. "You piece of shit. What are you doing here? You need to go to hell and pay for your sins. You killed my son."

She began beating on Bryce, her knuckles pummel-ing him as fast as she could deliver the punches. Maya, shocked, took a moment to respond, but she quickly jumped in and pulled Kay off. Maya twisted her arm behind her back, trying to gain some control. She didn't blame anyone for being irritated with him and part of her wanted to unleash Kay on him, but Maya had to do her job.

"What the hell?" Maya said. "Calm down. Kay, I need you to calm down."

Kay was breathing hard and Deputy Glen had Bryce pulled away to a safe spot.

"Kay. Calm down. If you'll calm down, I'll release your arm. If you can't calm down, I'm going to have to handcuff you. Got it?"

Kay nodded.

"Okay, I'm going to let go and we're going to walk outside," Maya said, giving a glance at Deputy Glen, who nodded in acknowledgment.

They walked through the doors and once they were outside, she said, "What the hell was that? You want to explain to me why you went ballistic?"

Kay started to cry again and pulled a tissue out of her pocket. She blew her nose, sounding like a foghorn, and then stared at Maya, fire still burning in her eyes. "That guy sold drugs to Avery."

"What? Why didn't you tell me this earlier? This would have been good information to have when I was asking questions about Avery."

"I couldn't. I mean, I didn't want to admit that he maybe had a problem. I blew it off and pretended that he was just being a stupid kid, but then I saw him spiral-ing out of control the last time he came home. We had a big fight over it. I wanted him to get help, he told me he was fine. I said things I regret and now those are my last words to him." Kay started sobbing again.

Maya waited her out, relating to the pain of knowing that you'd never see someone again. Never getting to say what you should have or wanted to. She thought briefly of Josh and how she'd left things. Maybe this was a sign that she should quit running away from pain and instead face it head-on.

She shoved her personal thoughts away and focused back on Kay. "I'm so sorry. I know this is very difficult. Tell me more about Bryce being a drug dealer. How do you know for sure it was him selling?"

"I caught them once. Bryce had come home with Avery. I was wondering what a guy who was a couple years out of college wanted with a freshman. I suppose they weren't that far apart in age, but they were at different points in their lives. Again, I was in denial. Bryce and Avery went to visit some friends. You know how small Pinecone Junction is. I was going to the Black Bear Café to get us all dinner and saw Bryce handing some baggies of stuff off to some older teenagers. The kids gave him money. I thought about calling the cops, but I didn't. Maybe if I had, Avery would still be alive…

"I confronted them that night and Avery told me to stay out of it, that I didn't know anything and didn't know what I was talking about. I told him that he needed to find new friends, get clean, stop before he got in too deep and it was too late. He blew me off and they left to come back here to Antler Valley. A couple weeks later, he disappeared. I wish I had stopped him. I wish I had done something," Kay said, with new tears flowing.

A car pulled up and another lady who resembled Kay was driving.

"Is that your sister?" Maya asked. Kay nodded. "Okay. Is there anything else I should know? Anything else that you can think of?"

"No."

"Then I want you to get in that car with your sister, go stay with her and let me do my job. But if there's anything you think of, call me. I'll answer. But if I hear that you were anywhere near Bryce or assaulting him again, I'll have to arrest you. I don't want to do that. I really don't, because I understand your grief and that grief makes us do things that we shouldn't, but I need you to let me handle this. Got it?"

"Got it," Kay said.

"Good. Then I'll keep you posted on any news in the case. You let me know if you think of anything else." Maya helped Kay to the car, opening the passenger door so she could get in. Kay appeared to have aged ten years in a short amount of time.

Maya closed the door and watched the car drive away. She understood the pain. Now it was time to figure out what Bryce had to do with this case. He had already pissed her off at the crime scene. But she had to be careful because he and the sheriff seemed a little chummy.

That made Maya even more suspicious of the sheriff. Did he realize his small-town reporter was supplementing his income selling drugs? Was the sheriff somehow involved in these murders? The thought that he could be the killer went through her mind, but she didn't want to believe that someone in law enforcement would commit these murders. On the other hand, things like this did happen and she needed to keep an open mind if she wanted to help bring justice to these victims.

Maya headed back inside to find out more. Deputy Glen and Bryce were still standing where she'd left them.

"I want to press charges against that crazy bitch," Bryce said.

"No, trust me, you don't," Maya snapped back.

"Why is that?"

"Because you really don't want me looking into your side business."

"Side business?" Bryce asked.

"You selling drugs, Bryce?"

"Excuse me?"

"Officer Thompson," Deputy Glen interjected. "You need to stand down."

"No, I don't, because if Bryce here is selling drugs and it links to a crime on national forest land, I promise I will make his life miserable, and I always keep my promises."

"That lady is nuts," Bryce said. "She accused me of selling drugs to some kids. I don't do drugs."

"Doing drugs and selling drugs are two different things," Maya said.

"I don't do either," Bryce shot back.

"Good, then I won't have to bust your ass."

"Okay," Deputy Glen said. "That's enough. Bryce, go find your uncle and I'll talk with Officer Thompson."

"Okay," Bryce said, giving Maya a smug look as he sauntered off. "I'll go find my uncle. The sheriff."

Once Bryce was out of earshot, Maya glared at Deputy Glen. "The sheriff is his uncle?"

"Yes, that's why I was trying to warn you. I don't like that kid either, but his mother is the sheriff's eldest sister. There's a good age difference between the sheriff and his sister, but we've all been instructed to look the other way when it comes to Bryce."

"Do you think he is selling drugs?" Maya asked.

"It wouldn't surprise me, but I'm telling you, you're better off staying out of it."

Maya put her hands on her duty belt and stared at Deputy Glen. "Staying out of things isn't my strong suit."

Chapter Twenty-Three

Taking a deep breath, Maya worked to calm her temper. Bryce being the sheriff's nephew was a complete shock, but maybe that was the reason he was sharing information with the kid? Although she knew that it didn't matter who it was—the sheriff shouldn't be releasing this information. He was pushing the line, and why? She didn't know. Didn't he want cases successfully prosecuted in his county?

Maya stayed in the front lobby, waiting for Rory to show up. Her mind shifted gears. She wanted to find this party and bust it, but they had to be careful. They would be outnumbered, creating a very dangerous situation.

Ben came out of the secure area in the back of the lobby. "I hear we had a situation with the mother and our favorite journalist?" he prodded.

"Yes. And did you know that our favorite journalist is the sheriff's nephew?"

"I just found that out too." Ben shook his head. "I've been in touch with the local FBI field office. Agent Kessler will be on his way here soon. I warned him about the situation here and he's agreed to come in as a consultant for now, but if we get a hit in ViCAP, then he can push to take over the investigation. Hopefully the way I've negotiated this doesn't come back on us, but with this town, who knows. What are you doing next?"

"I'm going with Deputy Rory Lopez out to an illegal party," Maya answered. "Deputy Lopez told me that these parties are happening quite a bit and from the evidence we've gathered, it could be where the killer is stalking and finding his prey. I'm hoping that I can bust the party but still get some of the participants to talk to me."

"How many people do you think will be there?"

"I don't know for sure," Maya said.

"Be careful. You'll be outnumbered. That could get dicey quickly."

"I'm hoping they'll have smoked a lot and will be laid-back and have the munchies," Maya said, trying to joke but knowing that Ben was also right. She was heading into a dangerous situation and her backup officer was a rookie.

"I'd go with you, but I have something I need to take care of. Maybe I can convince the sheriff to send some more deputies."

"That would be great," Maya said. "If he'll do that."

"I'll try, but if not, don't bust the party unless you're sure you can control the situation. I can be there quickly from where I'm going."

"Are you doing something with the investigation?" She knew it was none of her business, but she was curious.

"No, some personal things, but I'll be on call and can respond."

"Sounds good," Maya said, thinking she too needed to call Josh and deal with personal things at some point this evening.

A door from the back area opened and Rory came out, joining them.

"Ready to go?" Maya asked.

"I am," Rory said.

"Let me call the sheriff really quick and see about some extra deputies joining you." Ben stepped off to the side and pulled out his cell phone.

"Do you think we'll need backup?" Rory asked.

"We need to be careful. We'll be outnumbered," Maya said. "Backup would be good, but if it doesn't work out, we'll be careful. You know some of the participants, what do you think? Are they difficult?"

"No." Rory shook her head. "I think they'll be nervous about being busted, but I don't think they'll be aggressive."

"Okay," Maya said. "We'll be careful and take some precautions. I have Juniper and she might be able to help control the situation. I really don't want to bust and arrest them all. We just need information and I want them to stop these parties on Forest Service land. This will be their warning. Hopefully we can get that across to them."

Rory agreed as Ben came back over. "The sheriff says he doesn't have deputies to spare this afternoon. He said if you get in a tight spot, though, call dispatch and they'll send a few deputies your way, but otherwise you're on your own."

"That was nice of him," Maya said sarcastically, although she wasn't surprised. "Thanks for asking."

"Be careful," Ben said. "I'll take care of what I need to, but like I said, let me know if you want me to come out there."

"Thanks," Maya said. Then to Rory, "Let's go."

Maya followed Rory out of town. The scenery quickly switched from houses to wide-open meadows. The sun glinted off the snow, creating small sparkles. A few miles later they started climbing in elevation up a mountain pass. The trees became thicker and they passed a sign designating that they were now in the national forest.

The party location was a camping area that wasn't too far up the pass. Rory had mentioned that there was a good place to park where their patrol vehicles wouldn't be spotted. Maya pulled up next to her.

She stepped out and heard music in the distance. Before she closed the door, Juniper whined and put her golden eyes up to the opening in her compartment. "Don't worry, girly, if I need you, you'll know."

"What's our plan?" Rory asked.

"Let's see if we can tell how many people are here right now and determine if it's a good idea for us to break up the fun. It's early, so hopefully no one is too drunk and ready to fight."

Maya and Rory picked their way closer, using the trees to help give them cover. Their boots sank into the snow and the temperature was dropping as the sun started to set. Maya could see her breath. She was ready for warmer weather.

They approached an area where they had a good visual of what was going on. There were only a few people there and they had a small speaker set up on a log that was probably Bluetoothed into someone's phone. A fire was already going strong in a pit and the attendees had beers and were passing around a vape. Maya thought it was probably a marijuana vape based on the odor.

"What do you think?" whispered Rory.

"I'm counting about five people. You see anyone I'm missing?"

"Nope, coming up with the same number."

"Let's go ahead and announce ourselves. We can handle five people," Maya said with a confidence she wasn't sure she was feeling. She had promised Josh a while back that she would wait for backup in situations that warranted it. This might be one of those situations, but she wanted to shut the party down before more people arrived. Plus, the sheriff had said he wouldn't send deputies unless they were needed. And she could always call Ben, although who knew how far out of town he was.

Maya put her hand on her Glock and said, "Let's go."

Rory nodded and they came through the trees. "Forest Service law enforcement!" Maya yelled. "Stop what you're doing, put your hands up."

"Antler Valley Sheriff's Office," Rory said. "Put your hands up. Now!"

"What the hell, Rory?" one of the girls said.

Maya figured that was Rory's friend. She felt for the young deputy. The job was hard to mix with outside friendships for just these reasons.

"I need you to all put your beers down and show me your hands," Maya repeated. "We just want to talk."

Nobody moved or followed instructions. Maya was about ready to repeat her instructions when a group of another five people arrived. They'd walked in from the other direction. Now Maya and Rory were severely outnumbered. They glanced at each other.

"Anything gets crazy, call for backup," Maya instructed.

Rory nodded. Maya could tell she was trying hard to be brave, but this was not going as planned.

"Once again, I need everyone to show me their hands," Maya said.

The partiers stared back, no one moving or talking. No one complying either. She was debating her next move when a snowball from off to the side came at her and smacked her in the face. She turned toward her attacker and another guy used her moment of distraction to rush her.

He pushed Maya backward and she struggled to stay on her feet. She worked to gain control over him, but he was a big guy and she could tell this would be an exhausting power struggle—one that he wasn't going to back down from. Maya reached down to a remote on her duty belt and hit the button.

"Now's your chance to back off," she told the guy as she continued to try to gain control.

He laughed, reached toward Maya's gun and said, "I think you're the one in trouble."

Chapter Twenty-Four

Just as he was about to pull Maya's Glock out of its holster, brown fur flew in from the trees, nailing him in the bicep and knocking the guy off Maya.

Juniper latched on and had a good grip with her back teeth. She stayed on the bite even as the guy tried to push her off. The more he pushed, the more Juniper shook her head, biting down harder. The guy screamed out in pain.

Maya caught her breath for a second and made sure Rory was okay. Someone had rushed her too, but with the distraction of Juniper, Rory had been able to get the upper hand and had the person handcuffed.

A couple other people appeared to be thinking about rushing at them, but watching Juniper shake their friend like a rag doll had made them stop in their tracks.

"Out," Maya said to Juniper, giving her the command to release her bite. But Juniper's adrenaline was pumping. She hadn't taken a bite in a while. She flicked her eyes toward Maya, asking if she really had to let go.

"Get your dog off me!" the guy squealed in pain.

"Juniper. Out," Maya said again, firmly.

Juniper finally released, but stayed by Maya's side, ready to engage again if the guy even gave her a threatening look. Maya handcuffed the guy and inspected his bicep. He'd probably need to go to the hospital and get stitches. His thick winter jacket had provided some padding, but was still completely shredded. Juniper had bitten through the clothing. Once Maya had control over him and the situation, she would administer first aid.

"I need all of you to set your items down and line up over there," Maya said, pointing to an area with enough room for them to stand side by side. Much to her relief, this time, everyone complied. Once everyone was where she wanted, she hauled the guy Juniper had apprehended to his feet. She told Rory to call for backup, medical and to notify Ben of the situation.

"Are you going to apply pressure to my injuries?" the guy asked. "Or am I going to bleed out?"

"You're going to make it," Maya said. "And that means after you go to the hospital and get medical care, your next stop will be jail."

"You'll be sorry you did this," the guy said. "My dad's a lawyer."

"Well, if your dad is a lawyer, then he can explain why assaulting an officer and trying to take my gun is a problem and lands you in jail."

The guy shut up and Maya had him go sit down on a log. She didn't need him passing out and hitting his head. She praised Juniper, who continued to watch the guy in case he tried anything. Juniper loved nothing more than apprehending someone and given a chance would gladly take another bite. Feeling like things were under control, Maya addressed the group.

"Thank you for listening. Despite what you might think, we're not here to arrest you. We need information and we need you to be honest. The only ones getting arrested right now are these two gentlemen who assaulted officers. I don't want the headache of paperwork and arresting all of you. If you cooperate and answer my questions truthfully, then K-9 Juniper, who's trained to find narcotics, won't check any vehicles or belongings. Got it?"

The partiers nodded and mumbled some agreements.

"Good. I'm going to pat you all down, get your names and contact info, and then I have some questions," Maya said.

Rory was already watching the two guys in handcuffs, so Maya went and made sure that no one had a weapon or anything else that could be dangerous. She wrote down all their names, asking for IDs to verify the names. She wanted to run everyone through the system. One of them could be the killer. Rory's friend was muttering something about her being a snitch.

"She's not a snitch," Maya said. "This is all on me." She hoped that it would help to take some pressure off Rory with her friends. When Maya finished taking down everyone's information, she said, "So I know you've got some beer and marijuana here. Is there anything harder?"

No one answered.

"C'mon, I need some answers. Like I said, I don't want to arrest all of you. It would be a headache. I already have enough paperwork to do with these two," Maya said, pointing at the guys in handcuffs. "I need to know if you are buying illegal drugs, who you're getting them from. The beer and marijuana I know already. Those items are available anywhere. Although I should remind you that marijuana is not legal on federal land, but I'm going to ignore that tonight. I just need some-one to give me your source."

"We have a couple different sources," one guy fi-nally said.

"Hey man, shut up," his friend next to him said.

"She said she wouldn't arrest us."

"You want to believe a pig?"

"Hey," Maya interrupted. "You, stay quiet. You, tell me more."

"There's a couple sources in town to get more stuff."

"Will you give me names?" Maya asked.

The guy glanced nervously at his friends. "Maybe."

She realized she wasn't going to get more out of him in front of his friends. She decided to ask one more question and then let them all go. She had the contact information for this guy and could follow up later. "Is one of those sources Bryce Riley?"

The guy shrugged and nodded. "He has sold us stuff. He said it was for a story he was doing about drug use in the Colorado mountains, especially in resort towns. He wanted it to be about law enforcement look-ing the other way. But he had some good stuff and I may have bought some of it. To help him with his story, of course."

"Of course," Maya said, finding Bryce's twist on drug dealing interesting. Could he also be killing to get a better story? "Okay, thank you. One last question. Have any of you seen your friends accept a ride home from these parties from someone they didn't know?"

The same guy who had been cooperative spoke up again. "I noticed one of my coworkers getting in a ve-hicle with someone at the last party. He hasn't been seen since."

"What's your coworker's name?" Maya asked. The guy answered, giving Maya his friend's name. She turned to Rory, speaking quietly. "Is that our latest missing person?"

Rory nodded.

"Can you give me a description of the guy he went with? Or the vehicle?"

"No, I really don't remember. It was dark and I didn't notice much other than I thought it was odd they were leaving the party early."

"Okay, thanks. I appreciate it," Maya said. "I want you all to get out of here and figure out a spot that's not on Forest Service land for your parties in the future. Go the old-fashioned route and party in town at someone's house. I'll be keeping an eye on your get-togethers when I'm out patrolling. I really don't want to have to arrest all of you.

"I need to warn you too, there's a drug being sold called Gray Death. Be careful. It's potent and extremely dangerous. It could kill someone quickly. It's full of fentanyl and even carfentanil, which is even more lethal. I don't want to have to tell your families that you died from doing this drug. Be safe. Go home."

Maya felt like a mother lecturing these young adults, but she could only hope that maybe one of them would listen and be careful. Once everyone left, she made sure the fire was out. Even in the wintertime, fires could be a problem.

In the distance, Maya heard sirens. The medical response was here along with some backup. Of course, thanks to Juniper, they didn't need backup anymore. Juniper stood guarding the two men, hoping they'd make a run for it, but they'd learned their lesson.

Suddenly, Juniper's head whipped around and she went on alert, growling. Maya peered into the trees to see what Juniper was upset about.

A dark figure took off through the trees, running fast.

She knew Juniper could catch the person, but she wanted a backup officer before they started tracking. "Juniper, down. Stay."

The Malinois listened, but Maya could tell that she was itching to go after the person running.

"Don't worry, girl. We'll get someone to back us up and then we'll track them."

He had been planning on attending the party and observing. Seeing who was next. Who deserved it. But then he'd learned that Maya and the other deputy would be there.

Smart move, Thompson.

He had no doubt that Maya suspected he was coming to these parties and was hoping to get IDs on everyone there and research them. He knew he probably shouldn't have been there at all, but then he'd changed his mind. He had to see Maya. She made him feel something he wasn't used to feeling. He'd never cared for someone this much and had been a little worried about her when she was attacked.

Just as he was thinking about intervening, her dog had come out of nowhere and latched on. It'd given her the upper hand.

The dog was good. One of the best he'd seen. And the partnership that Maya and the dog had was impressive. He better keep that in mind, but unlike the others, he didn't want to hurt Maya.

He wanted a different relationship with her. Something more.

Could she ever accept who he was and what he had done? Maybe she'd understand that some people just shouldn't be in this world. He had listened while she had told these idiots out here partying that it wasn't legal. That they should go to someone's house.

He liked that idea. He liked the thought of cleaning up.

In his mind, Maya was perfect. He had to win her over, but in order to do that, he had to be careful too.

He had cautiously made his way back to his vehicle, making sure to walk where the others had. Having an understanding of working dogs, he knew that if he stuck to a well-used path and there was no scent article, then it'd make it harder for the dog to find him.

He knew her K-9 could find someone with a scent article, but she was also trained to find the "hottest" or most recent scent. The more people who walked on the path, the more the hottest scent was disturbed and the harder it was for a K-9 to track.

Good thing he knew all this from his work as a handler.

He'd enjoyed talking with Maya while they worked together. She'd given him some shy smiles. It was a start. He imagined what it would be like to have her long legs wrapped around him.

He had to stop the images in his mind before they went too far and he lost focus.

Yes, even though when he was a teenager, a therapist had told his mother he had no feelings, and was not capable of loving someone. But he did have feelings… and they were for Officer Maya Thompson.

He would stay close and keep an eye on his phone—she was probably going to need him tonight. Or at least he'd done his best to make sure she would.

Now it was time to see if his plan would work.

Chapter Twenty-Five

Maya and Rory each took their respective arrestees and handed them off to deputies who'd arrived as backup. The guy Juniper had bitten did need some stitches and went off to the hospital in handcuffs.

Maya wanted to start tracking whoever had been lurking in the woods right away, but she needed a backup officer. She'd considered Rory, but she didn't have the experience.

Maya missed Josh once again. He had become a great backup officer and she trusted him. Not only that, she missed talking to him and having him wrap his arms around her. Somehow, she always felt safe around him, but she had been able to take care of herself before she'd met Josh. She had to do that now.

Deputy Glen pulled up and parked. He had done a good job out at the crime scene. He knew how far to stay back and didn't seem put off by taking commands from her. The number one rule of backing up a K-9 team was that the handler was in charge. It didn't matter if the backup officer outranked the handler. Some guys would have a problem with that—especially with a female K-9 handler bossing them around.

Maya texted Ben and gave him an update. She had

halfway expected him to show up with all the radio chatter, but he obviously had other things to do. She received a text back that he would be there soon. She mentioned that she wanted to try a track with Juniper that started on national forest land.

Where it takes Juniper and me, who knows...

She received a quick thumbs-up back and headed over to find Deputy Glen and Rory. She figured Rory could learn from the experience and that way if she did end up at the Western River Sheriff's Office as a deputy, she already had some training that might help Maya.

She spotted both deputies standing with the sheriff. *Great, just what I need.* Approaching with Juniper by her side, she stopped a little distance away so that Juniper didn't get agitated by the sheriff. Juniper's adrenaline was already up from taking a bite and she might be ready to latch on to someone again without much provocation.

"I have a request," Maya said to the sheriff, deciding direct was best. "There was one person who left the party on foot and evaded us. I am going to track them and would like Deputy Glen and Deputy Lopez to back me up."

The sheriff chomped his gum, crossed his arms and stared at Maya. She held his gaze, not backing down. She wouldn't give him that satisfaction. "Fine," he said.

Then he turned away. Maya and Juniper walked off and the two deputies followed. Maya headed to the area where she'd seen the person take off. There were footprints in the snow, which made it easy to cast Juniper out and have her find an odor.

"Are you ready?" she asked the two deputies. "When Juniper catches a scent, she's off. Be ready."

"Got it," said Deputy Glen.

"I haven't done this before," Rory said.

"I know," said Maya. "Just stay behind Deputy Glen, let him direct you. You just never want to get in front of the dog or the handler. And you especially never want to get in between a dog and handler. If I give an order, you take it and listen. I'm not worried about that when it comes to you, though. You're a good officer, rely on your training."

"Got it," said Rory, a look of determination on her face.

"Good," Maya said. "This is good experience if you want to work K-9s."

They headed over to the area near the trees where Maya had seen the person before they ran off. She spotted the footprints in the snow and cast Juniper out, telling her to "go find 'em and seek."

Juniper happily put her nose to the ground and found the odor quickly. She took off and Maya followed her, throwing a little slack in the leash to make sure she didn't pull Juniper off the scent by accident.

The track Juniper took them on went directly parallel to the tracks in the snow. Maya knew this was from the humidity and the way the scent was coming off the snow. They came to a spot where the wind had blown the snow completely off the ground and the footprints disappeared. This was when Maya was grateful to have Juniper, as she never wavered, and she continued on confidently following the scent, tail up in the air.

They came up to a paved road and Maya was shortening the leash to make sure Juniper didn't dart out in front of a car. Once she was on a scent, Juniper wouldn't think about running out in front of a vehicle. She was in her zone, so it was up to Maya to help protect her dog.

Juniper threw on the brakes and Maya almost ran into her. Whipping around, Juniper went over to the side of the road and went along a drainage area. She stopped, turned back around and went to some bushes that had collected trash and dirty slush from the plows clearing the roads. Juniper lay down and stared at the bushes.

"Good girl," Maya said.

The tricky part about Juniper's alert was that it was difficult to differentiate which pieces of trash were evidence.

"Juniper is doing an evidence alert here," Maya said. "I don't know on what since there's a ton of trash."

The two deputies came over and stared at the bushes with Maya. "I'll call one of our crime scene guys and have him process and take everything," Deputy Glen said.

Rory continued to peer into the bushes and put on gloves as she moved some branches around gently, so she wouldn't disturb anything but could see better in the thick greenery. "I think there's some gloves, sunglasses and a hat back in there. Maybe our suspect took them off."

"Could be," Maya said.

"The crime scene tech will be here soon," Deputy Glen said, hanging up from his call.

"I can stay here and watch this area," Rory said. "You two can continue on with the track."

"I don't know if it's a good idea to leave you alone," Maya said. "I don't like that. With the number of victims this guy has had, it might be better to wait for backup."

"I'll be fine," Rory said. "Plus, I think I see the tech vehicle now."

Maya peered down the road and agreed that she could see a sheriff's van coming toward them. "Okay, but be careful and stay vigilant."

"Will do, thanks," said Rory.

Maya praised Juniper for her great work and then told her to "go find 'em" again. Juniper enthusiastically went back to work and it only took a few seconds for her to get back in odor.

They continued down the side of the road and came to the edge of town where there were some apartments near a trailer park. This was where many of the ski resort workers along with other seasonal employees lived.

Juniper started to cross the road, and since there were no cars coming, Maya crossed with her. They went down the drainage ditch on the other side and trudged through deep snow that was black from the road and plows. Climbing up to the other side, she was glad she had on her boots. Her legs cramped from the hike back up, but she pushed through it. If her dog was willing to track through this, so was Maya.

They ended up on the back side of the apartment building and Juniper pulled Maya around the front, staying perfectly on track. She could hear Deputy Glen's footsteps behind her.

Juniper paused at a staircase, sniffing and working a scent cone, and then proceeded up the stairs. Maya was proud of her as they hadn't practiced a ton of hard-surface tracks. It wasn't something that was common out in the woods.

Taking a sharp left, Juniper went to a door at the end of the walkway and sat, staring. Maya, breathing heavy from running with Juniper, said to Deputy Glen,

"This is where the track ends. We need to find out who lives here."

"I know who lives there," said Deputy Glen.

"Who?" Maya asked.

"The sheriff's nephew, Bryce."

Chapter Twenty-Six

Josh sat at his desk staring at the mountain of paperwork in front of him. He'd barely made a dent. He couldn't focus as thoughts of Maya and how he'd screwed up kept going through his mind. Pulling his personal cell phone out, he checked again to see if Maya had called or texted, but there was nothing. She must really be mad. He didn't blame her. But she also had important work to do and he kept telling himself that was the other reason she hadn't called or texted.

He tossed the phone back onto his desk and turned around, staring out the window. The sun was starting to set. Josh would be happier when the days became longer and he wasn't driving to and from work in the cold and dark.

A knock at the door startled him and he turned back around. It was the front desk deputy. "Sorry to bother you, sir, but there's a lady here to see you."

"Did she give her name?" Josh asked.

"Amber Zielinkski."

Josh sighed. The last thing he wanted was to see Amber, but if he didn't, she would throw a fit. Maybe this was a good time to work on setting some boundaries with her. "Okay. Bring her back."

The deputy nodded and returned a few minutes later with Amber. Josh thanked him and then shut the door. "What do you want?"

"That's not a nice way to greet your ex-fiancée," Amber said.

"Look, Amber, let's get something straight right now. I broke up with you for a reason. It wasn't working. I'm not in love with you. We're over. Done. I'm in love with Maya."

Amber's face turned red and she balled her hands into fists. Taking a deep breath, she said, "Fine. I think we could still work, but if that little tramp is truly who you love, then so be it. But I'm here for another reason too."

"I truly do love Maya and don't ever, *ever* call her a tramp again. What's the other reason you're here?" Josh asked skeptically. He knew Amber was the type to play games and he didn't trust her at all. When they were engaged, she'd often made things up to get attention or get under someone's skin.

"I'm working in the state attorney's office in Chicago. There's a case that's going to be appealed. I thought you should know."

"Why? Was it one of mine when I worked patrol or something?"

"You were the first officer to respond. The defense attorney discovered you were under the influence and tampered with evidence. He wants to have the case thrown out and the prosecutor's office may file charges against you."

Josh stared at her. He had gone to work high a few times before he was fired. His sergeant had suspected that and made him take a drug test. Of course he'd failed even though he'd thought the drugs would be out of his system. But he had never tampered with evidence. Ever.

"You and I both know that I had issues with drugs and alcohol, but I've never done anything to tamper with evidence," he finally said.

"I thought you'd want to know and I wanted to see your reaction."

"My reaction? Do you really believe that I would do something like that?"

"I don't know who you are anymore, to be honest," Amber said. "I thought we'd be married by now and have some kids. I didn't think you'd break up with me, but you did. So who knows what else you're capable of, especially when you were having drug issues. You might have needed money to buy your drugs. Maybe you were paid off to tamper with evidence."

"Amber, what the…" Josh didn't even know what to say. She had always been one to do whatever it took to get what she wanted, but did she really believe that he would have done something like this? "I never tampered with evidence. Ever. And I never stole money for drugs."

"I really wish I could believe you, but I just can't. I didn't want to tell your family and break their hearts. Especially your mother. She's such a dear. But I did want you to have a heads-up and I'm sure someone will be in touch with you soon. Unless…"

"Unless what?"

"I could help you out. Make paperwork disappear, that sort of thing. Make it hard for the defense attorney to prove you were under the influence and that you tampered with evidence."

"I don't want you to do that. That's not who I am and that's no different than what I'm being accused of. I'll accept the consequences of my time spent under the influence, but I won't accept being accused of something I didn't do. It seems like Chicago politics have worn off on you." Josh stared hard at Amber. She batted her eyelashes back at him. She always wanted something. What was it? For all he knew she was bluffing and none of this was true. "What do you really want? Why are you blackmailing me?"

"I want us back together again. We were happy. I was happy."

"But I wasn't. I'm sorry, Amber, we were not meant to be."

"I disagree. We had a perfect life together."

"If you call being with someone who was snorting coke and drunk every night a perfect life, then you also need to get help. I wasn't a good boyfriend or fiancé."

"But that's the thing. You're clean now. We could be so good together."

"I'm sorry," Josh said. "I love Maya. She's the one for me. You need to let this go and move on with your life. Find someone else. Be happy with whoever that is."

"You're the one who makes me happy and I'll prove that to you if you give me a chance. I can make you happy too," Amber said.

Josh sighed. He knew they could talk about this all night long and Amber would just keep going in circles. There was no point in trying to reason with her. "We're done. Over. Get that straight. You can leave my office now."

Amber stood and headed toward his door. "This isn't over. I'll win you back somehow."

"No, it is over. There's nothing you can do to change my mind," Josh said.

"Nothing?"

"Nothing."

Amber smiled and said, "Then I hope Maya enjoys dating a felon who's going to spend time in the Illinois prison system and probably be beat to death because he used to be a cop. And I hope nothing happens to Maya either."

"You stay away from Maya and leave her out of this. You hear me?"

"Heard," Amber said. "Just don't think that this is over. If I can't have you, no one can."

Maya stared at the apartment door Juniper had tracked to. Everything kept leading back to Bryce. Now FBI Agent Kessler really needed to get here because the sheriff and his department wouldn't be able to continue this investigation since Bryce was his nephew.

"We need to get a warrant," Maya said, petting Juniper and telling her what a good girl she was. They were in a dangerous spot, so they backed away and headed downstairs.

"I'll call a judge and get one," Deputy Glen said. "I should also call the sheriff."

"Okay," Maya said, pulling out her phone and sending Ben a text with the address of where they were and a quick summary of what was going on. He answered that he would be there quickly as he was in the area.

There was another text from Josh saying he really needed to talk to her. Having calmed down, she texted him back that she would call him later. She noticed there was still nothing from Lucas and double-checked her email, but there were no DNA results yet.

"I have a warrant," Deputy Glen said.

"That was quick," Maya said.

"Technology. Our courts have switched everything over so that we can do this electronically. It's been nice to get warrants this quickly. Helps a ton with our cases."

"I bet," Maya said, making a mental note to tell Pops he should consider talking to the courts in Pinecone Junction about that. Juniper leaned up against Maya's leg and stared back up at the apartment. "You did so good, girly."

Juniper answered with a tail wag. Ben and the sheriff pulled into the parking lot about the same time. The sheriff jumped out of his vehicle, face red, chewing gum like crazy, and stomped toward Maya. He appeared ready to unleash some nasty words when Juniper stepped forward and gave a low growl, stopping Sheriff Jackson in his tracks.

"I'd stay there if I were you," Maya said. "I can keep a short leash on her, but with the way you're coming at me, Juniper may not have much patience."

"How dare you put me in this position?" the sheriff snapped.

"How dare I? Really? I let Juniper track, she followed her nose and this is where we ended up. I had no idea who we were tracking and I certainly didn't know that it would lead to your nephew's apartment. But Deputy Glen already secured a search warrant."

"You know I can't help with this search," the sheriff said.

"I am aware of that," she said as Ben came over.

"Everything okay?" Ben asked.

"No," said the sheriff. "Your officer and her dog tracked to my nephew's apartment and now we need to search it. But obviously since this is a conflict of interest, I can't do anything."

"I'll help search it," Ben said. "And if we find anything, we'll have to let Agent Kessler know. He'll probably have to take over this investigation."

"I know," the sheriff said. "Where is the FBI anyway? I thought they'd be here by now to help us out."

"Agent Kessler was held up. He'll be in later this evening."

"Great." The sheriff threw up his hands, exasperated. "Well, let's get this search going. He's a spoiled brat of a kid, so let me go up and help talk to him. But I won't go in and do anything."

Maya was surprised to hear the sheriff admit Bryce was spoiled, but she didn't disagree. He and Ben headed up the stairs with Deputy Glen, who knocked on the door, everyone standing to the side. It was a dangerous position to be in. If Bryce had a gun, there was nowhere for any of them to go. Police officers didn't call doors the fatal funnels because they were safe.

The door opened and Maya could see the sheriff talking to Bryce. Bryce argued for a few minutes, but the sheriff held his ground and finally walked his nephew out, keeping a hand on his arm as he steered him down the stairs. Bryce glared at Maya and Juniper but didn't say anything as he and the sheriff stood off to the side in the parking lot.

Some of Bryce's neighbors had heard and noticed the activity and were peering through windows. Bryce seemed embarrassed, but it didn't stop his swagger. It didn't take long for Ben and Deputy Glen to start coming out with evidence bags.

Rory pulled into the parking lot and came over. Maya filled her in and Rory said she would also go help. It didn't take long for her to exit with more evidence bags. Ben came down the stairs and over to Maya.

"We've found drugs and signs that he's selling them. There was also a lot of Narcan in his apartment. I didn't have a chance to fill you in, but the coroner called me with two pieces of important information, one of which was that the tox screen showed that the victims not only had a heroin, fentanyl and carfentanil mixture in their systems, probably Gray Death, but also Narcan. He thinks someone was deliberately overdosing the victims and then bringing them back to life."

"That's awful," Maya said. "Can he prove that?"

"No, it's just a theory based on the tox screen."

"What was the other important piece of information?" she asked.

"The coroner has discovered biological evidence from more than one person on the bodies."

Maya was silent for a moment, processing that. "You mean there could be more than one killer?"

"That's exactly what I mean. The killer might have a partner. We need to do some more work to eliminate other sources, but it appears the same extra DNA profile is on all the recent victims."

"Assuming the suspect does have a partner, do you think it could be Bryce?"

"I don't know. We're not finding any evidence with blood or anything like that, although we still have a lot to search and that apartment is a pigsty, but maybe Bryce is learning the tricks of the trade, so to speak. Or maybe he's convinced the killer to let him join him to get a better story. Who knows, but I wanted to make sure I kept you up to date."

"I appreciate that," Maya said, taking in her surroundings. An idea came to mind. "You know, if you were committing or helping with a homicide, would you leave the evidence in your apartment? I mean, I know some murderers do, but that's usually when it's a crime of passion or something like that. These killings were very premeditated. And I know that the crime scene didn't have a ton of evidence because of the snow, but it appeared that the murderer was careful. Minus a few pine needles."

"Where are you going with this?" Ben asked.

"What would you do with evidence?"

"Throw it away."

"Exactly," Maya said, pointing at the dumpsters behind the apartment complex.

Ben followed her gaze and groaned. "There's four big dumpsters there."

"But what if we could narrow it down to one?"

"How?"

"Call in Tanner and Finn," Maya said. "An HRD dog will be able to tell you if there are human remains, including blood, in those dumpsters."

"I'll call him now."

"Great. Hopefully he can get here soon," Maya said. She stared at the dumpsters. Would they be lucky enough to find bloody clothing or other evidence? If so, was Bryce the main killer or an accomplice? It seemed like with this investigation, questions kept coming up, but very few were being answered.

Chapter Twenty-Seven

About twenty minutes later, Tanner and Finn pulled into the parking lot. Maya was a little worried as her patrol vehicle was still back at the parking spot from the party and she couldn't put Juniper away. Hopefully Juniper would behave herself and Finn wouldn't be distracted.

Tanner got Finn out and put on his working collar. Maya noticed Rory was bringing down another brown paper bag marked *Evidence*. As Rory passed Maya, she asked, "What did you find now?"

"You know the manila envelope that the sheriff received the other day?"

"Yeah."

"These match that one. Same brand," Rory said. "And I should mention the evidence Juniper found in the bushes matches the hat and sunglasses our mystery guy wore in the security footage. Bryce is denying it, of course, and saying someone set him up."

"That's convenient, to have someone set you up," Maya said.

"Yeah, that's what I thought too. When I get done helping with this, if you and Juniper need a ride back to your vehicle, let me know."

"Thanks," Maya said, thinking that she didn't want

to walk back to her vehicle in the dark. Especially with Juniper. "I'll probably take you up on that."

"I better get this stuff logged," Rory said. "I'll find you before I leave. It might be a while."

"No problem," Maya said.

Tanner now had Finn ready to go and was heading her way. He stopped a good distance from Maya when he saw Juniper.

"You think you can get along with Finn?" Maya asked Juniper.

Juniper whined and looked up at Maya and then back at Finn.

"At least try," Maya said. Juniper grunted in response.

"Where would you like us to start working?" Tanner asked, keeping his distance.

"I'd like you to run the dumpsters over there," Maya said, pointing to behind the apartments. Juniper's track had taken them past the giant trash containers, but she was following the fresh scent. If Bryce had dumped any evidence with blood or other human remains in the dumpsters earlier in the day or week, it wouldn't be the same track Juniper was following. Finn was their best bet.

"Okay," Tanner said. He and Finn headed over to the dumpster. Tanner started directing Finn around the area, getting his nose in different spots up high and down low.

"Good job," Maya said, proud of her students. She could tell Tanner had been practicing as Finn wasn't looking at him nearly as much and was out in front of him, working the scent.

Tanner was doing an excellent job getting Finn's nose into different areas with good airflow and by asking him to go up and down, the dog was getting into different air shelves and flows. Maya thought of scent literally like a bookshelf. You had to get a dog to check up and down because odor might rise or fall and then sit there depending on airflow and temperature.

Finn suddenly changed his body language and began working a scent cone. Juniper let out a yip as she realized that he was going to find something and she was jealous. Finn circled back around and then sat and stared at the end of a dumpster.

"Good job," Maya said.

Ben had come back over and nodded. "I think I'll find a rookie deputy to get in the dumpster."

"Leave Rory alone," Maya said. "She's my ride back to my vehicle and I don't want her to stink like old food and garbage."

"Got it," Ben said with a chuckle. "I think there's another newbie around here somewhere. The sheriff hired several new recruits recently."

Tanner praised Finn and took him away from the dumpster. Maya was about ready to tell him that she could put out a hide so that Finn could get a reward, but as they were walking in their direction, Finn suddenly put his nose up and pulled on the leash in the opposite direction from where Tanner was headed.

"Go with him," Maya said, interested in what Finn was smelling.

Tanner listened and followed his dog. Finn walked toward some vehicles in the parking lot and went up to a rusty two-door coupe that had its bumper tied on with bungee cords.

"Have you worked a vehicle before?" Maya asked.

"I have," Tanner said.

"Then go ahead and do a detailed search of that car.

Get his nose in areas with good airflow like the wheel wells, door cracks and the trunk area."

Tanner followed Maya's instructions and Finn worked the vehicle. She was impressed with how much better the dog was searching. Finn went around to the trunk area. First the yellow Lab put his paws up on the back of the trunk and air scented. Then he jumped down and tried to almost crawl under the vehicle. Maya knew that meant there was a good odor and it was dropping down. Finn pulled himself back out from underneath the car and sat.

"That's a good alert," Maya said. "I'll get Ben to see who owns that vehicle and see if we can take a look in the trunk."

"Okay," Tanner said, praising Finn again. The yellow Lab wagged his tail, appearing pleased with himself. "I'll just wait here."

Ben was still busy with the other rookie deputy and the dumpster. Maya found Deputy Glen instead and filled him in on what was going on.

"I'm pretty certain that's Bryce's car," he said. "I'll double-check and then get his keys. I'll contact the judge and DA too and get another search warrant."

"Sounds good," Maya said. "Never hurts to have a warrant, even with a dog alert."

She and Juniper went back to their spot and waited. Tanner was brave enough to come a little closer with Finn, and this time Juniper tilted her head out of curiosity.

"I think she's warming up to him," Maya said with a smile. "Poor Finn. Juniper is a tough one."

Tanner laughed. "Luckily Finn gets along with just about anyone. He's laid-back when it comes to other dogs."

Deputy Glen came back over. "That is Bryce's car and I have his keys. I also did get a search warrant even though with the dog alert we should have probable cause."

"Let's see what's in the trunk," Maya said.

Deputy Glen popped open the back. Maya peered inside and saw some black trash bags. The deputy put on some gloves and opened the bags.

"Bloody clothing," he said. "Lots of blood. And bloody rags."

"Were any of the victims stabbed?" Maya asked.

"Yes, the coroner found some stab wounds, but also signs that maybe some of the limbs were dismembered. You might need lots of rags to clean that up. I'll start going through all this and bagging it for evidence. We'll need to see if the blood matches any of the victims."

"I'll tell Ben that we need to arrest Bryce and hold him until Agent Kessler gets here," Maya said, heading over toward the dumpster.

She and Juniper stopped a little distance away to avoid the smell of trash. A baby-faced deputy was sorting through garbage. He'd pulled out more black trash bags and they had them lined up near the dumpster. Ben saw her and came over.

"We found bloody clothes and rags in Bryce's car," Maya reported.

"Finding similar stuff here," Ben said.

"I think it's time we arrested Bryce and took him in for questioning."

"I agree," Ben said.

Maya glanced at Deputy Glen, who had started searching the cab area of Bryce's car. He motioned for her to come back over. When she was close enough to hear, Deputy Glen held up some papers and said, "I found these in the front seat. They're letters to Bryce from the killer. Looks like our suspect wanted Bryce to run an exposé on him."

"I'll get some evidence bags," Maya said. "The FBI will want to analyze those."

She headed over to Ben's patrol vehicle to gather more bags. As she approached, she could hear Bryce still arguing that he'd been set up. Sheriff Jackson was telling him to shut up and not say another word. Maya knew that the sheriff was Bryce's uncle, but she was annoyed that he was giving him legal advice. It would only make this case more difficult.

She also had a funny feeling that maybe Bryce was somewhat telling the truth. He may have been the local drug dealer and he was the type who'd want the scoop on the serial killer story. A story like this could make or break a journalist's career, and if Bryce was selling to make extra money, it could mean a better job for him.

But that didn't make him a killer. The clothing and evidence all seemed too easy. Maya couldn't believe she was agreeing with Bryce even a little bit, but it did seem like maybe the killer was toying with them.

It was a game Maya didn't want to play.

Chapter Twenty-Eight

Serial killers often insert themselves into the investigation. It was a line that he'd heard over and over when he'd attended law enforcement conferences. And why not insert yourself, especially when you blended in by taking part in the investigation? That was the irony of the whole thing. He was right there. And no one suspected him. That made it even better.

Control.

That was the key, and by taking part in this circus that everyone thought was leading toward identifying him, he had complete control. Really, everyone should be thanking him. He was taking care of a problem.

Everything was going according to plan. This town was the best one he'd been in yet. The other towns where he'd done his environmental clean-up work, as he liked to think of it, the law enforcement had never caught on. Eventually he'd discovered Antler Valley, a bigger town that desperately needed his help, and he was happy to comply.

His side job taking care of people who caused problems wasn't always easy. He'd saved certain pieces of evidence—mostly bloody clothing—as what he liked to think of as an insurance policy. That insurance policy had paid off today in setting up the little prick of a journalist. He prided himself on thinking in the long term and reading people well. Bryce was arrogant and self-centered. That had made it easy to mess with him. Easy to set him up. He was a real pain in the ass who needed knocking down a few pegs.

He'd succeeded with his plan. He'd decided to find a needy journalist when he read about the Zodiac and how that psycho had communicated with the media. There were others who'd done the same, of course, like Jack the Ripper and Son of Sam. He knew that if he started using the journalist, the little prick would think that he was in the same league as the others. People like the journalist were entitled and thought the world owed them. Bryce thought he was all high and mighty when he started receiving letters with inside information. Little had he known what was happening.

Bryce, the idiot, thought he was being provided real information. But would he be that stupid? No. That's how killers got caught, and he had more work to do. Important work. He wouldn't ever be caught.

He'd set up the evidence but then wondered how to get the cops there. An anonymous tip? Instead, the party out in the woods had worked out better than expected. Maya had no idea how much she and her K-9 had just helped him. He couldn't have planned it better. He had hoped for this outcome knowing that Bryce would show up and sell something.

The kid had become greedy and wanted more money instead of looking for a job elsewhere and getting out of this town where millionaires and billionaires ruled. The kid thought that selling drugs was a way to make more money. Such an idiot, although if you were going to sell drugs, it was smart to do it where your uncle was the sheriff and could be blackmailed into bailing you out.

He wondered how things were going to play out now. He knew the truth about the sheriff. Being an idiot seemed to run in the family. But that made it easy for him to keep the upper hand. He knew how this would all work. The stupid kid would get a defense attorney and claim his innocence. Would the idiot get convicted? Maybe. Maybe not. He didn't care. If nothing else maybe it would make the little prick more humble. It would be good for him.

There was only one thing causing him concern. His partner had texted him on their burner phone. The coroner, who his partner had assured him was worthless, had actually found biological evidence from two other people on one of the bodies. They would of course run DNA. His would not be in the system. He didn't know about his partner, but that was his partner's problem.

There would be no way for the biological evidence to lead back to him. His DNA profile was nowhere to be found. And by the time the backlogged labs ran any of the evidence, he'd be long gone anyway. Until then, he was going to enjoy the show.

Especially Maya Thompson.

Chapter Twenty-Nine

Maya and Juniper hitched a ride with Rory back to their vehicle and then headed to the sheriff's office. Maya gave Juniper some love and put her blanket in her compartment. There was a good chance that by the time she came back out, Juniper would have shredded the blanket, but Maya didn't care as long as she didn't eat it. Sometimes Juniper snuggled in and slept in it too, so she kept buying cheap blankets and throwing them away once they were destroyed.

Heading in the entrance, she saw Agent Kessler standing by the front desk. She had first met the agent when he'd helped investigate a local drug trafficking ring in the national forest near Pinecone Junction. Doug had been involved with the trafficking and Agent Kessler had questioned Maya too, thinking that she might be taking bribes. She hadn't been happy, but now, looking back, she knew he had been doing his job and covering all his bases. She respected that he hadn't had tunnel vision and assumed a law enforcement officer couldn't be guilty. They were still humans, after all. Which made her wonder again about the sheriff. Could he be the killer? Or was he just a jerk?

The agent spotted Maya, gave a small wave and came over to shake her hand.

"I'm glad to see you here," Maya said, noting that the agent had circles under his eyes and appeared tired.

"Good to see you, Officer Thompson," Agent Kessler said. "I'm looking forward to working with you on this case and seeing your K-9 again. She's a sweet dog."

"She is," Maya said. "Well, as long as you're not a suspect."

Kessler laughed and agreed. His usually perfectly pressed suit was wrinkled with part of a stain showing on his shirt, although his jacket covered up most of the spot.

Feeling Maya's gaze, he said, "My wife and I just had our first baby. She's one month old. I was helping this morning feeding her and that's how I got this stain. I grabbed a fresh shirt and was going to change, but somehow the day got away from me. I think the jacket covers up most of it."

"Congrats on your baby girl," Maya said, thinking that she'd heard through the grapevine that Agent Kessler and his wife were expecting. "And I wouldn't worry about the stain. It's the least of our worries around here right now."

"Yeah, I agree. I went and questioned the suspect that was arrested tonight."

"Did you find out anything interesting?" Maya asked.

"No, not really. He was answering some of my questions and then his uncle came in and told him to stop answering until he got a lawyer. The kid listened and that was that, but I did push this case into ViCAP."

"Did you get any hits?"

"I did, actually," Kessler said. "This case matches some cold cases in Wyoming, and Utah as well."

"So that gives the FBI jurisdiction," Maya said, feeling relief. She wanted to find this killer and not only stop him before he murdered someone again, but also bring him to justice for the lives he'd taken. It didn't always help bereaved families' grief, but it did give some closure. "To be honest, I've been concerned about how this case has been handled by the sheriff's office and now there's a conflict of interest with the sheriff and his nephew."

"Your criminal investigator filled me in," Kessler said.

Maya realized that Ben was nowhere to be seen. Not that she was his boss or in charge of him, but she figured he'd be here to talk with Agent Kessler. "What did you think of Bryce Riley?"

"I thought he was a cocky little son of a bitch. The kind of kid that if my daughter ever dates, I'll ground her for life."

Maya had to suppress a laugh. Everything he'd said was true. She didn't disagree. "At least you have a few years before you have to worry about that."

"True," Kessler said. "But you know, for how much that kid rubbed me the wrong way, I think he's just spoiled. Probably has gotten his way his whole life. Despite that, he just doesn't seem right for these crimes."

"What makes you say that?" Maya asked. She agreed and thought again that all the evidence was too easy to find, but she wanted to hear Kessler's observations.

"The kid is certainly needy and, in a sense, enjoying every minute of this, but it's probably because he thinks he's going to write the next bestselling true crime book that will be made into a movie or documentary and he'll be set for life. That doesn't make him a killer, though.

"This killer is methodical. Smart. There's very little evidence. It's almost like he knows the system and investigations. For all we know, he could be a cop or have some kind of job in law enforcement. Maybe a degree in criminology. Who knows. If this is the same suspect in the cold case murders in the other ski resort towns, then he seems to wait until the time is right to murder someone. Assuming it is the same person, it also means he's killed in different areas, which makes me wonder, was he visiting those ski resort towns? Living there? Could he be a seasonal worker with family in law enforcement? If he is a seasonal worker, that could be hard to track too. They don't stay in one place too long and there's literally hundreds of workers going from ski town to ski town. Makes it like finding a needle in a haystack.

"There's so many questions to answer, but I do know that he's meticulous and controlled. I saw Bryce Riley's apartment and car. There's nothing meticulous or controlled about either of them. In fact, his life is a mess, both literally and figuratively. He made no effort to hide the drugs he had or the Narcan. Maybe he's the partner, but I even question that. Our suspect wouldn't work with someone who was so messy."

Maya let what Agent Kessler had told her sink in and added, "I wonder if it is the same person. It would be nice to see if the cases are all connected. Hopefully DNA or some other evidence can help us with that. If they are related, we really need to stop him. It'll only be a matter of time before he's compelled to kill again."

"I agree. I sent the files to our BAU," said Kessler, using the acronym for the behavioral analysis unit. "They said they'd look them over and have something

to me as soon as possible. Of course, they're like everyone else and have a ton of cases to get through. Because
of the number of people this suspect has killed, I tried
to push for a rush, but we'll see."

"That'll be good to get a profile," Maya said. "What
about the DNA off the biological evidence?"

"I'm getting that to the lab at Quantico, but DNA can
take a while. I'm trying to put a rush on it, but again,
there's other cases that the FBI deals with that take pre-
cedence. Especially now with all the counterterrorism
stuff we're dealing with."

Maya nodded, thinking about her own DNA sample.
The impatient side of her wanted results now so she
could find out if Eric Torres was her father. Same with
this case. She wanted to know if this murderer was by
some chance in the system. He wouldn't be, though,
unless he'd been previously arrested. There were also
ancestry databases, but they now required court orders
for law enforcement to submit DNA. That could take
too long.

"Let me know what I can do to help," Maya said. "Juniper can find narcotics too, so we can use her not just
for tracking and evidence searches, but also to see if we
can locate the source of these drugs. If we can find the
big dog dealer, then maybe we can find out who's buying from him."

"That sounds great," Kessler said. "I appreciate it.
That's part of what created the match in ViCAP. This
suspect seems to always use some sort of drug with fentanyl to subdue his victims. The victims all had Narcan
in their system too. Large amounts of it. But this case
is slightly different from the others."

"How so?" Maya asked.

"The cases here in Antler Valley are the only ones that seem to have another person involved. I'm guessing it's either it's a copycat team or the killer has found a partner."

Having one killer on the loose was bad enough, but the possibility of more than one was frightening. "Juniper and I have found some Gray Death in the area."

"I read in the case file that you found a baggie of it with one of the victims," Kessler said.

"That, but I also had a bust over near Pinecone Junction. A homeless guy who was camping illegally. Juniper alerted on his vehicle and we found Gray Death. All the guy would say was that the devil sold it to him. But Gray Death would fit our killer's purposes. Although it's so potent, I would think he would need to know something about Narcan doses or else he would kill his victims quickly."

"Maybe he's escalating," Kessler conjectured. "I have an idea that I've run by my boss. I'm waiting to get the okay."

"What's that?" Maya asked.

"I want to let Bryce Riley go with the stipulation that he gives us his dealer's name and becomes a CI."

"You trust him to be a confidential informant?" Maya asked.

"As much as I trust any of them. But I'm also hoping that we can keep an eye on him and maybe he'll meet up with someone that will give us a lead. Even if he's not the partner, the killer has contacted him through those letters. The killer seems to want Bryce to write his story. So maybe they're meeting up. If we can keep an eye on Bryce, then maybe he'll lead us to at least one of our suspects."

"I think that's a good idea if your boss approves it,"
Maya said, thinking about the killer and his partner
knowing law enforcement techniques and protocols.
That meant they knew how to manipulate the system.

She needed to be very careful about who she trusted.

Chapter Thirty

As Maya and Agent Kessler caught up more, Ben came into the sheriff's office and suggested they grab some dinner over at the local brewpub. Maya's stomach was rumbling; she wouldn't mind having some food.

As they headed inside the restaurant, she saw that the sheriff, Tanner, Rory and Deputy Glen were already seated and waiting for them. She didn't mind the group except for maybe the sheriff.

"Deputy Glen is going to tail Bryce for us," Ben said, filling Maya in as they sat.

"That'll be good," Maya said.

The sheriff studied his menu, but finally piped up. "Bryce is a stupid kid, but he's not a murderer. I don't like that you're using him to try to get to the killer."

"We're out in public," Agent Kessler said. "Let's table any conversation about specifics until later." Maya agreed and was relieved that Kessler put an end to the sheriff discussing the investigation.

"Wish we were out of uniform," Deputy Glen said. "I would buy everyone a round."

"You can do that when this case is solved," Ben said. "We'll celebrate when we catch this son of a bitch."

"You think you'll be able to get him?" Tanner asked.

"Yes," Agent Kessler said. "At some point, everyone makes a mistake and gets caught. And with the help of the BAU, we will probably have a better feel for his victims. That'll help too."

"I've heard of that," Deputy Glen said. "Victimology. Is that the right term?"

"It is," Agent Kessler said.

"You know what I think?" the sheriff asked. Maya really didn't want to know what he thought, but she knew that it was a rhetorical question. "I think these victims died from their addictions, which is their own fault," the sheriff continued. "If they would go get help and just quit using, my job would be a lot easier."

Maya was relieved when the waitress came over to take their order and interrupted the sheriff. Once she was done, though, he started in again. "Addicts need to know that they bring this upon themselves. It's their own damn fault."

Maya couldn't stand it anymore. Her temper flaring, she spoke up. "Keep in mind, Sheriff, at least one victim was stabbed, so their addiction didn't kill them. Not to mention, addiction is a disease. It can be hard to control and it doesn't mean you deserve to have something bad happen to you. It really doesn't mean that you deserve to die because you battle it."

"What do you know about addiction?" the sheriff asked.

"More than you think. I'm an alcoholic myself. Used it to self-medicate because of my PTSD. I've been sober for six months now, but it continues to be a struggle. I go to regular meetings and every day I work to not take a drink," Maya said, noticing that Ben seemed to tighten up next to her. Maybe she shouldn't have been so open, but she hated it when people judged addicts without understanding. "Maybe you need to learn more about addiction before you make such rash statements."

"Maybe you shouldn't be a law enforcement officer," the sheriff shot back.

"Who are you to judge that? I never drank at work. I've always passed my random UAs. Just because I have a disease that I struggle with doesn't mean I shouldn't have my job. My AA group has several people from different law enforcement agencies. It doesn't make us bad people or bad officers. Being sober gives me empathy and makes me a better officer. Shouldn't we all have a second chance?"

"Whatever you say," the sheriff said.

Everyone sat in silence. Maya was relieved when a few minutes later the server brought their food and everyone began eating. She felt her phone buzz and checked it, wondering if it was Josh. She really wanted to talk to him. But the caller ID said *Lucas*. Did he have the DNA results?

"Excuse me," Maya said, standing up and heading outside into the bitter cold night as she answered her phone. "Lucas, tell me you have some news."

"I do," he said. "Are you ready for this?"

Maya's heart rate increased. Her breath formed a cloud in the frigid air. "I think so."

"Eric Torres is your father."

She gripped her phone. "For real?"

"For real. It's a ninety-nine percent match. Doesn't get any better than that."

"I can't believe it."

"When you get back, I'd like to get that letter from you. I'm planning on visiting Abigail and having a little chat. I'd like to have it with me to help find out why she wanted you to know this now."

"Of course. I'll get it to you when I get back."

"When do you think that'll be?"

"No idea," Maya said, sighing. "This case is complicated. Working long hours and I feel like we're not making much progress."

"I understand. Hope you get a break in the case soon. Oh, and Tree Cop?"

"Yeah?"

"If Eric Torres contacts you, let me know. Okay?"

"I will."

"You okay? This is tough news. Maybe call Josh and talk with him about it or something."

"It's tough, but I can handle it. Catch you later," Maya said, and hung up. She went back inside, trying to stay calm. She had to focus back on her current case for now and let Lucas do his thing investigating Eric. He was right—she wanted to call Josh. She should call Josh now, but she wasn't ready to discuss this with him. Not yet. Maybe later, after she processed everything.

They all paid and Deputy Glen said he'd go release Bryce and tail him. The sheriff just grunted in response to that, threw cash on the table and left, muttering something about going to his sister's house and telling her that Bryce had been arrested. Tanner said good-night to everyone and mentioned that he and Finn were available if needed. Rory also headed out to go back on shift. That left Maya, Ben and Agent Kessler.

"Well, that was fun," Kessler said.

"Yeah," Maya muttered. "At least we had dinner."

Ben crossed his arms and faced Maya. "I didn't know you were an alcoholic."

"It's not something I usually blurt out," Maya answered. "I just couldn't stand hearing the sheriff act like those victims deserved what they got because of their addictions."

Ben nodded. "Fair enough. Let's get back to work."

"Gladly," Maya said, standing up and putting cash on the table for her dinner. She'd be happy when she could go back home. And if she didn't need an AA meeting before this, now she really needed one.

Anger coursed through him. How dare she hide this from him? He should have known that Maya Thompson was too perfect. An alcoholic? She was no better than the rest of the people he was trying to eradicate. She was no better than his father. Or his mother.

He'd been stupid to put her on a pedestal. That was his fault. He should have learned more about her first. She'd just seemed so perfect.

How could she be an addict and be in her position of power? It was like his father. His father had been a very rich man. Family money that went back to his grandfather striking it rich through investments and hard work. His father had never worked hard. He'd just spent money and slept around. And he'd been a cop. He'd liked the power, and when his father drank, he would make sure that everyone knew he was the man of the house. No, cops were not allowed to drink. There were no second chances in his mind.

He had to do something about this.

Pulling out his phone, he texted his partner. Maya could not go on being a cop and a drunk. He needed to stop her. It didn't matter that she claimed she was sober right now. He knew how it worked. His father had proved that you could stop drinking for a while, but it only took one little thing to push him right back to his old ways.

Maya had to be stopped and he was the one to do it. It might distract him from his cause, but he could take a break for this purpose.

Maya Thompson needed to be taught a lesson. Even if it meant she died.

Chapter Thirty-One

Josh headed out of his office for the night. The visit with Amber had only given him a headache. But his concern right now was wondering if Maya would forgive him.

It was one of those things that couples went through, right? They'd been living together for four months and never had a big fight. It'd been bound to happen; he just was wishing he hadn't been the one to start it. But he would talk with her, apologize and figure things out. He knew one thing for certain—his house seemed empty without her and Juniper.

God, his family was driving him nuts. His mother had been sweet and loving ever since Josh walked out on lunch and kicked them out of the house during dinner. She'd doted on him and reminded him how much she loved him. Josh appreciated all that, although an apology would be nicer. He was reminded of why he'd left Chicago to come out here to the middle of nowhere in the mountains of Colorado.

At least he knew his father would do a good job as an attorney for Pops. Thanks to Maya, Pops had become more than a boss to Josh—he was like a second father. The investigation had continued, which mainly meant there were long days of Pops being asked questions.

Josh had seen him a couple times and he had aged and seemed exhausted.

Pops had asked about Maya, but Josh had skirted around the question for now, just saying that she was busy with her case. Pops wasn't a fool, though, and Josh suspected that he knew Maya and Josh had been fighting before she left. He had to make things right with her.

When he'd met Maya, it was like lightning had struck. Not only was she beautiful, but she had a strong side. She was passionate about what she did and she was down to earth. At the time, Maya had still been struggling with her addiction, but she had worked hard to get herself sober and continued to take her AA meetings seriously. That took an inner strength that Josh understood.

As Josh reached the front door, deep in his thoughts, he heard his cell phone ringing. The caller ID showed it was from a federal prison. There was only one person who would be calling him and he didn't feel like talking with her, but the cop side of him knew that he should answer. Abigail had called a few times and never really divulged any useful information, but all conversations were recorded and who knew what she might let slip. Josh didn't know why she kept calling except for the fact that deep down she was still a detective and she knew he was in love with Maya. She'd tried to get under his skin with that fact before.

Josh stopped in the lobby and answered the call. He listened to the usual voice asking if he would accept a call from the federal prison from inmate Abigail Harper and agreed.

"What do you want now, Abigail?" Josh asked.

"Someone sounds grumpy. Did I catch you at a bad time?"

Josh sighed. He couldn't let her get to him. If she wasn't going to say anything useful, he'd end the call. "No, this isn't a bad time."

"Good, because I was just wondering about Maya."

"I'm not going to talk to you about her. If that's why you're calling, then I'm hanging up."

"So protective," Abigail said. "I admire that. I only wanted to know one thing."

"What's that?"

"Did she receive my letter?"

Josh hesitated. Letter? Maya hadn't said anything about receiving a letter from Abigail. Although with everything going on, maybe she'd forgotten to tell him. He knew that she had mentioned talking about something before his family showed up. "I don't know if she received your letter."

"Oh, I hope you two are doing okay."

"We're fine," Josh said, doing his best to sound convincing. Were they fine? "Why are you so interested in this letter?"

"Because I want to know how she took the news."

"What news?"

"I might have let it slip that Eric Torres is her father."

"What?" Josh said. He worked on composing himself. He couldn't let Abigail ever have the upper hand, but he also needed to keep her talking. "Why would you send a letter to her about that?"

"I thought she'd want to know the truth. That she has one parent still alive. I have my sources out there still. I heard she asked that investigator friend of hers to run her DNA. Are the results in yet?"

Was any of this true? He took another deep breath. "I have no information for you. Good night, Abigail."

Before she could say anything else, Josh hung up. He had to talk to Maya tonight and find out more, but he knew she would be out late working. Would she keep something like this from him? He was disappointed, but after everything with Amber, maybe he deserved this. But if Eric really was Maya's father, why would Abigail want her to know? Why not tell her sooner? That part worried Josh, but there was nothing he could do about it until he spoke with Maya.

He stepped out into the cold night, making a mental note to get the recording of that conversation from the prison. It might end up being evidence if Abigail tried anything.

As he headed home, his stomach started growling. His family had decided to go explore Fort Collins for the evening, which meant he could do the bachelor thing and go to the Black Bear Café. He could get a meal to go, but the thought of going home to an empty house didn't seem appealing. It only made him miss Maya more, even if they were upset with each other. Josh parked and headed inside.

The place was packed. It seemed like the entire town had come out to eat. Everyone was probably there to go out one last night before the big storm that was forecast to hit. The storm had slowed down and was not expected to move in now until tomorrow afternoon. The delay helped with getting prepared for the snow but meant that the snow totals would be higher as the storm stalled out over the mountains.

Josh peered around for an open table, but there were none. He saw a couple open seats at the bar—not the best option for him, especially when he had so many triggers going on. He finally decided that he could sit at the bar and overcome the urge to have a drink. It would be part of him working on his sobriety.

After sitting down, Josh ordered his meal without looking at the menu. He and Maya ended up here at least a couple times a week. Since it was really the only place to eat out in town, he had the menu memorized. His food came quickly and he was enjoying his meal and lost in his own thoughts about Maya, Amber's blackmail and his possible problems back in Chicago. Was Amber telling the truth? Or just making things up to manipulate him?

His thoughts were interrupted when he heard someone behind him say, "Is this seat open?"

He closed his eyes and rubbed his temples. *Amber.* Not at all what he needed right now.

Josh turned around and saw her standing there in her designer clothes clutching the expensive purse that she no doubt had "needed." His first thought was to tell her to go away. The problem with that was, he knew how she'd act. She would pout and throw a fit, raising her voice so everyone around her could hear.

In Chicago he wouldn't care. Sure, there were people who knew him at the bars there, but it was the city, where loud didn't matter as much, as long as there wasn't a fight. Even then, most bartenders in Chicago would just tell someone to take it outside unless it seemed serious.

But Pinecone Junction was another world. Here, this would become *the* gossip for days. If he pulled someone over, they would question him about Amber and why she was upset while he wrote the ticket. They would pry about whether or not she was a girlfriend and if Maya knew. In fact, some of the patrons were already staring at him with interest, including one of the town busybodies. Josh figured the busybody was getting ready to take notes or even record everything on her phone to show Maya later. He had no doubt that Amber had thought all of that through. If nothing else, she was very smart.

"Sit down," Josh said, gesturing to the seat next to him. This was not good, but he didn't feel like he had a choice.

Amber ordered a glass of chardonnay and then a couple shots of Jack Daniel's.

"Mixing Jack and chardonnay?" Josh asked.

"No, silly, the Jack is for you. It's your favorite."

Josh took another bite of food. She was right, of course. That was how he had always started his nights. Couple shots of Jack with a line of coke. Not something he was proud of at all. Anger stirred. Was Amber seriously trying to get him to lose his sobriety? Just to add to her blackmail? She was shallower than he thought.

"I don't drink or do drugs anymore. I've been clean since I left Chicago and I am staying that way." Josh swore the town busybody was leaning in closer. He'd tried to keep his past quiet and that meant people wanted to know more about what had brought him to Pinecone Junction. It was no one's business that he'd had issues. He was clean and healthy now. That's what mattered.

"Oh, whatever," Amber said, as the bartender delivered the drinks.

Josh pushed the shot glasses away from him, noticing that people were still watching out of curiosity. The whole town knew he and Maya were together. He lived at the edge of town and it hadn't taken long for them to realize that her patrol vehicle was there permanently after her cabin burned down. Someone was bound to call or text her.

Amber reached over, put a hand on his leg and started rubbing it. "I miss you," she said.

"Take your hand off me," Josh said, moving his legs off to the side. "Look, Amber. We're over. It's done. It's been done a long time. I'm a different person. I'm sober, and I don't know how many times I have to tell you this but I'm in love with Maya. Not you."

Amber gave him her pouty face, her lips coming together tightly, but she removed her hand from his leg and took a big gulp of her wine. "You used to be fun, you know," she said.

Please don't start screaming at me. I don't think I can handle that tonight.

Josh's phone rang. It was one of his new deputies out on duty. While he was hoping it was nothing serious, he was also glad for the distraction.

"I need to take this," he said, hitting Answer and turning away from Amber. He walked over toward the bathrooms, where it was a little quieter and he could hear better. The deputy had a couple questions about some protocols that Josh was able to answer quickly. When he turned back around, Amber had slid the shots over to his spot.

"I told you," Josh said, sitting back down. "I don't do that anymore. Why are you trying to get me to drink?"

"You were more fun when you drank," Amber said.

"Trust me," Josh said. "I wasn't."

"You could just drink with me and not do anything else."

"Amber, I said no. I'm serious about this," Josh said.

He needed to finish his dinner fast and get out of here. He'd head home where he could be by himself, and he wanted nothing more than to call Maya and hear her voice. At some point he wanted to tell her that Amber had threatened him, that he too might be under investigation but he didn't know for sure. Maya was strong. She would help him through anything in the days ahead, just like he would always be there for her. He wanted to know if she had received a letter. Had she run her DNA? Were there any results? He wished she had told him so he could support her, but she was strong. She might be okay with it if Eric was her father, but she might also struggle knowing that her biological father was a felon on the run.

He turned his attention back to Amber. Not only was she threatening his sobriety, but she also knew from being engaged to Josh that he was still in uniform, which made it unacceptable to have any kind of alcohol. Knowing Amber, she was trying to get him fired.

Nice. Really nice. If you cared about me at all, you wouldn't do something this shallow. This is one of many reasons why I broke up with you. I'm sure you're just trying to get back at me because of Maya. No one expected me to like it out here or succeed out here. They all thought I'd be back to Chicago within a few months.

He signaled the bartender and when he came over, Josh pushed the shots of Jack toward him. "I can't drink these. Sorry. Put them on my bill."

"Yes, sir," said the bartender, taking the alcohol away.

Josh wolfed down the rest of his food and gulped the rest of his soda. He motioned to the bartender again that he was ready for his bill.

"Go back home and move on with your life," he said

to Amber. "Leave me alone. I'm with Maya now and I'm happy. You need to find someone who will make you happy."

"You made me happy."

"No, I didn't," Josh said, hoping the bill would come soon and he could just get out of here. "We weren't good for each other. You wouldn't have been happy being a cop's wife."

"You've always said that, but I would have been happy with you. You say you're in love with Maya, but then where is she? She's not here right now. I am."

"She's working," Josh said, feeling like this was going down a bad road. The less he said about Maya, the better. "But that's not the point. The point is, she makes me happy. You never did."

He knew the words were fighting ones, but Amber just turned away and finished her wine.

"Be careful driving," Josh said, grateful to see the bartender heading his way with the bill.

"Or what? You'll pull me over? Is that a threat?"

Great. Just more of the crap Amber liked to pull. She'd probably add this to the case in Chicago—if there even was a case. Everything that came out of her mouth seemed like a lie. "No, I'm not threatening you. Just be careful. That's all."

Josh paid, glad to be leaving. As he stood, the room spun and some sweat popped up on his forehead. He started to walk and his feet didn't quite go where he wanted. He tripped and ran into the back of someone's chair. Josh heard himself trying to apologize, but he couldn't form his words. His speech was slurred.

"So sorry," Amber said to the person whose chair Josh had run into. "He's had a little too much."

"What?" Josh said, again hearing his speech slurred and unrecognizable. "I need…"

"You need some fresh air," Amber said, guiding him out, continuing to apologize for his behavior with little giggles. "Get some shots in this guy and look what happens."

Josh struggled to get outside. Maybe some cold air would help. Was he going to be sick? His vision continued to blur and he couldn't do anything when Amber grabbed his keys to his patrol vehicle.

"Looks like I'm actually the one who's safe to drive, Officer," she said.

Josh grabbed the railing and felt the stares coming from inside the restaurant. Shit. He just needed to get out of here. Amber guided him to the passenger side of his patrol vehicle. He fell into the seat, sweat beading up on his forehead as his stomach churned.

Amber got into the driver's seat and Josh reached for his radio, wanting to call for medical. He didn't know what was going on. She took the radio out of his hand and put it back in its holder and said, "You'll be fine. I'll get you home and you can sleep this off."

"What did you do?" Josh asked, his words slurring again. She must have drugged him, but he was already so foggy that he couldn't think straight or do anything.

"Just reminding you of how much fun you can be when you have a little something to take the edge off."

Amber drove out of the parking lot. Josh struggled to stay awake. Why was she doing this to him? He knew she was spoiled and manipulative, but he hadn't realized she would threaten his sobriety, job and life by drugging him. It must have been something in his drink. Probably when he took the call from his deputy.

He'd had a Pepsi tonight. If she'd slipped something in there, he wouldn't have been able to tell.

He couldn't think straight. His eyes were heavy. He just wanted to sleep. Everything was going dark.

After pulling into his driveway, Amber helped him out of his vehicle. She leaned in close, her lips next to his ear, and whispered, "I want you to feel the pain and embarrassment I felt when you dumped me. I want you to know what it's like to have everyone gossiping about you behind your back."

Josh wanted to say something but couldn't form the words. He remembered entering the house through his front door. He remembered seeing his phone ringing and the caller ID saying *Maya*.

Then everything went black.

Chapter Thirty-Two

Maya woke up early the next morning. It was still dark outside and Juniper was snoring on the bed next to her. She was probably going to regret letting Juniper sleep with her in the motel when they went back home. But for now, it was comforting.

Especially with the news she'd received from Lucas last night. Eric Torres was her biological father.

So many different emotions had hit Maya all at once. Her long-standing question had been answered. She understood that her mother had been having an affair with Eric and that was probably one reason Zoey hadn't put him on Maya's birth certificate. But her father was also a felon and wanted by the Marshals. He had saved her life, but had committed crimes. Feeling confused and overwhelmed, she had called Josh last night, but he hadn't answered and hadn't called her back. What would he think? Would he be upset with her for not telling him?

Stepping out of bed, Maya pulled on a sweatshirt and turned up the heat in the room. The wind gusted outside, the first sign of the big storm coming in. She might end up being stuck at the motel for the weekend. Or she might be able to get back home and then come

back to Antler Valley on Monday. She wasn't sure yet
if the investigation was on hold until test results came
in. She'd have to ask Ben.

Although she felt a little uneasy about that too. After
she had spilled her guts at dinner about being an alcoholic, Ben had been more reserved and standoffish.
Maya decided not to worry about it, though. She was
clean and going to AA regularly. She could pass a random drug test at any time. If Ben wanted to judge her,
then so be it.

She left Juniper snoring on the bed to go to the front
office and get some coffee and another complimentary
pastry. She grabbed two cups again. It was the minimum
amount of caffeine she needed to get her day started.
She would find more on the way into the sheriff's office.
Maya had already learned that this sheriff's office didn't
have good coffee. She was kind of spoiled at her home
office where she had bought her own coffee machine
and could have a good cup of joe anytime she wanted.

It was early, but Maya decided to call Josh and see if
she could catch him at home. Sometimes he went into
work early depending on the amount of paperwork Pops
gave him. With Pops's investigation going on, she didn't
know how much Josh had on his plate along with having his family in town. Josh was right—she didn't understand the demands of a normal family. She'd never
had one. She needed to cut him some slack and figure
this out with him. Josh was the best thing that had ever
happened to Maya besides Juniper.

The phone rang a couple times and then Josh picked
up.

"Hey there," she said.

"Hey," Josh said. "It's good to hear from you."

His voice sounded funny. Not quite like himself. Concern came over Maya and she put aside telling him about the letter and DNA results. "You okay? You don't sound quite like yourself."

"No, I don't feel good this morning."

"You staying home from work?"

"No, I'm actually already at work," Josh said.

"Oh." Maya hadn't known him when he was a drinker, but he almost sounded hungover. Maybe he had the flu or something. "I'm sure Pops would give you the day off if you need it."

"No, I'm good. I'm sure I'll feel better soon."

Maya clutched her phone. She remembered saying that too when she'd been a heavy drinker. She'd wake up feeling crappy, but if she gave it a few hours she would be back to normal.

"How's the investigation going?" Josh asked.

"It's kind of crazy," Maya said, filling him in.

"Be careful over there. Don't do more than you need to. You're a Forest Service officer offering support. You don't need to save the day."

Maya took a sip of coffee. What was up with him today? "I'll be fine. I know how to take care of myself. This is my job, and just like yours, it has its dangers. We know that. I have Juniper too. She'll let me know if there's any problems."

At the sound of her name, Juniper opened one eye, saw that Maya wasn't going anywhere and went back to sleep.

"What's going on?" Maya asked. "Something is up with you. I tried calling you last night and you didn't answer. Besides feeling like you have the flu, what's wrong?"

There was silence on the other end of the phone. Her

anxiety heightened. Josh was never like this with her. He was always open and honest. Of course, he'd failed to mention he'd been engaged previously, so maybe she didn't really know him as well as she thought. On the other hand, she hadn't told him about the letter from Abigail and that her father was a wanted felon.

"Nothing's wrong. I'm sorry, I have a lot on my mind today. You don't sound like yourself either. Is it the case or something else?"

Maya hesitated, then said, "There's something I need to tell you."

"I may already know."

"What? How?"

"I received a call last night from Abigail," Josh said.

Maya tried to judge how upset he sounded, but since he already didn't sound like himself, she couldn't get a good read over the phone. "What did she tell you?"

"That she sent you a letter with some shocking news. Did you receive a letter?"

"I did."

"Did that letter say that Eric Torres is your father?"

"Yes," Maya said. Dizziness from anxiety swept over her and she massaged her forehead as a headache started. She had an answer to a question she'd had her whole life, but it hadn't made her happy like she'd thought it would. Instead, she felt uneasy. "I didn't want to bother you with all this while your family was in town. You had enough on your mind."

"Did you get DNA run?"

"Yes."

"Do you have results?"

"I do," Maya said. "Lucas called me last night..."

"And?"

"He is my father." A wave of apprehension swept over her again. Did she owe Eric, not only for saving her life, but also because he was her father? Would he ever be in touch again or would he always be on the run? Did she want to know him and have some sort of relationship? None of the answers to her questions were easy.

"How are you doing with that news?"

"Good and bad," Maya said. "I mean, I'm happy to know the truth, but I don't know how I feel about *him* being my father."

"I understand," Josh said. "It's big news and will be a lot to process. I'm here for you, though. Tell me what you need."

"I'm still getting used to knowing the truth. I thought, though, that you'd be mad at me for not telling you."

"I'm not thrilled that you kept it from me, but after everything with Amber, I know I've kept things from you too. I'm sorry for that and when you get back, let's sit down and talk. Tell each other everything. Right now, I just want to make sure you're okay with the news about Eric."

Maya could still tell from the tone of his voice that something more was wrong. She didn't feel like talking more about Eric. For now, telling Josh was enough. Sort of like a first step in processing the news. "I'm good. And I agree, when I get back, we'll sit down and discuss everything more. I feel like you're not yourself this morning. Is there anything else going on with you? Some other news? Your family bugging you? Your ex-fiancée being a pain?"

Josh paused. "No. Yes. There are things going on and we'll chat more later. Just know for now that I've spoken with my family and they understand how I feel about you. I told them that I love you, because I do, Maya. I've never felt this way about anyone else and I want to be with you forever."

Maya didn't know what to say. She'd never trusted anyone or allowed anyone into her life, but Josh was different. "I love you too. I want nothing more than to be with you too. This time away has made me realize how much I miss you."

"You have no idea how that makes me feel."

"No," Maya said. "I think I do. What about Amber? When I get back, will you tell me more?"

"Yes. I'm so sorry that I didn't tell you about her. Let me make it up to you somehow."

"I have some ideas," Maya said. Her tone became playful, but she felt like Josh was holding back regarding his ex. What wasn't he telling her? "You sure you're okay?"

"I am. Look, I'll fill you in about everything in the past, but I'd rather do it in person. I better get back to work. I have a huge stack of paperwork in front of me."

"Okay. Talk later?" she asked.

"Definitely." Maya thought Josh's tone changed and he was closer to sounding like the man she knew and loved.

"I love you, Josh."

"Ditto," he said and then hung up.

Maya sat on the edge of her bed. He was definitely holding back. But on what and why, she didn't know. That bothered her more than the results of her DNA test.

Chapter Thirty-Three

Josh hung up with Maya and leaned back in his chair, staring at the ceiling. He should have told her about Amber's visit to his office, her threats and everything that happened last night. At some point someone was going to tell her that he'd appeared drunk or high or both at the Black Bear Café and that Amber had driven him home. It should come from him first, but he had chickened out.

Plus, he didn't really know what had happened last night other than he suspected Amber had put something in his drink like Rohypnol, otherwise known as being roofied. She always had an endgame. Did this have something to do with the case in Chicago being appealed? Or with Maya? Or both? The words that she'd whispered in his ear kept running through his head. She'd been high-maintenance when they dated, but either she had kept this nasty side to her hidden or she was having some sort of breakdown.

Josh was now glad that Maya was gone, because he needed to handle Amber while she couldn't go after her. Would Amber hurt her? Josh didn't know, but he did know he'd never thought that Amber would spike a drink and apparently she had.

His head pounded and he popped a couple ibuprofen,

realizing that he used to live his life this way. If nothing else, he knew that he never wanted to go back to being that person. He liked who he was now and a big part of that was Maya. He should have told her the truth about what was going on, but he was afraid of losing her.

His thoughts were cut short by a knock on the door. Pops entered his office.

"You're here early," Josh said.

"The same could be said for you," Pops answered. "Mind if I take a seat?"

"Please, sit down."

The sheriff pulled a chair up and they sat in silence, eyeing each other. Josh didn't like the expression on Pops's face. He knew his boss well by now and knew when Pops was upset. The longer it took for Pops to start talking, the more Josh was worried.

"Anything you want to tell me?" Pops asked, breaking the silence.

Josh wondered if there had already been calls about last night at the Black Bear Café, but he decided to play dumb for now. He didn't need to start more problems if Pops was talking about something else. "No."

"Sure?"

"Yes."

Pops stared out the window behind Josh and then brought his gaze back, looking straight at Josh. A shiver went through Josh. Pops's eyes were the same intense green as Maya's, and like her, her grandfather could look straight through him.

"I received some calls last night. Complaints about you being drunk in uniform at the Black Bear."

Josh closed his eyes, took a deep breath, and then opened them. Pops hadn't looked away. "I wasn't drunk."

"Were you high?"

"No."

"Then what?"

Josh started to answer, but then stopped. He didn't know what. Roofied? Some other drug? So, then he really was high? Maybe it had been a reaction to food? He didn't know. "I don't know for sure, to be honest. I suddenly felt ill and I suspect that Amber drugged me. Maybe with roofies. She could have mixed in something more too. I really don't know."

"One of the calls said that you had shots of Jack. I looked at your tab and it looks like you paid for a couple. I need you to be straightforward with me: If I have you take a piss test, will you pass it?"

"I don't know," Josh said, hoping honesty would help, but understanding that it made him seem more guilty. "I didn't drink the shots. Amber bought them for me and I asked the bartender to take them back, but I didn't want him to be out the money for the shots. I told him to put them on my bill. Ask him."

"I will follow up with him. As for the test, I need to know that you're sober right now since you're here and in uniform. I hope you do pass it. You're going to go pee in that right now." Pops pulled a random UA container out of his coat pocket and set it on Josh's desk.

Josh's heart sank. What if he didn't pass it? How long were roofies in the system? Did she mix them with something else? He couldn't remember right now with his head pounding, but he was certain it was recent enough that if that's what Amber had drugged him with, he was going to light up this drug test.

"You think you're going to pass?" Pops asked.

"I honestly don't know," Josh said.

"You're serious about being roofied?"

"I am," Josh said. He didn't know if Maya had told him anything about Amber. It would be better if he told Pops more. "My parents brought a family friend with them."

"Yeah, that tall blonde gal."

"That's the one. Well, that tall blonde gal and I used to be engaged and she wants to get back together. I told her no. I love Maya. I think she drugged me out in public to get me fired as payback for dumping her."

"Well, shit. Go pee and then we'll talk more. I'd like to believe you, but I wish you'd called me when this happened. It's harder to deal with this because you didn't come to me. I trusted you—the least you could have done was trust me. Now you've put me in a bad spot because depending on what this test says, I may have to suspend you and start an investigation, which is just great timing with the investigation going on with me. This could get us both fired. You better hope you don't have a positive test result."

Josh picked up the cup and went down the hall to the bathroom. Pops was right—he should have called the moment he woke up. He only appeared guilty because of the way he'd handled this whole situation. To make matters worse, Pops followed him and watched him take the test to make sure he didn't try to cheat it. Feeling humiliated, Josh finished and handed the cup to him. He washed his hands and went back to his office and waited. The test Pops used was a rapid one that they kept on hand in case of officer-involved shootings or anything else where they needed to find out if an officer was sober at the time of an incident. Josh should know soon if he still had drugs in his system.

Coming back in the office, Pops set the cup down. The test strip on the side was bright red, indicating a positive test.

"Based on this test you have several substances in your system. I'd really like to believe you, but with the way you handled this, I can't. If what you said happened with Amber is the truth, then you should have told me and not come to work while you're still under the influence. Right now, I don't know if you've fallen off the wagon or what. I hope you're telling me the truth because I gave you a second chance, and if this is how I'm repaid, saying I'm disappointed is an understatement. I'm putting you on paid leave pending further investigation. Go get a full blood panel from Doc Clark. That way if she did drug you, we'll have a better idea of what she used."

Josh stood and started gathering his things. Pops was right—he needed to go get a better test. He'd swing into Doc Clark's office, the local general practitioner as well as coroner, on his way home. Then he planned on searching his house to see if anything was missing and finding Amber to confront her. He also needed to call Maya.

As if reading his mind, Pops spoke up again. "Sit back down," Pops said. "I'm not done."

Josh followed orders. It was best to not say much right now until he could gather more evidence and figure out what had happened to him.

"Until I know if you're telling me the truth, stay away from Maya. Got it? She's finally getting better and recovering. She doesn't need you messing her up or your ex-girlfriend tormenting her. Call her and break up with her. Or tell her to stay in Antler Valley for longer. I don't care, but she's not staying in your home."

"With all due respect, sir," Josh said. "That's between Maya and me. She's an adult and so am I. I'll let her know what's going on and she can make her own decision. Our relationship is between us."

Josh and Pops stared at each other, neither wanting to back down. Josh's jaw tightened and his hands balled into fists. He needed to calm down now before he did something he'd regret, but he couldn't break eye contact with Pops.

A knock on the door broke the tension. Josh's dad, Spencer, stood outside. Josh figured he was here to get Pops and continue the questioning and investigation. This was supposed to be the last day of interrogating Pops. After that, from the investigation, it would then be determined if Pops would go to trial.

"Am I interrupting something?" Dad asked.

"No," Josh said. "I was just heading home."

"The sheriff give you the day off?"

"No," Josh and Pops answered in unison.

"I think I'll have several days off, actually," Josh said. "I've just been put on paid suspension."

Dad stepped into Josh's office. "What do you mean? What's going on here?"

Pops pointed at the cup of urine sitting on the desk. "Your boy just peed hot."

"What? Josh, why? You've done so well. What happened?" Josh was a little surprised at his dad's reaction. In the past, his dad would have told him how disappointed he was and how Josh was a screwup.

"I didn't deliberately do any drugs," Josh said. "I think my soda was spiked."

"Really?" Dad said. "This is just like you, son. Be a man and take responsibility."

That was more like usual for his dad. Josh should have known better.

"I'm telling you both the truth," he said, placing his badge and his service weapon on the desk next to the drug test.

"Like I said," Pops piped up as Josh was walking past him out the door. "Stay away from Maya."

Josh stopped and turned to look at both of them. "I love Maya more than anything in this world. I would never hurt her. It would be good for you to remember that."

Chapter Thirty-Four

Caffeinated, showered, dressed for work and with Juniper exercised and fed, Maya realized she still had about fifteen minutes to kill before she had to leave. In the tense conversation with Josh, she had forgotten to ask about Pops. Rather than bug Josh again, she decided she'd call Pops herself. She hadn't seen or talked to him for a few days.

Pops picked up quickly. "Hey there, Maya Bear."

"Hey, Pops. How are you?"

Pops hesitated, which worried her. He only did that when he didn't want to give her bad news.

"What's wrong?" she asked. "Is the investigation not going well?"

"No, the questioning is going very well. Spencer is a great attorney and I think I'll get through this without having to go to trial."

"That's great news," Maya said, feeling some relief. She couldn't imagine the stress of a trial, much less Pops getting convicted and going to prison. "I get the feeling that something else is going on then. What's up?"

Pops hesitated again and then said, "I just put Josh on paid suspension."

It was Maya's turn to be speechless. Josh hadn't mentioned a suspension when they'd just talked, but she had felt like he'd been holding back. She finally managed to get out, "Why? What happened?"

"I don't want to be the one to tell you this, but I guess it's better you hear it from me."

"Pops, you're scaring me. What the hell happened?" She gripped her phone harder and sat down on the edge of the bed. Juniper, sensing the strain in her voice, jumped up next to her on the bed and slapped a giant paw down on her leg. Maya petted her absentmindedly.

"Sorry, Maya, I didn't mean to scare you. Josh was seen in uniform at the Black Bear Café intoxicated or high. Maybe both. I'm not sure. He just failed a UA. Big-time. He lit it up like I haven't seen in a while."

Maya was speechless again. Juniper gave her a quick lick on the cheek. "I'm sure there must be some mistake or some reason. Josh is serious about staying sober. He would never jeopardize all the work he's put in."

"I don't know, Maya. All I know is that I need to investigate. Based on the drug test, it appears that Josh mixed cocaine with some roofies. I know from the initial interview I did with Josh before I hired him that cocaine was his go-to drug, but I didn't know about the roofies. I supposed that could be something new. He might have mixed them to offset the upper effect of the cocaine."

"I know about the cocaine, Pops. And I know that sometimes users mix cocaine and roofies, but I'm telling you, Josh wouldn't do this."

"Are you sure about that?" Pops challenged. "I thought I knew him too. He was my chief deputy, for Christ's sake. But Maya, drug tests don't lie and we're not talking about one witness here. There were multiple. I don't know what's going on except for that Josh is suspended."

She flopped back on the bed, regretting that as Juniper lay across her chest, pinning her down. Maya gently asked her to move and sat back up.

"There's more," Pops said. "It gets worse."

"How could it get worse?" Maya asked. Although she already had a feeling she knew. It had to have something to do with Amber. That's the only thing she could think of that would make things worse.

"He was seen leaving the Black Bear with his ex-fiancée. She apparently spent the night at his house. Josh's mother was coming over to bring him some breakfast pastries early this morning and saw Amber leaving. She told Josh's dad, elated, thinking that they were getting back together."

Maya took a deep breath. This couldn't be happening. The Josh she knew wouldn't do drugs and wouldn't cheat on her. She had to give him a chance to explain himself, although it had better be a damn good explanation. If she had managed to get into another relationship with someone who cheated, she figured she would swear off love forever. She knew he'd been holding out on her this morning.

She glanced at her watch. She might have time to call Josh again before she had to leave.

"You still there?" Pops asked.

"Yeah, I am," Maya said. "I'm just trying to come to grips with everything you're telling me. What was Josh's version of the story? Did you ask him some questions?"

"I did, but I'm having a hard time believing him. He

claims Amber drugged him. I think it's an excuse for losing his sobriety. I'm sorry."

"I am too," Maya said. "But I don't think Josh would throw away all the work he's done to stay sober that easily. Amber could have drugged him. I need to talk to him and find out more. I'm going to let you go and give Josh a call."

"Think about something for me, will you?" Pops said.

"What's that?"

"Maybe you should take a time-out with Josh. If he's going down a bad road or this ex is going to cause problems, I don't want to see you affected. You've done so well and I want you to stay healthy."

"I can take care of myself, Pops," Maya said. She knew he was telling her this out of love, but she was also irritated that he was stepping into her personal life. "This is between Josh and me."

"He said the same thing," Pops said.

"You know, at one point you were happy that Josh and I were together, but you have to realize that, in any relationship, there's going to be ups and downs. We'll work through this."

"I just want you to know that I'm there for you," Pops said. "If you decide you need to move out, then you and Juniper can always stay with me until your cabin is done."

"We'd kill each other, Pops. We're too much alike."

"True."

"Look, I need to get going. I appreciate you telling me everything so I wasn't blindsided. I know you have to do your job and investigate as Josh's boss, but as Josh's girlfriend, I need to be there for him. Got it?"

"Got it," Pops said.

Maya could hear the resignation in his voice. She said her goodbyes and then hung up. Juniper had managed to drape herself across Maya's lap. She hugged her dog and thought about everything she'd learned. She didn't have much time, but she needed to talk to Josh.

Maya had just unlocked her phone when a call from Ben came in. She answered it.

"Thompson, I need you to join me at Saddle Rock Falls immediately," Ben said. "There's been another homicide."

Chapter Thirty-Five

It didn't take Maya long to get to the crime scene since the famous ice-climbing area was not far from her motel. She had wanted to visit the falls on her trip, but this was not the plan she'd had in mind.

Ben hadn't said much more other than it was linked to their case, the killer was escalating and she needed to get there right away to help.

Maya parked next to Agent Kessler's unmarked FBI bureau car, or "bucar." There were other emergency responders' vehicles from different agencies in the same area. In the law enforcement world, when there were this many first responders, the saying was "the world has arrived."

Before Maya stepped out of her vehicle, she took a deep breath, still shaken by what Pops had told her about Josh. She wanted to contact Josh and find out his side of things, but there wasn't time for a phone call. She picked up her cell phone and wrote:

Pops filled me in on what's going on. Are you okay? I'm worried about you. Let's try to talk to later. I love you.

There were other things Maya wanted to text, like,

What the hell were you doing with Amber and did she hurt you? Or did she get you to use drugs again? Instead, she put her phone back in her pocket, trying to give Josh the benefit of the doubt. She grabbed her heavy coat as clouds had moved in and the wind was starting to pick up. The weather was putting a time constraint on getting this scene processed.

Once this massive winter storm moved in, it would destroy or cover up evidence. She would do everything she could to help. Maya had wanted to try to go home for her day off, but with this murder, it appeared she would be staying in Antler Valley longer. Exiting her vehicle, she heard Juniper start yipping and even giving a howl or two.

"I'll let you know if you're needed," Maya said to a very unhappy Juniper. "I promise."

She made her way over to the crime scene tape. Ben was waiting for her and, again, didn't seem like himself. She wondered what was up or if it was her imagination. On the other hand, this case was starting to wear on her. Why wouldn't it do the same thing to him?

"Wait until you see this," he said. "The victim is Bryce."

"What?" Maya asked. "Seriously?"

"Seriously."

Ben logged her into the scene—standard protocol to keep track of everyone who went behind the crime scene tape. Maya followed behind Ben, being careful about where she was walking to avoid interfering with any possible evidence. When they arrived at the falls, she stopped in her tracks trying to process the scene in front of her.

The victim hung from some climbing ropes, red blood

contrasting against the ice. He had an ice pick lodged in his torso and a note pinned to him. Her breathing became shallow and fast. Had their plan to use him as a CI gotten him killed? If he had been set up, they may have done exactly what the killer wanted. Bryce may have been safer remaining locked up. Maya closed her eyes and worked to slow her breathing. She used to get upset about her reactions, but as she learned more about PTSD and worked with her therapist, she was starting to accept them. She knew she had to work on staying in the moment, which would help her anxiety.

Maya had to process what she saw, but even in Afghanistan she hadn't seen a horror like this. The amount of blood and violence showed that the killer had been angry. Actually, angry didn't even cover it.

"It's bad," Ben said.

"That's one way to put it," she said. All she could think to ask was "What does the note say?"

"The investigators said it read 'He got the exclusive interview.'"

"That's awful," Maya said.

"I know."

"Wasn't Deputy Glen supposed to be watching him?"

"He was," Ben said. "According to the deputy, somehow Bryce slipped out without him seeing anything. There was a back window with a fire escape in his apartment. Maybe he went down that way."

"Unbelievable," Maya said as Agent Kessler came over and joined them.

Overhearing, Kessler added, "It *is* unbelievable. This killer is taunting us. The only good thing about this escalation is that I was able to get our ERT up here immediately. This case was just bumped up a few notches in importance."

"I'm glad your evidence response team could come process this," Maya said. "I know you've been studying the other cases that ViCAP matched to this one. Did the suspect in those crimes ever do something like this where he taunted law enforcement?"

"No," said Agent Kessler. "His MO is changing. He's evolving, and that's not good."

"Maybe that means we're getting closer to him," Maya said. "We're doing something that's setting him off. We need to go through every little detail in this case. Maybe something we're overlooking will lead us to him."

"I agree," Kessler said. "I'm sending crime scene photos and information to our BAU at Quantico. I'm hoping they'll see something that we've missed."

"Possibly," Ben said, jumping back into the conversation. "All we know for sure is that Bryce Riley wasn't the main killer. Maybe he was the partner and when we arrested him, the killer decided he needed to be taken care of. Have you heard from Quantico about the DNA samples?"

"Not yet," said Kessler. "I did my best to put a rush on it, but of course all of us think our cases are the most important and need to be bumped up ahead of everyone else's. Hopefully I'll hear something soon."

"What if I get Juniper out and see if she can find a fresh odor to track?" Maya asked, changing tactics. Juniper had the ability to track the suspect and find evidence. Juniper tracking was something that Maya didn't need to wait on like DNA testing. They could do it right now. She took in the number of people processing the scene. "There's a lot of people here who could have disturbed a scent while processing the scene, but maybe if I try the perimeter outside of the crime scene tape, she'll be able to pick up an odor."

Agent Kessler shrugged. "It's worth a try, and if it leads us to where the suspect parked, then maybe we can get tire tread or some other kind of evidence."

"I agree," Ben said. "It's worth a try."

"Okay," Maya said. "I'll go get Juniper."

She hoped that they could find something. This killer was only becoming more violent, and who knew who was next on his list?

Chapter Thirty-Six

Juniper was thrilled to have the chance to work. She danced around as Maya wrestled her to put on her snow booties, Doggles and tracking gear. With the temperature dropping and the wind picking up, Maya hoped Juniper could catch a scent. The steep cliffs would block some of the strong wind and make the track less difficult.

After finishing up with all of Juniper's gear, Maya let her out on the leash as they headed back to the crime scene. Happy to be out of the vehicle, Juniper jumped around in the snow, tail wagging, enjoying her freedom.

Maya went back over to Agent Kessler and Ben, but stayed outside the crime scene tape so that Juniper didn't destroy any evidence. Deputy Glen had joined them.

"I asked Deputy Glen to back you up again," Ben said. "I'll come along too, but I'll stay back."

"That sounds good," Maya said. Juniper fidgeted by her side, ready to work. "Let's see what Juniper can find."

There were two sides to the crime scene due to the high cliffs. Eventually there were steep trails on either side that hikers used in the summertime and snowshoers often enjoyed in the wintertime. Would the killer have used either of those trails? If he'd driven in, that evidence and the track would be long gone with the number of responders on the scene. Maya could only hope that Juniper would pick up some odor and maybe they would be able to find something useful to the investigation. She was starting to feel helpless, which she didn't like.

Taking Juniper over to the north side first, Maya cast her out around the trail and worked to get Juniper into areas where there might be a scent. Juniper put her nose to the ground and worked well, but never showed any interest in a fresh track.

Maya wished she had a scent article to use, but that wasn't an option for this. Instead, she was hoping that Juniper could find a fresh scent from the killer. The weather made it hard with both the wind and the temperature. The cold would make the scent harder to find. At least the high cliffs provided a windbreak.

Maya cast Juniper out to one last area, but there was still no interest or indication that there was a fresh scent. She called Juniper back over to her and praised her dog for checking the area so well.

"I don't think there's a good scent to track here," Maya said to Deputy Glen and Ben. "At least nothing fresh."

"Okay," Ben said. "It was worth a try."

"There's one more trail over on the south side of the cliffs," she said. "Let's try over there."

The trio hiked back around the crime scene and up toward the trail on the other side. This path was much steeper and used less by hikers and snowshoers. Maya saw what she thought were fresh snowshoe tracks. She cast Juniper out and unlike the north side, Juniper's tail poked up in the air, her body tense and rigid as she worked back and forth in a scent cone, pinpointing the odor.

Maya tried not to get too excited. Yes, there was a fresh track, but that didn't mean it was their killer. Although with the site back by the ice-climbing area, she couldn't imagine someone snowshoeing on this path and not seeing Bryce hanging from the ice falls. It had been a climber who had called police when he arrived early that morning.

Juniper brought her nose up in the air, catching some of the scent off the breeze, and then took her nose back to the ground, near the tracks, sniffing around for a moment. Maya saw the change in her dog and was ready to go with her. The first time they tracked, Juniper had taken Maya by surprise with the way she took off like a racehorse out of the starting gate. Maya had become accustomed to her dog taking off and was ready.

Juniper did exactly that and Maya called over her shoulder, "She has a good scent."

Bounding up the steep trail, Juniper didn't seem to be tired at all. Maya, on the other hand, felt like she was sucking in air. Her calves and thighs burned as she pushed through the thick snow to stay with Juniper up the path. She'd put on the long leash so at least she could give Juniper some slack and not interfere with her track.

Glancing over her shoulder, Maya could see that Deputy Glen and Ben were also feeling the burn of the incline, struggling to keep up with them. Maya didn't want to get too far ahead just in case this was some sort of trap by the suspect. He'd already proven that he liked messing with them.

The path flattened out and widened. Juniper slowed, her nose back off the ground as she switched to air scent-

ing. She stopped and Maya was on high alert. Could
the suspect be in the area? Had Juniper switched to air
scenting because the suspect was somehow trying to
come back around and ambush them?

Deputy Glen must have thought the same thing as he
had his gun pulled but pointed down in low-ready position. Maya turned her attention back to her dog, which
was the point of having a backup officer. That way she
could watch Juniper's body language and not worry
about being ambushed by the suspect. Watching their
surroundings was the backup officer's job.

Juniper continued to work the scent but seemed to
be struggling to maintain it. Maya was about ready to
start casting Juniper out again when the Malinois put
her nose back to the ground and took her over to a tree.
She lay down and stared up.

"Is she tired or something?" Deputy Glen asked.

"No," Maya said. "I've taught her that she should lie
down for an evidence alert and sit for a narcotics alert.
There's probably evidence in this area."

Maya praised Juniper, gathering up her leash. Ben
and Deputy Glen came over and started checking around
the area where Juniper had alerted. Ben saw the evidence first.

"Even though it took us a minute to locate that, our
suspect wanted to make sure we found it," he said,
pointing toward a plastic bag pinned to the tree Juniper had alerted on.

"He knows K-9s," Maya said.

"I agree," Ben said.

"What makes you say that?" asked Deputy Glen.

"As a former handler," Ben said. "He left that evidence in the perfect location for Juniper to find. The

wind threw her off, but he made it easy for Juniper by putting these pictures right at her nose level."

"Exactly," Maya said. "And maybe even more disturbing, he knew we would use Juniper to try to track him. He understands dogs and he knows our investigative techniques."

Maya didn't add in her thought that the suspect might be in law enforcement and could even be one of the two men she was with right now. Ben had been acting weird and had disappeared when they had busted the party. Could he have planted the evidence in Bryce's car? Did she really think that he was capable of these crimes? And she really didn't know Deputy Glen. Had he had other intentions when he offered to be her backup officer? The evidence had shown that there was more than one killer. Maybe they were working together. At least Maya had Juniper to help protect her, but she had to be careful. She'd feel better when she was no longer alone with Ben and Deputy Glen.

Ben photographed and logged the bag hanging on the tree. After putting on gloves, he took the pictures down and stared at the one on top. Then he carefully opened the bag and peeked at the others. He pulled out a note, raised his eyebrows as he read it, and then put it back in the bag.

"Are those pictures of the victims or something?" Maya asked.

"No," Ben said. "They're pictures of the sheriff having sex with women who aren't his wife."

"Oh," Maya said, not totally surprised. Somehow the sheriff cheating on his wife just fit him. "What did the note say?"

"It said, 'Your sheriff is a dirty man. He should pay for his crimes.'"

"I agree," Maya said. *So why did the killer leave those for us? Is he trying to make the sheriff look guilty? Or does he have another motive?*

She thought about the manila envelope and the sheriff's angry but also embarrassed reaction. "It's possible the suspect has been sending these pictures to the sheriff to try to control the investigation. Now that the FBI is in charge, maybe this is his way of still trying to influence the case."

Ben nodded as he pulled out another picture and note. "I think he does want to control this investigation. I don't know for sure, but I'm assuming this is a picture of Agent Kessler's wife and daughter taken from outside their home."

Maya glanced at the picture. She'd never met Kessler's family, but the baby in the picture looked about a month old. "We'll have to ask him to know for sure. What does the note say?"

"It says, 'The FBI will never catch me, but I know what matters to our favorite agent.'"

"Then that has to be his family," Maya said. "We need to warn him ASAP. Let's see if there's any more to this track and then get this evidence back to Agent Kessler and the evidence team."

"Sounds good," Ben said. "Deputy Glen, you up for continuing on?"

"I am," the deputy said.

"All right," Maya said, and she praised Juniper for the evidence find again. She didn't voice any further concerns since one or both officers with her could be their suspect.

She also didn't know how tired Juniper was getting, although her dog appeared ready to go again.

All Maya knew for sure was that she would have to watch her back.

Chapter Thirty-Seven

Feeling anxious, not knowing now who she could trust, Maya went ahead and cast Juniper out to see if they could find the track again. Juniper immediately went back out, and with plenty of energy, found the scent again and continued up the snowy path. From the flat area where the evidence had been left, Juniper remained on the trail that started another upward climb.

Maya was starting to get concerned about the depth of the snow and, as they climbed in altitude, the danger of entering avalanche territory. Just as she was about ready to pull Juniper up, they came to another flat point in the trail. Juniper circled around an area that appeared to have snowmobile tracks. They took off in a direction that would be difficult to travel on foot, so the person riding the snowmobile would have to be an advanced rider with the slope of the hill and terrain.

Maya praised Juniper, proud of her dog and how well she had worked. "I think we need to stop here. The conditions aren't safe to continue and follow these tracks."

"At least we know how he got to the crime scene," Deputy Glen said.

"I think he was setting this up for us again, for Juniper to track," Maya said.

"I agree," Ben chimed in.

"Why do you two say that?" asked Deputy Glen.

"Because there's no blood and no signs that he had Bryce with him here," Maya said. "If Bryce was already dead, there would have been blood and drag marks. If Bryce was alive and came with our suspect this way, there would have been an extra set of prints in the snow. My guess is that he drove to the crime scene and left Bryce for us to find. Then our suspect decided to play another game with us knowing that I'd want to use Juniper."

She wanted to add that this game was starting to feel personal. An uneasy feeling came across her and she shivered. All she could hope was that, being on a snowmobile in this area, the killer might trigger an avalanche and bury himself.

Mother Nature taking him out would be divine justice in Maya's mind.

He walked around near the crime scene, keeping an eye on all the activity. One of his best works of art, if anyone asked, but of course they wouldn't. He was just glad to be rid of the little snot journalist. He was starting to be a pain in the ass and he was tired of writing the letters. He had asked his protégé to lure the kid out and then they'd taken care of him.

Even better, he'd decided to toy with Maya and her K-9. It'd worked perfectly, of course. His plan had been spot-on. Maya was beginning to suspect something, though. He was sure of that. Did she suspect him? Or was it his partner that she was starting to realize was always around?

His partner, or protégé as he liked to think of him, had learned well and was ready to go out on his own.

Time to let him be free and see what happened. That meant he might be ready to move on himself. Maybe move out of Antler Valley. He'd be sad as he felt like there was still work to be done here, but the fact was, there were people in every mountain town that needed a reminder that they too could be extinguished just like they were killing the environment.

He wondered if anyone would put together that hanging the journalist at the falls was symbolic of the fact that it took longer every year for the waterfalls to freeze due to climate change. In fact, there was now a push with the town to create man-made ice falls just like ski resorts made snow. Thanks to climate change, the falls didn't freeze properly and snow totals were less. The snowpack was dwindling and water in the West would soon be liquid gold. Trees would die, animals would go extinct, and no one cared. Instead, humans just tried to pretend like nothing was happening and re-created nature with things like fake icefalls and snow.

Except for him. *See, Mother?* He did have feelings. He had empathy. Just not for human life. But how could he keep his mission going if he was caught? He reminded himself, though, that he was part of this crime scene right now, blending in, and no one suspecting anything.

But there was one more human he wanted to take care of before he left. He worked to calm the anger that surged through him at her betrayal. Maya. Here he'd thought she was different. That she cared for the forest and had a perfect life.

Then he just continued to find out more and more. His partner had filled him in too. Not only was she an alcoholic, but she'd fought in Afghanistan as a Marine. The military only polluted the world more, in his eyes.

Bombs, missiles, drone strikes, planes, tanks—the list just went on and on. And what had they accomplished in Afghanistan?

Nothing. Absolutely nothing except ruining another country.

He worked to control his anger. If he didn't, he would make a mistake. Maya was a hypocrite. A liar. She had seemed like a good person and then she'd turned on him.

She would pay for this.

But the damn dog was always by her side. He couldn't get to Maya when the dog was in the patrol vehicle either because she had the remote popper that could open the door. He needed some support. He would ask his protégé one more time for some assistance. Maybe he could repay his partner's kindness by helping him find his first victim. He knew who his protégé was eyeing. He didn't understand why, but he could help kidnap that person too.

Between the two of them, they could take down their victims. He could prove his point with a grand finale that included letting the world know his mission. Then he would move on to another town.

His work never ended.

Chapter Thirty-Eight

Josh arrived home and threw his keys onto the counter. He flopped down on the couch and sat back trying to comprehend everything that had happened to him in the past twelve hours.

He'd stopped by Doc Clark's office on the way home and waited for an opening to get a blood test and another urine sample. He wanted to know exactly what he had been drugged with. Then he would confront Amber on why. He didn't understand. Roofies were generally used as a date rape drug. Did Amber really just want him to move back and get back together with her? Or was it for something more? He needed to find out more about the case she was using for blackmail. Was she somehow being forced by someone else connected with that case to come after him? Or was she really having a mental health crisis? Were some of her high-maintenance traits signs that she had problems and he hadn't noticed because of his own issues?

When they'd dated, he'd thought he'd been in love with her. They'd known each other since high school and their families were friends. His mother had been ecstatic when they were dating, already saying things like she had another daughter. But the financial strain of Amber's lifestyle had started wearing on Josh.

He'd been living paycheck to paycheck and his job was stressful and time-consuming. His father had continued to put pressure on him to get off the street and into the courtroom. Josh had resisted. Nothing about law school appealed to him. Even with the stress of the job, he had loved being a cop. He'd felt like he was on the front lines, making a difference, trying to help those who could maybe be coerced into making better decisions and arresting the ones who needed to go to prison to make the streets safer.

He'd known his family hadn't understood at all. Amber had kept hinting for him to go to law school as well. Josh kept telling her he would think about it. Mom had given him her mother's engagement ring and continued to push for him to ask Amber to marry him. Josh had figured maybe if he were engaged, everyone would get off his back. Looking back now, that had been the dumbest idea ever, but at the time he'd thought it would help. So, he'd popped the question. Amber had been thrilled and said yes, and then things got worse and his downward spiral began.

They'd gone out to stores to register. Amber had wanted the most expensive items. Josh hadn't. He'd wanted to register for things that made a home a *home*, not things to have big dinner parties and wine and dine with rich people. That day he'd realized that his life would never mesh with Amber's. She didn't want to be a cop's wife. She wanted to be the arm candy for a governor or senator or a fill-in-the-blank bigwig. He'd asked for the ring back and returned it to Mom. His mother had been upset, his father furious he'd put the family through such an ordeal. His sister had once again been the one and only support he'd had through all this. She'd just listened.

The week after he broke off his engagement, his partner was shot and killed.

Josh had self-medicated through everything until he hit rock bottom. He hadn't known if he would ever be able to be a cop again or even hold down a steady job. But he'd gone to rehab and it was there that he'd realized he did still want to be in law enforcement if anyone would ever hire him. And he'd needed to leave Chicago and be away from everything that had triggered him.

Now the everything was here, including Amber.

Amber didn't do anything, though, without an endgame in mind. He kept coming back to the question, why drug him? What did she *really* want?

Josh stood and started walking around his house. What would she need from him? He wasn't rich. The house had simple furnishings and he'd redone the place himself to save costs.

He continued to pace around the house. Nothing seemed to be missing. There were reminders of the life he and Maya were building together all over, like photos from hiking trips. Juniper's dog bed that was duct taped together since she loved constantly ripping it apart. Maya's clothes in the closet. The smell of her still lingered in their bedroom.

When he'd moved to Pinecone Junction, the last thing he'd wanted was a relationship. His goal had been to live the bachelor life and be on his own. Then one day he'd walked into the sheriff's office for work and seen Maya standing there talking with her grandfather. At the time, it was more like fighting rather than talking. She'd applied to be a deputy and Pops had ripped up her application. She'd stood up to him like no one else Josh had ever met.

Then she'd stomped out past him, barely acknowledging his presence. And yet he'd fallen for her. Hard. They'd worked together when she got the job as a Forest Service officer. In the beginning Maya would hardly give him the time of day, which had only intrigued him more. The more he learned, the more he realized she was hurting just like he had been. He'd realized she'd needed a friend and so had he. And that's where their relationship started, only his feelings for her had continued to grow, and when she moved in with him, for the first time in his life, he was happy. And in love.

God, he missed her right now.

He went out to the garage. Everything was in place there too. His gaze landed on his gun safe. Shit. He kept the gun safe combo and lock in a certain position so that he'd know if anyone ever tried to break in. Maya knew that and had the combo so she could store her personal weapons in there too. Amber probably also knew the combo, because it was the same gun safe he'd had in Chicago. When he and Amber had lived together, he'd wanted her to know how to handle the guns and properly store them, but she didn't know about Josh's lock protocol.

The lock and handle weren't in the correct position.

Josh opened the safe. Everything was there except for one gun—his personal Sig Sauer. Why would Amber want that? And now that she was armed, did he need to be concerned that she was going to do something rash like go after Maya? Maybe that's why she'd drugged him. Would she go after Maya and frame Josh for shooting her? And then add to his list of offenses by making sure the case in Chicago was sent to appeals? If that happened, would he appear guilty of all the crimes? Was Amber capable of killing Maya?

Maya had texted him this morning, but if Amber had a gun and was coming unhinged, he had to warn her. He pulled out his phone, dialed and hit Call.

It went to voice mail. Josh left a message and then hung up.

He was worrying too much. Amber wouldn't do something like going after Maya, would she? Sure, she was shallow and materialistic, but did that make her a cold-blooded killer?

He called his mom. She answered right away.

"Hi, Josh," she said, her voice curt. "I heard about everything that happened. What are you thinking? You just got your life back together and you've been clean—"

"Mom," Josh cut her off before she could launch into lecturing him. "I'll talk with you more about this later. Where's Amber?"

"After the way you treated her, she left town."

Shit.

Josh cut his mother off again before she could tell him how rude he'd been. "Where did she go? I need to know. Now."

"She went to Antler Valley. There are some stores there that she wanted to check out, and she thought maybe she'd ski until we head home. Your sister and I are going home early. Your father is going to have to stay longer."

"Okay, thanks," Josh said, adding a "Love you" before he hung up. He'd worry about his mother later.

Did Amber know where Maya was? He closed his eyes and tried to remember everything he'd said in front of Amber. He didn't know for sure, but at some point, he might have let it slip that Maya was in Antler Valley.

Maybe he was being paranoid. Except last night his ex-fiancée drugged him and stole his gun and was now headed to the town where Maya was working. No, that wasn't paranoid.

He hit the call button again and every time it went to voice mail, he hung up and called back.

"Pick up, Maya. Pick up," he muttered, as he dialed her number again, grabbing his keys to his personal vehicle.

He needed to get to Antler Valley and find Amber before something bad happened.

Chapter Thirty-Nine

The wind had picked up more and was gusting at times. Maya had on her heavy winter gear but was standing in place to help guard the crime scene and log investigators in and out. This was going to be a long day. She and another young deputy had taken turns watching the scene and logging techs in and out.

She had put Juniper away after her track, making sure she had water, her heater was on and that Juniper was comfortable. Maya was proud of her dog—she'd worked well—but she was concerned that the suspect seemed to know K-9 work and was using Maya and Juniper. Ben had been a K-9 handler and Deputy Glen certainly knew K-9s from being a backup officer. There was also Tanner. He'd been very involved in this case. Could one of them be the killer? She had the feeling too from the lack of evidence at the scenes, including this one, that the suspect knew law enforcement techniques or even was an officer, making him that much more dangerous.

The pictures had been a warning. If the killer wanted Sheriff Jackson out of the way, he'd succeeded. With those pictures, the sheriff was probably going to be suspended by the sheriff's committee, or lose the upcoming election. His wife, once she caught wind of the scandal, might file for divorce. At least in Maya's mind, she *should* file for divorce.

There was also the matter of Agent Kessler's family. He had confirmed that was his wife and daughter in the photo. Looking grim, he had excused himself to call his family and then his boss. The suspect had crossed a serious line. No one threatened the family of an FBI agent. The FBI would probably give Kessler's family some sort of protection and they'd make the case a higher priority. The only good news to come out of that was the DNA and other evidence would be processed quicker. Going after an FBI agent might end up being this killer's undoing.

Maya's pocket that held her phone vibrated. She looked at the caller ID.

Josh.

She'd have to get back to him later. This was not the time to discuss the issues back at home. Maya hit Reject and put the phone away. She logged in another person to the scene. Her fingers were freezing. The pen she was using was getting so cold it wouldn't write well anymore. She stuck that in her pocket too, hoping to warm it up.

Her phone rang again.

Josh.

He'd called three times in a row and hadn't left a message. Instead, he'd hung up and kept calling her back. Now concerned, Maya waved Ben over. "I'm sorry to bug you. Do you mind standing in for me for a few minutes? I need to take a personal call."

"Sure," Ben said.

Maya was relieved. Ben had continued to be standoffish after the track. She still didn't know what his deal was. She headed to her vehicle and answered when Josh called again.

"Maya, thank God. Are you okay?" Josh said.

She was taken a little off guard by Josh's greeting. "Yeah, other than freezing, I'm fine. Why wouldn't I be okay?"

"Good. I'm headed to Antler Valley. Trying to beat this storm coming in, but I need to talk to you. There's so much I have to tell you, but I know you're working and I don't know how long I'll keep a phone signal."

"Josh, what's wrong?" Maya asked again. She'd never heard Josh sound panicked like this. He was always so calm—the opposite of her. When she had a "redhead temper" moment, Josh was the voice of reason.

"It's a long story and it ties in with everything that happened last night. It's too much to tell you right now. Just do me a favor and keep your eyes open today when you're working. Amber is in Antler Valley and she has my personal gun."

"What? You think she's coming after me?"

"I don't know," Josh said. "I'd like to say that she wouldn't, but I don't know…"

His phone started cutting out, but then the signal came back.

"I'm at a crime scene all day today. It would be hard for her to find me here, much less get back to where I am, but I'll keep an eye out for her," Maya said.

"I'd like to see you tonight. Amber might know where you're staying. Is there somewhere we can meet to talk that would be hard to find?"

Maya thought for a moment and then an idea came to mind. "The Forest Service has some yurts not too far out of town. I don't believe any of them are being rented right now. They have wood-burning stoves and the basic necessities. I could meet you there."

"That's perfect," Josh said. "If you text me directions, I'll meet you there when you get done at work. I don't care how late it is. I'll get a fire going and be there for you."

"Do you think Amber would follow me?" Maya asked.

"I don't know," Josh said. "But you're a good officer and you're street smart. Just keep your eyes open. Once I fill you in we can figure out how to deal with Amber, but I want you to hear my side of the story. I should have called you when I failed my drug test, but I was so upset and I thought you'd be disappointed, so I didn't. I'm sorry you had to hear everything from Pops."

"It's okay," Maya said. "I'll get the whole story tonight and we'll figure out whatever is going on. I'm there for you."

"I love you so much, Maya."

"I love you too. I need to get back to work."

"Okay, see you tonight."

They hung up, and Maya texted Josh directions as promised. As she headed back to her post, she realized that Josh was the first person she'd ever trusted, other than her grandparents. Whatever was going on was serious and if he was worried about Amber finding Maya, then there was more to the story.

"Everything okay?" Ben asked as Maya took her spot back. Deputy Glen was in the process of logging out of the scene with evidence. Ben signed him out and Maya took back her clipboard.

"It is," she said. "My boyfriend is coming tonight

and we just have some things to discuss. When we're done here, do you mind if I take the rest of the evening off and maybe tomorrow too? I can always be on call."

"That's fine," Ben said, as Deputy Glen left. "You've been working hard. Finish your shift today and then go enjoy yourself."

"Thanks," Maya said, relieved that he seemed like he was back to his normal self. "I appreciate it."

"No problem. I need to get back to some other things right now. Let me know before you leave."

"Will do," Maya said, now wishing that her shift was over and she was already at the yurt. She hadn't known how much she missed Josh until she'd heard him on the phone. Maya wanted nothing more than to hear Josh's side of the story. She craved being curled up next to him, her body fitting snugly next to his, his arms wrapped around her.

Feelings hit her that she didn't know what to do with. She'd pushed them away for so long, denied them, but now that she'd been away from Josh, she realized she was completely in love with him.

And that scared her more than anything.

Chapter Forty

As Maya continued to stand guard at the crime scene, the first snowflakes started coming down, soft and small. She had often heard the phrase "small flakes, big snow." It seemed like this system was going to follow through on that saying. It would still be a while before the heavy snow hit, so Josh would have time to get here and Maya and Juniper would have time to get to the yurts.

Agent Kessler spotted her and came over. "The joys of the job, huh? Nothing like the nonglamorous side of law enforcement guarding a crime scene."

"Yeah, not like on television, that's for sure," Maya said with a laugh before switching topics to a more serious one. "How's your wife and daughter? Are they safe?"

"They're doing fine. My wife was understandably shaken. When I took on this job, I agreed that I would leave the job at the office, but this was tough. I don't think either of us ever worried about her being a target. This is a very unusual case. She and our daughter are at a safe house and they have agents with them. My wife is handling it well considering everything, but the sooner we can catch this bastard, the better."

"I agree," Maya said. "Any word yet from the lab?"

"I did just get some information. The toxicology reports from each victim from Antler Valley came back— they did have Gray Death and Narcan in their systems. Looks like the same batch of Gray Death based on the tests they ran."

Maya nodded. That confirmed their suspicions. If they could catch Bryce's supplier, maybe he'd turn out to be the killer, or at least know who the killer was.

"But the really big news," Kessler continued, "is that there's a DNA profile match between the other cases out of state. It's the same guy. The bad news is that he's not in the system. But at least we have that evidence to link him to when we catch him. Should help with a conviction."

"What about the second person's DNA?" Maya asked.

"That doesn't match anything from the other cases, and so far, there's no hit in the system for that profile either. The partner is new or somehow they managed to keep their DNA off the victims in the other crimes."

"That's pretty tough to do," Maya said, thinking about how DNA could come from so many different sources. To say the tests had improved over the years would be an understatement. DNA testing could even come from touch now. A suspect keeping his DNA off a body was not impossible, but much more difficult. "I bet he met his partner here and they just started working together."

"I would lean toward that too," Agent Kessler said.

"And the killer, or killers, know K-9s," Maya said, telling him about the track and evidence find that seemed set up for Juniper.

"We should make a list of everyone with K-9 experience," Kessler said.

"Done," Maya said, handing him a sheet of paper. "I even included myself to be fair."

Kessler laughed. "Glad to hear that. Although I don't want to interrogate you again. You were one tough cookie."

"You were an FBI rookie at the time," Maya said with a grin.

"All forgiven?" Kessler asked.

"Yeah, all forgiven."

"Okay, now that you're off the list, let's take another look here." Agent Kessler scanned the list Maya had made that included Ben, Deputy Glen, Sheriff Jackson, the chief of police and the local K-9 search and rescue handlers, including Tanner. "Really? You added your criminal investigator here too?"

"I did. Ben worked K-9s in a previous job. I don't know much about him. What do you know about him?" Maya asked.

Kessler frowned and said, "Nothing, really. He's new. I've never worked with him before, but he seems good. You really think he's a suspect?"

Maya shrugged. "I don't know. I guess I added him because of the K-9 experience he had and the fact that he's been out of the loop a couple times since we've been here. That timing correlates to things happening in the case. It could be a coincidence."

"I trust your gut instinct," Kessler said. "I'll look into him."

"Thanks," Maya said.

"I'll also look into this list of people and see if any

of them were in the other ski areas when the other murders happened."

"You mean besides the sheriff?"

"Don't worry, I've been digging deeper into his background," said Agent Kessler. "So far, what I've gathered is that he made trips out of town to be with these women. Told his wife it was for work. He's a real ass, but I can't place him in those areas when the crimes happened, except for the murders up at the ski resorts in Wyoming."

"What if our killer saw him there, took the pictures and then came here thinking they could do whatever they wanted because they had blackmail?" Maya asked.

"It's a possibility. I'll look into it more and talk to the sheriff. He may be a jerk, but when we told him about his nephew's death and the photos, he at least started cooperating with us and answering questions. I'll see what he knows. He also gave us his DNA without any hassle, so I don't think he's involved. If he was guilty then he wouldn't have done that, but I'll get those results soon too. I better get back to the investigation. I'll keep you posted," Kessler said.

"Sounds good," Maya said, dusting some of the new fallen snow off her jacket and moving around to stay warm. She would rather be out working Juniper and doing something with her to help this investigation than standing here in the cold watching people go in and out of a crime scene.

Maya thought about the track today with Juniper and where it had ended. There was obviously some way for a snowmobile to get out of there. So where did that trail go? If this were Pinecone Junction, she would have a pretty good idea of the area since she'd grown up there and knew most of the trails. She even knew the local inholdings.

Inholdings. Why hadn't she thought about that? Inholdings were small pieces of private property in the national forest. The Forest Service had bought properties as the years went by, but there were still some small slivers of private land. They could end up literally being surrounded by national forest.

If a family didn't want to sell the property and had passed it down over the years, there could be some inholdings in this area. Maya needed to find a map of this part of the forest. She had a bunch in her patrol vehicle that she had gathered before she left.

"Hey," she called out to a young deputy who was also guarding the scene. He and Maya had backed each other up all day and given each other breaks. He turned toward her. "Mind if I take a quick break? You good watching all this?"

"Sure," he said. "Go for it."

"Thanks," Maya said, handing him her clipboard. She almost jogged back to her vehicle. Juniper, still napping when Maya opened the passenger door, opened one golden eye and the shut it again, tired from tracking through the snow.

Maya found where she had tucked the maps for safe-keeping and pulled out a couple different ones until she found the one that she wanted. She spread it out on the passenger seat since the wind was gusting outside. Finding the ice-climbing area on the edge of the map, she ran her finger along the trail where she and Juniper had tracked. She followed a route that seemed logical and it didn't take her long to get to a small marking on the map for private land.

It could be where the killer was staying.

Maya pulled out her phone, glad that they were close enough to town that she had a signal. She debated calling Ben. What if he really was a part of this? Did she believe that he was really a killer? Maya finally called him. She needed more to go on to suspect him of being a killer. There could be some other explanation for him leaving and he was the best person to find out who owned the inholding since it was the Forest Service that maintained those records.

He answered on the third ring and Maya filled him in. She agreed to bring the map back with her and show Ben and Agent Kessler. After hanging up, she went back to her spot guarding the scene and waited until they came over. Maya turned her back to the wind to try to block it some as she showed them the map and pointed out the inholding.

"I think it's worth checking out," Kessler said.

"I agree," Ben chimed in. "I can see if I can get a hold of someone in the lands and realty management department. They would have the records as to who owns that property."

"That could take a little bit," Maya said. "What if I took Juniper and drove back into this area? It looks like there's an access road not far from here. I could see if it looks like anyone is living there. Maybe I could see something that would help us get a search warrant."

"I like that idea," Ben said. "Except you're not going alone. You need a backup. Deputy Glen seems to be doing a good job and Rory has some experience with you. Why don't you see if one of them wants to go with you?"

"Sounds good," Maya said, hesitating. "You know, I haven't seen Rory today. Is she off?"

"No idea," Ben said. "But Deputy Glen is here. I can go get him for you if you want."

"That would be great," Maya said.

"Keep us posted," Agent Kessler said, heading back to the crime scene. He paused and turned back around. "And be safe."

"Thanks," Maya said.

Ben returned with Deputy Glen. "I filled him in on what's going on," Ben said.

"I'd be happy to go with you as backup," Deputy Glen said.

"Thank you," Maya said. "Let's get going. I'd like to get up there and check things out before this storm hits."

"Isn't your boyfriend coming into town?" Ben asked.

"Yes," she said.

"If you get to this property and don't see anything suspicious, call it a day. You've been working hard. Go relax. We won't be able to do much with this storm dumping snow and we're waiting on a bunch of lab stuff, which could take a while. If you see something on this property, let me know. We'll try to get a search warrant and move on it quickly, so you can still meet up with your boyfriend tonight."

"I appreciate that," Maya said. She and Deputy Glen headed back to their vehicles.

"Do you mind if I stop by the motel and pick up a few things?" Maya asked. "It's on the way."

"Works for me," he said.

Maya wanted to be prepared with an overnight bag

for her and Juniper's items in case this inholding didn't pan out. She didn't know which she wanted more—to have this property be nothing so she could see Josh, or to have this be where the killer resided so that they could finally catch him.

Chapter Forty-One

He paced around the barn, waiting. The wind made the old building creak and groan. Cold seeped in and he put on his hat and gloves. He didn't care though how chilly and miserable the barn was—it was the place where he had fun. The place that no one knew about. His own special spot.

Checking his burner phone over and over, he hoped he'd receive word soon from his protégé that the plan was in motion and going smoothly. He could hear the cries down the aisleway from his latest catch. She had fought hard and he liked that, but she had another purpose—a reward for his partner if his partner brought him Maya.

His phone dinged and as he read the message, he trembled with pleasure. He couldn't have planned this any better. He'd been working on the plan with his partner to get Maya alone and it had proven to be very difficult. His partner had texted earlier that Maya was planning on meeting up with some boyfriend later that night.

That only ignited his anger more.

She had said nothing about a relationship until now. He'd been kind and compassionate and she hadn't cared one bit. Maya Thompson was just like everyone else—a fraud.

His partner texted asking if he should try to grab Maya at the crime scene when she took a break from guarding. No, he had insisted that they wait and have some patience. The nice thing was Maya didn't suspect either of them, and that made things easier. Now his patience had paid off.

Maya was coming to him.

It didn't get any better than that. He studied the picture he'd taken of Rory before he'd headed out to the crime scene. A little going-away present for his partner and protégé. His partner had worked hard for him while he'd been in Antler Valley and he appreciated it. He needed to leave and have a fresh start. His partner didn't need to come with. Time to part ways.

But he liked having options and insurance. Capturing Rory wasn't just a reward for his partner. He knew you couldn't always trust someone to do their job. He needed to know that Maya would remain motivated to continue looking for him. Otherwise she might go visit her boyfriend and then his plan wouldn't work.

He couldn't give away his location, but Maya was smart and according to his partner, she was on the right track. His partner promised that he would continue to encourage her to check out the inholding area she had discovered. Kidnapping Rory would help make sure that Maya changed her plans and would continue to hunt him. And when she did, he had a plan for the damn dog too. If he did this right, he could have some fun with Maya and be gone before anyone realized she was missing.

Using his burner phone, it was time to give Maya a little more incentive to head this way—the picture of Rory being bound, gagged and crying seemed perfect.

Excitement coursed through his body as he loaded the image to the text message and hit Send.

"Enjoy the photo," he said to himself. "See you soon, Maya Thompson."

The snow had let up, but Maya knew that was just Colorado weather teasing them. The big part of the storm would arrive in a couple hours. She checked her phone quickly to see if Ben had been able to find out anything about who owned the inholding, but there was nothing.

Nothing from Josh either, but she kept his warning in mind. She glanced at her mirrors, but no one was following her. What the heck was the deal with Amber? Was she unhinged enough to come after Josh and then Maya? She wanted to know the rest of the story.

Pulling into the motel parking lot, adrenaline surged through her. The door to her room was open. She parked down away from her room, trying to stay out of visibility from anyone who might be in the room. Maya picked up her radio. Before she got out and did anything, she needed to radio dispatch. Deputy Glen was parked next to her and she needed to let him know what was going on.

"FS 28," Maya said. "There's a break-in at the Saddle Rock Falls Inn. My room. Please send backup."

The local dispatcher acknowledged Maya and said another deputy was on the way. Maya asked Deputy Glen to switch channels so that they wouldn't clog up the main dispatch channel.

When they were both on the other channel, Maya said to him, "I may have an idea of who broke into my room. I'd like to clear it with Juniper, but I'd like to wait for backup."

"Who do you think did this?" he asked.

"My boyfriend's crazy ex," Maya said. "Supposedly she's armed and in the area."

"Okay. If she's possibly armed, then I agree we should wait. Switching back to the main radio channel."

Maya set her radio mic down and also changed back to the dispatch channel. She opened the door to Juniper's compartment and the Mal stuck her head through, staring at the open motel room door with her.

"If the crazy ex is in there, you have my permission to bite her," Maya said.

Juniper gave a small whine in response.

"You're also getting your Kevlar vest for this. I don't need something happening to you."

Juniper gave Maya a slurp on the face.

"Glad you're in agreement."

They didn't have to wait long since another deputy was patrolling in the area. He arrived and shut down the emergency light bar before pulling into the parking lot. Maya was glad that he'd come quiet. If an officer arrived with their lights and sirens going, that could tip off a suspect and start a problem like the suspect shooting at them. It was better if they could have the upper hand with anyone in the room by surprising them.

She opened her door and stepped out of her vehicle, making sure she kept an eye on the room in case of an ambush. She headed over to where Deputy Glen and the other officer were waiting to discuss their plan when Ben pulled in. He got out of his vehicle and joined them.

"I heard the call and figured since I was close, I'd come," he said to Maya. "Any idea who might be in there?"

"My boyfriend's armed ex is one possibility," Maya

said. "Otherwise, it could be something related to this investigation since the suspect likes to set up scenarios involving Juniper."

"Neither of those possibilities are great," Ben said.

"Exactly. I want to go ahead and use Juniper to help us clear the room."

"Works for me," Ben said. "You take the lead since you have the K-9."

"Sounds good," Maya said.

"If Ben backs you up, then we can cover the back," Deputy Glen said. "Just in case anyone tries to run."

"Okay, let me get Juniper ready and then let's go," she said.

Juniper started jumping up and down as Maya approached. Maya didn't need her tipping off anyone in the room by barking or yipping in excitement. She leaned close to Juniper's compartment and told her, "Quiet."

They'd been working on the command, but it was a hard one for Juniper. Much to Maya's relief, her dog understood and didn't make any noise. She put on the dog's Kevlar vest and then let Juniper out of the vehicle. They'd also been working on hand signals so that they could work silently. Maya started using the signal asking Juniper to stay by her side. Juniper followed the command perfectly.

Maya, Juniper and Ben approached the room once the other deputies went around back. She kept Juniper by her side. They approached the door. Entries were very dangerous. Suspects could be hiding in numerous places and had the upper hand. Maya and Juniper stayed off to one side. Ben was on the other, his gun drawn and ready. He nodded to her.

"Forest Service law enforcement!" she yelled. "Come out with your hands up or I'll send the dog."

No answer.

Juniper remained quiet, but Maya decided to give her the command to bark. Juniper happily agreed and let out a ferocious growl and bark.

"Forest Service law enforcement," Maya yelled again. "If you don't come out with your hands up, I'll send the dog."

Again, nothing.

Ben nodded. He was ready.

Maya told Juniper, "Go get 'em. Go find the bad guy."

Juniper took off like a shot with Maya and Ben behind her. Sometimes a K-9 cleared a room by themselves, but this time, Maya wanted to back up her dog. If there was someone in there with a gun, like a jealous ex, she would be ready to make sure her dog wasn't shot.

The motel room was small and Juniper quickly cleared the main area and then the bathroom. She came back to Maya and gave her a look that said she was disappointed there was no bad guy or gal to bite. Maya was relieved that no one was waiting in there, but the state of her room was another story.

Someone had been in there and they'd wanted her to know.

"Good grief," Ben said, staring at the wall near the bed.

Maya holstered her weapon and shook her head. "Nice, huh?"

"I'd definitely say that's a crazy ex."

The wall had been spray-painted in red with the words, *He's mine. You're going to pay.*

Maya radioed the other deputies that all was clear

and then called Juniper back over to her, snapping on a leash and reflecting on her relationship. She loved Josh, of that she was certain, but she hadn't signed up for this kind of stuff. They needed to figure this out.

"I better go back outside so that I don't contaminate this crime scene any more than I have," Maya said. "When this nut job is found, I'm definitely pressing charges."

"I don't blame you," Ben said.

They both stepped back outside, joining the other deputies. Deputy Glen put a call in to their crime scene unit and then started running tape around the area. Maya rubbed on Juniper, telling her how good she was, when another gust of wind hit. Some clouds had built up over the mountains and were moving around, the weather shifting. Maya's cell phone buzzed. If it was Josh, she was going to let him know she was now running behind and it was Amber's fault.

Instead, as she opened the text message with a picture attached, her stomach flip-flopped and adrenaline surged.

Chapter Forty-Two

Ben saw the change in her and said, "What's wrong?"

Maya showed him the picture sent from what was probably a burner phone.

"Is that Rory?" he asked.

"Yes. Did you find out anything about the owner of that property?"

"I'm still waiting on a phone call back, but it shouldn't take long."

"We need to do something," Maya said.

"I agree, but we have no idea where she is."

"I'm forwarding the picture to Agent Kessler and then I'm heading up to that property. There's nothing else I can do here except stand around and wait for crime scene techs to come process my room," Maya said.

She loaded Juniper back up in her patrol vehicle but left on the Kevlar vest. If they were going to check out this property and Juniper needed to be deployed, it was better for her to have it on.

"Deputy Glen is going with you," Ben said, coming up behind Maya. "If Rory is there, then this killer might be setting a trap. He's smart and cunning. It's good to have backup."

"Okay," Maya said, not certain if she was relieved

or not. It was good to have backup, but she still questioned who she could trust. At least Ben seemed like he was back to his old self, but the way he'd reacted when she'd talked about her drinking had put her on guard, along with the fact he'd been gone when she suspected some of the evidence might have been planted. Deputy Glen had at least been a reliable backup officer so far.

"I'll work on finding the property records," Ben said. "And I'll see if Agent Kessler needs me to follow up on other leads to find Rory."

"That'll be good," Maya said. "I'll report in when we get to this property."

Getting into her vehicle, Maya quickly texted Josh about her hotel room and her suspicion that Amber was the culprit. Then she added that a local deputy had possibly been kidnapped and she didn't know if she'd make it to the yurt or not. How could she spend a night with Josh when Rory had been kidnapped? She'd keep him posted. She really wanted to find Rory before the weather moved in and made the search that much more difficult.

Setting her phone down, Maya thought about Josh and how much she missed him. She wanted to see him and talk through everything going on, including Amber. And Eric Torres being her father. She'd only been gone a few days and yet it felt like a lifetime.

Maya peered back up and saw that Deputy Glen and Ben were also texting people. They too were probably letting people know that plans had changed. She put her vehicle in Drive. The access road to the property wasn't too far away from the motel.

He received the next text message from his partner. He knew he'd been right in taking on his protégé. It had ended up being so easy to get Maya to come to him. He should have manipulated her earlier so he could have had more time with her, but he'd enjoy what he had.

Anger still pulsed through his body, but he fought it. He had to be careful he didn't get too upset. When you got upset, mistakes were made. He could almost hear his mother saying that.

He wanted to toy with Maya, make her beg, but his biggest obstacle was the dog. That dog would protect Maya to the death, so he had to figure out a way to subdue her. He didn't want to kill the dog right away because he could use the K-9 to make Maya suffer more later.

The problem was, she had told several people about the inholding. His partner was certain the FBI knew. He would only have so much time, although if he played things right, he could probably hold off anyone coming to check on her. He'd managed to catch her putting in her passcode on her phone. He'd learned a long time ago that it was very useful to be able to access someone's phone and email to convince family members that a person was still alive. Maya was no different.

His partner had overheard Maya talking to her boyfriend and there was perhaps a bit of a lovers' spat going on. Trouble in paradise, perhaps? He would read through her messages once she was subdued and figure that out. This was going to be fun.

The access road was hard to find, especially as the wind increased, blowing snow across the highway and creating a ground blizzard. Maya slowed down and finally found the turn. Like many roads back into the national forest, it wasn't plowed or paved. This one was almost like an off-road Jeep trail.

Maya hesitated as she really didn't know the road conditions, and once she turned, she was committed to driving this until there was either a good place to turn around or she found the property. She was about ready to do a U-turn and park on the other side of the road when she noticed tire tracks going in and out. They were fresh, but with the blowing snow they'd already been covered up a little bit, which was why she'd missed them at first.

That did it—she would turn down this lane and hope that it wasn't a mistake. But if another vehicle had driven it ahead of her, then that meant it led somewhere where you could turn around. Or at least she hoped that's what it meant.

Maya put her patrol vehicle in four-wheel drive mode and started down the road. Juniper had her head through the compartment door, staring straight ahead but staying quiet. It was as if she knew they were heading into a serious situation. The lane was bumpy, but not too bad as the snowpack had filled in some of the ruts. The vehicle still swayed as Maya slowly navigated, trying to keep a steady pace so that she didn't get stuck by stopping or going too fast and getting sucked into the shoulder. Getting stuck in snow was the last thing she needed.

The tire tracks turned off into a driveway that led to an old barn and house that had seen better days. The property wasn't in total shambles, but the buildings were still in need of paint and some care.

There was an area past the driveway where Maya could turn around and park. She decided to go there rather than drive down the lane to the property. Now that she knew that the property did have buildings, she wanted to be careful how they approached.

Deputy Glen pulled in next to her and also turned around. They stepped out of their vehicles, the wind blowing snow in Maya's face as more flakes started to fall. This was probably the start of the main storm, which meant conditions could change quickly and they would need to watch that as well. As she approached Deputy Glen, she noted that the lane leading to the barn was lined with ponderosa pine trees like the evidence they'd found on Kay's son, Avery.

"You want to drive up there and see if anyone is home?" Deputy Glen asked.

"No," Maya said. "I think we should see if there's any activity. There are tire tracks leading to the barn and house. It's hard to tell how fresh they are because of the weather."

"We could go knock on the door."

"No," she said. "I think we should just watch and if we decide to go onto the property, we should have a search warrant. That way our suspect doesn't have time to get rid of evidence. This guy is smart. We know that, and if he has any kind of a heads-up, we'll end up paying for it. Plus, I'd like to give Ben time to see if he can get the records on who owns this inholding."

"Okay. Your call," Deputy Glen said. "But I think we should sneak up behind these trees and get closer so that we have better visibility. Especially with this storm moving in."

"That works," Maya said. "I'm going to get Juniper just in case we need her. I'd rather have her with us."

"Good idea," Deputy Glen said.

"If the weather gets any worse, then we may have to leave and come back later."

"Hopefully we'll see something soon."

"That's what I'm hoping too," she said as she headed back to her vehicle. She let Juniper out and made sure she had on her snow boots and Doggles since the wind was gusting. She grabbed extra Narcan. If this was the killer's home, then she wanted to be prepared for any kind of drug they might encounter.

Maya and Juniper joined back up with Porter and, staying behind the trees, started trudging through the snow toward the barn. As they got closer, they stopped.

"What's up?" asked Deputy Glen.

"Did you hear something?"

"I thought I did, but I wasn't certain if that was the wind or a person."

Maya stayed still for a minute. There it was again. She was certain now. "Let's go. Forget the search warrant, we're going in. That's the sound of someone screaming."

Chapter Forty-Three

Maya and Juniper continued closer to the barn, stopping to listen again in case the sound of someone screaming was just the wind blowing, although Maya was certain about what she'd heard.

Even with all her winter gear on, she felt the bitter cold as a chill made her shiver. Juniper came closer. Maya was concerned about her being cold, but with her Kevlar vest, boots and Doggles, she seemed fine.

Maya listened again for a scream, straining to hear over the wind. As another gust whipped through the trees, it blew open a man door on the barn. The hinges creaked and groaned as the door swung back and forth.

Then she heard it again. A scream coming from inside the barn. She knew it wasn't her imagination either as Juniper tilted her head and stared intently at the open door.

"I clearly heard someone yelling," Deputy Glen said. "That gives us exigent circumstances to go in."

"I agree," she said, "but this could be a trap. We should get backup out here."

"I'll radio it in, but I think since we have Juniper, we'll be okay. What if something horrible is happening to the person screaming? It could be too late before backup arrives."

"True," Maya said, feeling her cell phone buzz. She was surprised she had service, but maybe there was a nearby cell phone tower. "I need to check my messages quickly. You go ahead and radio in for backup."

"Sounds good," Deputy Glen said.

Maya pulled out her phone as Deputy Glen called dispatch on his shoulder mic. The message was from Ben saying that he'd received the records on the inholding. The property belonged to Sheriff Jackson's family. Surprise washed over her.

She knew the sheriff was a jerk, but she really hadn't pegged him as a killer. Unless he was the other DNA source? Had the sheriff really been messing with them? Would he have set up the track to his pictures just to throw them all off?

Deputy Glen came back as Maya put her phone back in her pocket. "Everything okay?" he asked her. "You look shocked."

"No, everything is not okay," Maya said. "You radio for backup?"

"I did. What's wrong?"

Maya debated telling him. If the sheriff was the killer, could she trust his deputy? Should she share the information? Maybe if she told Deputy Glen what she'd just learned, she could gauge his reaction and figure out if she could trust him or not. The wind died down for a minute as another scream shattered the silence.

They needed to get inside and help the person crying out. She and Juniper needed Deputy Glen to do that. If she told him what was going on and he didn't seem shocked, then Maya would make an excuse to wait for backup, but she really didn't want to do that. Someone in the barn needed help and they needed it quickly. "Ben just texted me. This property belongs to Sheriff Jackson."

"What?" Deputy Glen said. "You don't think he's the killer, do you?"

"I don't know what to think," Maya said, trying to watch his expression. He seemed to be genuinely surprised. Another scream came from the barn. "What I do think is that we need to go see who's in the barn and we better hope it's not a trap. If Sheriff Jackson is our suspect, then he knows our tactics and that makes this that much more dangerous. He could be luring us inside."

"Good point," Deputy Glen said.

"I say we at least get to the door that's open and blowing in the wind. We can decide from there if we want to proceed depending on what we find."

"Works for me. I'll follow your lead."

"Sounds good," Maya said. Juniper nudged her with her nose. "Good girl. Let's go see what we can find."

Juniper was ready to go, an intense stare coming from her golden eyes. Maya was proud of how far her dog had come and the partnership they had developed. Right now, she didn't know what humans she could trust, but she knew Juniper was always going to be by her side and have her back. That gave her confidence.

The trio started the trek toward the barn. Maya's legs were stiff from staying in one spot in the cold, but she loosened up as they approached the barn. The closer they came to the old building, the more Maya could hear screams and shouts of "Help!" coming from inside. The building blocked some of the wind and she thought it sounded like Rory.

Hope surged through her. Maybe they had found Rory in time. But was this a trap?

Maya and Juniper came to the open door. She un-
pinned Juniper's leash and gave her dog the hand signal
to stay by her side. Juniper listened perfectly, making
Maya proud again. Juniper didn't seem to be sensing
anyone near the door and Maya carefully peered around
and then gave Deputy Glen the signal that they were
going in. He had his gun drawn, in low-ready position, finger off the trigger like all law enforcement was
trained to do.

"Forest Service law enforcement," Maya said, announcing herself before she entered. As much as she
didn't want to give away that they were here, a good
defense lawyer could get a case thrown out with little
technicalities like an officer not announcing themselves.
"If anyone is in here, come out with your hands up."

There was no answer other than sounds of screams
again, this time with a more panicked tone to them.
Maya couldn't make out distinct words, but she could
tell the voice was female. She hoped it was Rory.

As Maya entered the barn, she noticed stalls to the
left and then an open area to their right. The open area
probably had been for hay storage at one point, but now
the barn was eerily empty. The stalls had short fencing,
making them easy to clear and make sure no one was
hiding to ambush them.

She was trying to figure out where the screams were
coming from when Juniper put her nose up in the air,
taking in an odor. Her tail came up and her body language changed. Juniper's muscles tightened and she
headed back over to a corner. Maya signaled to Deputy
Glen to follow them.

Juniper continued following her nose to the corner.
Maya knew that depending on airflow and what Juniper

was smelling, scent could gather in a corner and provide a strong odor. Juniper followed her nose and made a sharp turn to a wall that had some storage cabinets with six doors side by side. She shoved her nose into some of the cracks of the cabinet doors and went down the line until she arrived at the end. Then Juniper sat and stared straight ahead.

"What did she find?" Deputy Glen whispered.

"When she sits, it's for a narcotics odor," Maya said, praising Juniper. "This could be where the suspect keeps his drugs. Normally I'd take a look, but we need to find the person who's screaming. We can come back here later."

Maya was glad she had grabbed some extra Narcan from her vehicle just in case they ran into any narcotics with fentanyl. She had it in her pocket. How much Narcan would it take to counteract the effects of drugs like Gray Death? She didn't want to find out, but at least she was prepared in case they were exposed.

"We need to figure out where those screams were coming from," she said, hoping the person would yell again. The only sounds were the creaking barn door and the wind blowing snow against the side of the building.

"Maybe there's a hayloft, or maybe there's an area with more stalls. Perhaps an old milking area?" Deputy Glen said. "We could only see one side of the barn, but it seems like the way it's built into the side of the mountain, it could have a lower area that opens up to the pasture."

"Good point. Let's look around a little more and go to the other side."

The trio headed to the back of the barn, which they had visually cleared. As the wind gusted again a wooden trapdoor rattled. Juniper gave a low guttural growl. Stepping off to the side to stay flush with the barn wall, Maya had a better view of the door in the floor.

She signaled to Deputy Glen, who still had his gun out, then gave Juniper the hand signal to stay by her side and went over to the trapdoor. Deputy Glen gave a nod, and Maya pulled up on the heavy wooden door. The hinges squeaked, stopping any chance of surprise. Maya let the wooden door flop open and stepped back in case someone was there waiting to ambush them.

Nothing.

"Forest Service law enforcement and Antler Valley Sheriff's Office. Come up with your hands up!" Maya yelled again, hoping that no one was standing right below them and could shoot up at them through the floor. She really didn't like this and was ready to back out and wait for backup, but then she heard a scream again. It was coming from downstairs. Where was their backup anyway? They weren't that far out of town. But based on the noise of the wind against the barn, the storm had moved in worse since they had arrived here. Could backup even make it down the road to this property?

"Let's check it out," Deputy Glen said. "I'll go first if you want."

Maya didn't like this at all. "No, I'll go first with Juniper. If there's someone waiting, she might be able to apprehend them."

"Okay, I'll cover you."

"Thanks," Maya said, testing out the first step. It seemed to hold her weight. The stairs were wide enough for Juniper to stay by Maya's side, which made her feel better. She didn't want her dog to be out in front of her in danger. They came down into an open area with tie stalls for milking cows, but this part of the barn had been remodeled.

Deputy Glen came down the stairs behind Maya. She turned around to signal that she was going to check an area down the aisleway. Another chill came over her as she stared at him. Juniper growled next to her.

Deputy Glen's demeanor had changed. He still had his gun out, but it was now pointed at them. His finger was on the trigger.

His eyes had darkened and appeared beady. Maya had once heard this change in expression called "snake eyes" and she could see why. She slowly stepped back, her hand on her gun. She could try to send Juniper, but she was afraid that Deputy Glen would shoot her dog before Juniper could bite him.

"I'd leave your hand off your gun if I were you," he said.

"What's going on? What are you doing?" Maya asked, still slowly stepping back, trying to put some distance between them and looking for somewhere she and Juniper could go for cover. She continued to step slowly back, trying to put space between her and Deputy Glen. As she came closer to a calf holding pen, she heard a noise off to the side. There was a narrow aisleway leading to what was probably once a feed room. Out of the corner of her eye, Maya spotted Rory chained and gagged against the wall, her eyes wild and scared. "You can quit pointing that gun at me, Deputy Glen."

"No, thanks," he said. "You can stop where you are. You have no options and you know it."

"Backup will be here any minute," Maya said.

He laughed. "You think I really called them? Why

would I do that? I logged out with dispatch for the night. Told them you were going off shift too. You walked into my trap perfectly."

She didn't know what to say. If she could keep Deputy Glen following her, maybe she could find somewhere to take cover, grab her gun and shoot him. She had to protect Rory. Right now, the large animal aisleway didn't provide any cover.

Juniper stayed by her side, and as they backed up, Maya noticed something on the ground. Juniper walked right on top of it, and before Maya could do anything, a net snapped up around her dog, lifted her off the ground and trapped her.

Juniper snarled and bit at the net, but it quickly tightened and made it so that she couldn't move. Panic ran through Maya, but she fought it. If she was going to get them out alive, she had to react.

Deputy Glen fired off a shot, the noise deafening in the barn, but he missed them both. Maya did the only thing she could think of to save herself and keep Juniper safe—she rushed him.

Chapter Forty-Four

Maya immediately regretted her decision. She'd been hoping to catch Deputy Glen off guard and surprise him, but it was like he'd read her mind. He attempted to grab Maya in a hold, but she knew the technique and slipped out of the way.

She came back at him, scratching at his eyes and trying to kick him where it counted, but he countered her moves and blocked her. She managed to get in one swipe down his cheek and draw blood. He let out a howl, and that gave her the advantage for a moment, but it also incited his temper and he came back at her, pushing her up against the wall.

Pinned, Maya didn't have a good way to fight back, and Deputy Glen held her with one hand and started choking her with the other. She worked to free herself, but he was bigger and stronger. What he didn't realize, though, was that Maya was a fighter. She'd never been in such a close quarters battle with another person, not even in Afghanistan, but she wouldn't give up and if he was going to kill her, Maya wasn't going to make it easy.

She couldn't reach her weapon. Deputy Glen's fingers clamped down more on her neck and she gulped for air. Her first reaction was to try to pry his fingers off, but he was too strong and he only tightened his grip more. Maya felt around her duty belt. She couldn't quite reach her pepper spray and was too close for a Taser.

Her fingers landed on her knife.

Hope surged through her as she worked to pull the knife out of her duty belt sheath. She struggled to breathe but stayed focused on her mission of getting a good hold on her weapon. What she wouldn't give for her Marine Ka-Bar fighting knife right now. Luckily, she always carried a folding knife that she could open one-handed. She'd done that for emergencies. Maya just hadn't thought that the emergency was going to be another officer choking her out.

She struggled to breathe, but Deputy Glen maintained his solid hold on her throat. Staring him down, she could see that he was enjoying choking the life out of her. Luckily that meant that the pleasure distracted him. Maya managed to pull the knife and get it open before he realized what was happening.

Grasping the handle hard, she knew she had one chance at this and very few options because of the body armor Deputy Glen wore. There was no way she could penetrate the vest, but she knew where the openings were. She estimated the vulnerable area where the ballistic vest opened by the armpits. Maya plunged the knife in as hard as she could.

Relief surged through her as Deputy Glen screamed in surprise and pain, releasing the hold on her throat. Maya gasped for air, seeing stars, but knowing she'd have to act rapidly. She pulled her Glock out of its holster, aimed at his head between the eyes, where she might hit the brain stem, and fired off three shots.

Deputy Glen stumbled back and then dropped to the

ground. He quit moving and lay still. Maya's breathing
came in short, rapid gulps as she worked to recover from
being choked. *I just killed someone.* Her hands shook
as she returned her gun to the holster. She worked to
slow her breathing.

He's dead. It was justified shooting. Maya kept telling herself that, trying to calm down.

Juniper.

She had to cut her down.

Maya stumbled past Deputy Glen's lifeless body, trying not to stare at him. There were enough bad memories etched into her brain—she didn't need another one.
She forced her feet to work and she went back to where
Rory was chained up.

"I'll be back," Maya said. "I promise. I just need to free
Juniper. If I have her, then it'll help us escape."

Rory nodded and Maya started back down the barn
aisle. She heard some whining and whimpers. *Hang in
there, Juniper. I'm coming.* Maya arrived at where she
had last seen Juniper, but her dog was gone. Where was
she? Whining and whimpering noises came from the
end of the barn and Maya continued.

She needed to find Juniper, get Rory and get out of
here. There was no backup coming for them. Ben was
probably waiting for her to check in. Maya tested her
radio and made a call to dispatch, but there was no response. She pulled out her cell phone, unlocked it and
tried to call 9-1-1, but there was no signal. Being in the
lower level of the barn meant that signals were probably being blocked by the stone foundation. Or there
could even be some sort of jammer device so that victims couldn't call anyone.

She put her phone back and continued to look for Ju-

niper. The fact that Juniper was missing scared her—
it meant that the other suspect was in the barn. Maya
pulled her gun back out.

She went back the way she'd come, toward Rory.
There were some doors that might lead to a supply room
or area where Juniper could possibly be kept. Maya
opened a door and saw Juniper still tangled in the net,
lying on the dirt floor.

"Juniper," Maya said, rushing forward, not thinking
about properly clearing the area.

The punch to the head came quick and without warning. She reeled back, falling to the ground. She fought to
get to her feet as quick as possible, but she was stunned
by the blow to the head and couldn't make her body
work. Juniper's golden eyes stared back at her and Maya
fought to get back up, but suddenly she was pinned down.

Desperately trying to move, Maya only ended up
flailing, her head pounding. She stared into the eyes
of another dog held captive with Juniper.

"Finn?" Maya said, as the realization hit her.

She turned toward her captor and saw Tanner's smile.
Only it wasn't the friendly, easygoing smile she knew.
This time it was sinister. He pulled her arm out and man-
aged to get a needle into her vein and plunge it before
Maya could do anything.

Tanner.

Tanner had body parts and tissues for training. He'd
most likely lied about the donations from the hospital.
His training samples were probably from victims. He
was involved in the investigation. The first search with
Finn had only been successful because Tanner knew
where he had stashed one of the bodies. Maya had even
offered to help him train and it gave him the chance

to learn how she worked Juniper, especially what she looked for and how she liked to set up training situations. He would have had perfect opportunities to set up the evidence properly. Sheriff Jackson would have to sign off on the training aids he had, so maybe Tanner was even involved with the blackmail.

He leaped off her and she scrambled to her feet, ready to fight, but her vision quickly blurred.

The last thing she heard was Juniper whimpering.

Chapter Forty-Five

Maya sat up and gasped for air. At first, she thought she was waking up from a bad dream. Then she saw Tanner's face with his sick, twisted smile and everything came rushing back. Her head pounded and her stomach roiled. She thought she was going to be sick, but managed to breathe through the sensation.

"Wake up," Tanner said, crouching down next to her. "Time to have some fun with you."

The cold seeped into her body she as lay on a concrete floor. Dust, mouse droppings and some moldy straw pieces surrounded her. Maya struggled to sit up and realized she was in one of the tie stalls. He must have dragged her there.

She stared him down, trying to figure out what to say back. What she really wanted to know was if Juniper was okay, but that would only give him more ammo against her. A weak point. How did you get a narcissist to do what you wanted? She had to play his game.

She tried moving her hand to push back her hair, but everything seemed like it was in slow motion. She was sluggish and her arm didn't want to work, but she soon realized part of that was she had chains around her wrists. They were heavy and made it hard to move in her drugged state.

"What kind of fun are you thinking of?" Maya finally asked.

"Oh, I don't know. Now that I know you're an addict, you might enjoy my special concoction."

"Drugs really weren't my thing. So sorry, not enjoying it."

Tanner smirked. "I was just kidding about having fun. I actually want you to suffer."

"Why? What did I do to you other than help you out with Finn?"

"You betrayed me."

"I betrayed you?" Maya asked. *Stay calm. Play his game. Buy yourself some time.*

"Yes." Tanner stood back up. He started to pace, balling up his fists as his face turned red. "First by not telling me that you were an alcoholic and then by hiding the fact you had a boyfriend. But what really pisses me off is that you killed my protégé. He was almost ready to go out on his own."

"I wasn't trying to hide anything from you. I had no idea that my personal life mattered so much to you. As for your protégé, he was going to kill me. Maybe I actually helped you out."

"Oh?" Tanner said. "How's that?"

"You obviously want to be the one to kill me or at least torture me. If I'd let him do that then you wouldn't have been able to have this conversation with me."

"Not a bad point, but you still betrayed me with your boyfriend and by being an alcoholic."

Holding some Narcan, Tanner continued to observe her, making her want to punch him in the face. She didn't have enough control to accomplish that and it would get her nowhere. Not to mention, she had to figure out how to get the chains off of her. They were just loose enough to have some freedom of movement, but not much. What she did have was the ability to maybe reason with Tanner and negotiate. If she could buy herself more time, then maybe Ben would realize she hadn't returned. Although he had told her to go meet Josh after she checked out this property. Would he assume she had left? She had to keep Tanner talking.

Josh would know that she hadn't arrived, but she had told him she might be late. Deputy Glen hadn't called in backup and instead probably radioed dispatch that they were fine and clocking out. There was a good chance no one would look for Maya and Juniper until it was too late.

But she promised herself that, at some point, Tanner was going to pay for this. She would make sure of that and she wasn't going to make it easy on him.

"I'm curious. Why does it bother you so much that I'm an alcoholic?"

"It's a sin. Wasteful. People only caring about themselves. It pollutes our world, especially our forests, with the amount of glass and plastic bottles. Everyone talks about the oceans, but nobody talks about the illegal marijuana grows with pesticides that kill wildlife and trees. The water that becomes polluted before it even reaches the ocean. All these people care about is making money and providing drugs so that parties can happen and people can have 'fun.' I care about our forests and I see people trashing them all the time. I thought you understood that and we were on the same page with our love for the forests, but then I discovered you're no different from everyone else who pollutes them. You don't love them like I do."

"I do love our forests and mountains. You're wrong there. I thought maybe your mother or father was an alcoholic," Maya said, immediately regretting the words.

Tanner's face darkened and he slapped her hard across the face. "Don't ever speak about my parents again."

There was enough slack in the chains to rub her jaw. That would probably leave a mark. At least she knew one of his weak points now. "I apologize."

"You should."

"What about Finn? You seemed to enjoy working him," Maya said, changing topics. *Just keep him talking. That's what I need to do until I can figure out the right time to make a move. I can get out of this.*

Tanner shrugged. "Yeah, he's fine. He was a good front for me. That's all. He's really not that great of a dog."

"The training you did was a good start."

"Probably because he had fresh training aids. I also worried that animals would scavenge and move my kills. He helped me find the dead heathens and make sure they stayed where they were supposed to. He was only a tool. Nothing more."

Maya shuddered, but worked to keep a poker face listening to him talk about his dog with no feeling. She had to figure out a way to save Finn too. First she had to get of this situation. How long would Josh wait at the yurt before he started looking for her?

"I'd love to know more about why you traveled around so much. What brought you here to Antler Valley? Is it where you grew up?"

Tanner only smiled that horrible grin. "Let's talk about you, not me. My travels don't matter."

"I just wanted to get to know you better, that's all."

He sat for a moment, studying Maya. She felt squeamish under his stare, but managed to not look away. A few seconds later, he spoke up. "I appreciate that, but what I really want to know about is your boyfriend. This Josh."

"He's nothing special. Just a fling, really." Maya was hoping her face wasn't giving her away.

"I think you're lying to me."

"What makes you say that?"

"For starters, I really enjoyed reading your text thread with Josh. Very touching. I hope he enjoys my message back to him. His heart should be breaking about now."

Josh arrived at the yurt and pulled out his phone. He didn't have enough cell service to make a phone call, but he was able to get text messages. One had come in from Maya about being held up. He was concerned when he read that one of the deputies she'd worked with had disappeared. With this weather moving in, a search and rescue operation could be tough.

He thought about leaving and heading into town to help look for the deputy, but decided he'd give it more time. He didn't think that a chief deputy on suspension from another county would be welcome.

There was another message from his mother saying that she didn't know where Amber was and she wasn't responding to messages. That concerned Josh as well. Would Amber really go after Maya? There was a time he would have said that she wouldn't have done such a thing, but he'd also never thought she would drug him. Part of him wanted to go find Maya right now, but he also knew she could take care of herself. He'd wait for her to show up after her work was finished.

He got out of his Jeep and went to the door of the yurt. He put in the combo for the lock on the door that Maya had texted him. Snow blew around him as the storm picked up in intensity. A squall came through, making visibility difficult. He almost couldn't see his vehicle through the whiteout conditions.

Managing to get the right combo entered, Josh stepped inside. The yurt was cold, but had a wood-burning stove with some firewood next to it. He braved the weather again, going back out to his car and grabbing his overnight bag and some old newspapers that he'd brought along.

He'd get a fire going and warm things up so that when Maya arrived, they could heat up the dinner he'd also brought. He just hoped Maya would make it here tonight. The last check of the forecast showed that it would snow all afternoon, evening and through the night. Sometime tomorrow morning the system would move out.

Since he had enough signal to get a text out, Josh sent one to Maya.

Be careful driving here. If you need to wait until morning, that's fine. It's more important you and Juniper are safe.

After sending the text, Josh worked on getting the fire built. He could see his breath inside the yurt, but at least he was out of the wind and that helped. His thoughts turned to how Maya was the best thing that had ever happened to him. He knew that she hesitated when it came to commitment, but he didn't care. He'd wait for as long as he needed to.

He didn't feel Maya's hesitation concerning commitment came from being with him, but rather her journey healing from the traumas she'd experienced. Josh understood, having lost his partner to a horrific shooting. It had taken him a long time to process that. Maya had spent a full tour in Afghanistan where she had lost not only her fellow Marines, but her K-9 as well. She still blamed herself for Zinger's death. Processing her trauma might take longer, but Josh would wait. She was worth it.

She and Amber were so different. He was relieved he hadn't married Amber and now he wanted his past out of his life so he could move forward. He also hoped he could get his job back. If Pops decided that he had deliberately become intoxicated in uniform, Josh would be fired and that would be the end of any kind of career in law enforcement. Pops and the Western River County Sheriff's Office had been his second chance.

There would be no third.

Josh's phone chimed and he picked it up. Maya had texted him back. As he read the text, he was crushed. It said: I won't b coming to meet u tonite. I need time alone. I can't b with u anymore.

When they'd talked on the phone, Maya hadn't sounded this upset. In fact she'd sounded forgiving, like she was the only one willing to listen to him. He was ready to chuck his phone across the yurt, taking his hurt out on it, but instead he sat down, staring at the message again. Maya had been the one person, other than his sister, who had stood by his side no matter what. And vice versa. Was she really that upset over

Amber and already judging him? Had her grandfather spoken with her and convinced her that she needed to break up with him?

He punched in his code and stared at the message again. As he did, worry spread over him instead of hurt. There were little things he noticed first, like the "u," "b," and "tonite." She always spelled out words and texted full sentences. The voice of the text didn't seem right to him. And he truly believed that Maya would try to come and talk to him. She was the type to break up in person, not over the phone. And definitely not over text.

He stared at the message over and over. It wasn't right. It wasn't Maya's voice or her style. Something was wrong. Was she trying to warn him and texting fast? Or if she was in trouble, was this some sort of code? Instead of lighting the fire, Josh grabbed his jacket and keys.

He didn't care how bad the roads were—he was going to the sheriff's office to find out what Maya's last known location was and the status of the missing deputy.

She was in trouble.

He could sense it.

Chapter Forty-Six

Maya woke up again, shivering violently. Her teeth chattered as she worked to remember what'd happened. Her mind was in a fog and she curled up as tight as she could to stay warm. She was lying on a cold floor. The wind howled outside and she could hear snow pelting the side of the barn.

Little by little, the memory of what happened came back to her. Her head pounded as she remembered. Tanner. Their conversation and the way he'd twisted things in his mind. He'd told her how disappointed he was in her. That he'd thought she was different from the others. That she cared for the forest the way he did. They'd discussed her relationship with Josh. Then he'd stuck her with a needle and she couldn't remember anything after that.

She hadn't had a headache like this since she drank. Pushing aside the pain, she forced herself to think. The chill hit her harder because Tanner had taken away her load-bearing vest and jacket. She had on one layer.

The storm.

There had been a nasty winter storm heading their way and it was now here, adding to the cold and explaining the creaking and groaning of the old barn.

Juniper.

Oh my God. Juniper. Panic flowed through Maya at the thought of Tanner doing something to her dog. She'd always heard that serial killers started out on animals. And Tanner didn't seem to really care about Finn. Would he hurt Juniper? Finn?

If he hurt Juniper, she didn't know how she would continue on. Juniper was tough. She wouldn't let Tanner near her without a good fight. She thought about the change that'd come over his face. The way his pupils had darkened in anticipation. He'd prattled on about the environment and saving it from people who partied and trashed the forest. Maya couldn't make sense of his logic other than that he thought by killing people, he was doing the world a favor. And she had struck a nerve when she'd speculated about his parents being alcoholics.

Back to Juniper. Her mind couldn't stay focused. He'd probably given her Gray Death, or the "special concoction," as he called it. She was lucky to still be alive, but Maya was also certain that he had plans for her.

Her only chance of surviving was escaping.

Think, Thompson. You're a Marine. You've got this. You have training. Use it.

Maya managed to push herself up to a sitting position, shivering uncontrollably. She was heading toward hypothermia. Maya made herself think through the symptoms just to take her mind off the cold.

Confusion. Slowed breathing. Slow pulse.

Crap, she could have all those symptoms from the drugs too. Back to figuring out how to escape. She'd worry about hypothermia later. Juniper. Figure out if Juniper was here first. Maya had a special whistle she used to call Juniper. She worked to get her lips to cooperate so that she could make the shrill noise. It took a couple tries, but then she managed a faint version of the whistle.

In the distance, she heard a yip. Relief flowed through her body and she allowed herself a momentary smile. Juniper was okay. She was out there. That meant that Maya needed to free herself, find her dog and get the hell out of here.

What about Rory?

Maya hesitated to call out. If Tanner was around, she didn't want him to know she was awake. She was about ready to say something when she heard footsteps coming on the concrete aisleway.

Think, Thompson. Get your brain in gear.

She stared at her wrists, her brain slowly putting everything together. Despite the cold, Maya felt like maybe the drugs were wearing off and she was able to reason better. Yes, she was chained, making it hard to fight back, but her hands were in the front. Tanner didn't know how to properly restrain someone. There was a reason you handcuffed people with their hands behind their backs. Her legs and feet were also free. If she could lure Tanner close, she might be able to use her legs and the chains to attack him.

Hopefully he'd have a key on him and she could free herself, but even if he didn't, she had enough play in the chains to probably defend herself.

Tanner was relying too much on the drugs to help him out. Luckily, she was coming out of the side effects. Now she just had to get him to come closer. The footsteps continued echoing through the barn, heading in her direction. As much as Maya didn't want to lie back down on the freezing floor, she forced herself to.

She had to pretend that she was sleepy and make him come over to her.

Then she'd make him pay for everything he'd done.

The Jeep fishtailed as Josh took a curve in the road a little too fast. He knew he was driving too fast for the conditions, but he didn't care. The more he thought about that text, the more he was concerned and convinced that Maya was in trouble.

Snow continued blowing across the road, making visibility about zero. The weather only complicated matters, but Josh kept going. He'd walk through fire for Maya.

Or in this case, drive through a blizzard.

He made it to the outskirts of Antler Valley and saw the flashing yellow and blue lights of the giant orange snowplows. They'd be working all night trying to keep the streets clear. With a storm like this, it was a losing battle. But it did help him gain some traction and he accelerated, making a move to get past the plows.

The sheriff's office was illuminated in the distance, and he made a quick turn into the parking lot. For a moment, hope surged through him as he saw a U.S. Forest Service law enforcement vehicle. His excitement passed when he realized it wasn't Maya's. It probably belonged to the criminal investigator she'd been working with. That worked too. Maybe he could answer some of Josh's questions.

After parking, Josh sprinted inside and saw a lone front desk deputy. Josh went to pull out his badge and then remembered—he didn't have one anymore.

Damn it.

"Hey," Josh said to the deputy. "I need to talk to the Forest Service investigator now."

"He's in a meeting," the deputy said.

"Then interrupt it."

"I can't do that."

"Believe me, you can," Josh said. "Tell them it's about the murders and Maya Thompson."

The young deputy stared at him and didn't move.

"Now," Josh said.

"Fine." The deputy picked up a phone and dialed an internal extension. Much to Josh's relief, he relayed the message, listened for a moment and then hung up. "The investigator will be here shortly."

"Good," Josh said, pacing back and forth. Every minute that went by could mean Maya was that much closer to losing her life. If she hadn't already. He forced that thought out of his mind. She was a fighter, and strong. She wouldn't go down easily.

"Can I help you?"

Josh turned around and saw a man in a Forest Service uniform. "Are you Ben Easton?"

"Yes."

"Josh Colten, chief deputy sheriff for Western River County. I'm also Maya's boyfriend." Josh held out his hand, shook Ben's, and hurried through introductions. He launched into how Maya hadn't shown up and the text Josh had received. He showed it to Ben hoping to better plead his case. He didn't mention that he wasn't the current deputy chief because he was on suspension. If Ben knew that, Josh would never learn anything about the investigation.

Ben cut him off, pulling out his phone. "That makes no sense. I received a message from Maya that there was nothing at the property she was checking out and that she was headed to meet you. She also said Deputy Glen was heading home for the night."

"Did Deputy Glen come in and clock out?"

"I don't know," Ben said. "Let's go find out."

"While we do that, fill me in more on this property," Josh said.

"It's an inholding—private property within national forest boundaries."

"Who owns it?"

"Ironically, the sheriff," Ben said.

"Where's he right now?"

"Here, in an interrogation room," Ben said, filling in Josh about the investigation and the pictures of the sheriff.

"We need to see what he knows and there's GPS on Maya's vehicle. Same with the deputy's vehicle. We need to ping those and see where they are."

"I agree," Ben said. "Getting someone on it now."

Ben went to a deputy standing outside the interrogation room and gave him orders to find out about Deputy Glen and have dispatch run the GPS on Maya's and Deputy Glen's vehicles. Then Josh and Ben entered the interrogation room.

"Are you charging me with anything?" the sheriff asked, arms crossed.

Josh took an immediate dislike to the man and thought Maya had actually been kind in her description, having just called the guy an asshole.

"Well, there's no charges for being a cheating husband," Ben said. "But there are charges for withholding information."

"What are you talking about?" the sheriff asked.

It was everything Josh could do to stay quiet, but

for now he needed to let Ben take the lead. He had no jurisdiction here, so it was best not to try to join in on the questioning. Josh didn't know how long he could take it, though, if the prick in front of him didn't start cooperating. Hopefully he didn't lawyer up.

"You need to tell us about your property out in the national forest," Ben said.

"Why?"

"Don't need to tell you that," Ben answered.

"Then I want a lawyer before I start talking," the sheriff answered.

Ben and Josh turned around and left the room. "Well, I guess that's that," Ben said.

Frustration built up in Josh, but he knew Ben was right. They couldn't ask anything more until a lawyer showed up, and with the storm raging outside, who knew how long that would take? Josh didn't know his next move. Everything that might lead to Maya would take time. They could ping her phone, but the phone company would want a warrant. There was only one thing left to do.

"Where's this property?" Josh asked.

"What?"

"The property Maya was going to check out. Where is it? I'm going there."

"You need to back off," Ben said. "In case you haven't noticed, we have a major winter storm and we don't know that Maya is at the property. She could have gone somewhere else, like back to her motel room to get some things now that it's not a crime scene anymore."

"What?" Josh asked. "What happened at the motel room?"

"Her room was broken into and ransacked. We believe it's completely unrelated. Maybe even random. We did get some prints, though, and will run them through the system."

Josh groaned. Amber. He would put money on it being Amber who broke into the room. "Try running the prints against an Amber Zielinkski from Chicago. She works in the district attorney's office. Her prints should be on file from her background check."

"Okay, I'll let the crime scene techs know. I don't suppose that's your ex-girlfriend?"

"Yes," Josh said with a sigh. "She's upset about Maya. You should also know that she stole my gun and headed for Antler Valley."

"Maya mentioned some of this to me," Ben said.

"I know. I can't believe she's doing this."

"Do you think she might have done something to Maya?" Ben asked.

"I don't know. That's why we need to see where her patrol vehicle is and if Juniper is still in it."

"Let's go see what the deputy came up with," Ben said, heading back down the hall toward the dispatch center. The deputy he'd talked to earlier was coming out of the room.

"I was just coming to find you," the deputy said. "I have some information. Deputy Glen logged out with dispatch for the night, but based on the GPS signals from their patrol vehicles, both Deputy Glen's and Officer Thompson's vehicles are in the same location in the forest near this private property."

The deputy handed Ben a piece of paper. Josh didn't wait for Ben to say anything. He turned and marched down to the interrogation room. He didn't care if he got in trouble. Hell, he was already suspended, so why not break the rule of talking to a suspect without their lawyer? The prick of a sheriff knew something more and Josh was going to get it out of him. He needed as much information as possible because he was going to find Maya and Juniper.

Chapter Forty-Seven

Closing her eyes, Maya forced herself not to think about the cold. She had to focus on getting out of this place. If she didn't get away from Tanner, then he would kill her and being cold wouldn't matter. She had the chains ready in her hands. She just had to get him to come near her.

Footsteps came closer and she felt Tanner's presence. He came over to her and nudged her with his foot. She had to stay quiet. Wait for the right time.

Be patient. Hopefully Tanner would make a mistake.

To her surprise, he pulled out some keys and unlocked one of her arms, leaving the chain dangling down. He was pulling out her arm and Maya cracked her eyes slightly. Tanner had another needle and syringe and was getting ready to give her a shot in the vein. If he was successful, she would be knocked out again and might freeze to death.

It was now or never.

Maya flung her legs out. She wrapped them around Tanner's torso, locking them in a hold. Disbelief registered on his face as his eyes darkened. She didn't have a good hold and she knew it. He knew it too and started wriggling, trying to grab an arm and pin her down. She tightened her hold. Before Tanner could get out of her grip, she took the chain dangling from her wrist and bashed him in the face. Hard. Over and over.

After what seemed like an eternity, but was probably only a few seconds, his nose started bleeding. She didn't let up even though she shook from exhaustion. She thought about Juniper and attacked him harder.

Tanner fell back in surprise. Maya couldn't hang on with her legs, but she lunged forward and hit him again in the face, pinning him down as best as she could. The drugs made her reactions sluggish, though. The cold made it hard for her to land punches that would knock him out.

Her breathing ragged, Maya tried to get a better grip, but Tanner managed to flip her over and climb on top of her.

"You're a fighter, aren't you?" he asked. "I like fighters."

Maya worked to get him off her, but he had the advantage. The chain, though, was still attached to her one wrist. Tanner was so intent on giving her the drugs that he didn't have the arm with the chain pinned down. She flung the arm toward his head, managing to catch him on the side of his face.

He fell back as the chain caught him in the eye. Maya took the opportunity to push him off and scramble to her feet. She couldn't outrun him. Not in her current condition. She had to incapacitate him somehow. Her body shook violently, but Maya fought through it. Barking in the distance distracted her for a second, but she realized it was Juniper, and that only increased her motivation.

Tanner managed to get to his feet before Maya could

stop him. They circled each other, and the same twisted smile came across Tanner's face.

"I loved you at first," Tanner said.

Maya didn't answer. He was only trying to get her distracted by his sick thoughts and mind games.

"I didn't want to kill you," Tanner continued. "You gave me no other choice."

He lunged toward Maya, and she managed to side-step and then kick his feet out from under him. She worked to pin him down, an arm across the back of his neck and knees in his back. If she could get the right hold on him, she could make him pass out. That would give her a chance to get Juniper and get back to her ve-hicle where she might be able to radio for help.

Tanner continued to thrash around, making it hard for Maya to get the proper hold on him. At one point he pushed her away and stabbed her with the needle, plung-ing the contents of the syringe into her thigh. Maya didn't know how long she had before it took effect since drugs weren't usually taken in the muscle. There was a reason users liked the vein—it was a quicker high.

With more determination, she hit Tanner with the chain, whipping him in the face over and over, giving her the chance to attempt the hold again to make him pass out. This time Maya was successful and relief flowed through her as his body went limp.

She wanted to restrain him, but she was starting to feel a little lightheaded. He should be out for a while. She had to find Juniper and get out of here before the drugs hit her system more.

Stumbling down the barn aisle, Maya started look-ing for Juniper and Rory, talking to herself, fighting the drugs in her system.

Find them.
Get out of here.
Survive.

Josh slammed his hands palm down on the interrogation table, making the sheriff jump.

"What the hell?" the sheriff said. "I want my lawyer."

"I don't care about your lawyer right now," Josh said, using his size to intimidate him. "I care about finding Maya and I need to know everything about your property, including what you did with her. You tell me where I'm going to find her."

"I don't know what you're talking about," the sheriff said.

Josh heard the door open and close behind him as Ben walked into the room.

"You need to stand down," Ben said. "Get out of here before you compromise this investigation."

"No," Josh said. "I won't leave here until we know why Maya's vehicle is still at the sheriff's property."

The sheriff suddenly went pale. "Her vehicle is still there?"

"Yes, and I'm heading there next, but I need to know about this property. Any information I have before I go helps me find Maya faster and prevents an ambush," Josh said. "Start talking. Lawyer or no lawyer. I don't care. I'll do what it takes to find her even if it means I have to kill you and spend the rest of my life in prison."

Ben tried to grab one of his arms, but Josh shook him off.

The sheriff finally held up his hands and said, "I'll tell you about the property."

Ben let go of Josh and they both stared at the sheriff.

"It has been in my family for decades. My father left it to my mother as a gift. They weren't married. My mother was his mistress. One of many, I think, but after she had two of his kids, my father decided that he needed to leave us something."

"What does this have to do with finding Maya?" Josh asked.

"I'll tell you, but you need to know the background."

"Get to the point quickly," Josh said.

"Turns out my father had other children with his wife. One of them, a half sibling, tracked me down. I wasn't certain at first who it was. I was receiving blackmail threats over my own indiscretions and the person threatened to tell my wife if I didn't give him what he wanted."

"What did he want?" Josh asked.

"He wanted to have use of the property, no questions asked. I was told I wouldn't be allowed to go there either."

"Do you know who it is?" Josh asked. "This lovely family member of yours?"

"I've figured it out."

"Then who is it?" Josh stepped in closer.

"Tanner Drake. And I believe he might be our killer."

"Why didn't you say something before?" Ben asked.

"I wasn't certain until he killed Bryce."

"Why?" Josh asked.

"Because Bryce was a decent reporter and had done some digging into his mother's genealogy. Bryce wanted to write an exposé. The stupid kid thought he'd become an instant bestseller since he was the nephew of a serial killer. I suspected something like this was going on, but Bryce wouldn't tell me or his mother the truth."

"Shit," Josh said. "So why would Tanner take Maya? I need to know more about what we're walking into."

"I don't know why he'd take her other than if she went to that property. She probably found where he was keeping victims and was going to arrest him. I'd check the barn first. He was obsessed with the barn. Said that's why this property was perfect for him."

"You better hope she's still alive," Josh said. "Or else I'll make sure you pay."

He stepped out of the room, Ben behind him.

"We need SWAT," Josh said. "Who knows what kind of trap we're walking into."

"I don't know if SWAT will be able to make it in or not with this weather. Plus, I'm not their boss. And the FBI has taken over this investigation."

"I don't care who you get," Josh said. "But find some backup. Now. We're heading out to that property. I don't care about this storm. We need to get there before it's too late. I'm heading there and I suggest you find some reinforcements."

He sprinted out to his Jeep. The storm was full fury as snow blinded him. He had to hold up an arm just to block the onslaught of flakes pelting his face. He had most of his gear in the back of the Jeep. He'd taken it from his patrol vehicle since he knew he'd have to turn that in too.

He opened the back door, put on his tactical vest, pulled out another personal handgun and grabbed a long gun, setting it in the front seat.

"Just hang in there, Maya," he muttered. "Keep fighting. I'm on my way."

Chapter Forty-Eight

Stumbling down the aisleway, Maya forced her feet to keep moving. *One step in front of the other*, she kept telling herself. *Find Juniper first.* Shivers made her body shake and convulse, but she didn't care. Right now, she was still alive and on her feet. That wasn't just half the battle—it was most of the battle.

She worked to remember the layout of the barn from when she and Deputy Glen came in, but her mind was in a fog. Maya gave her whistle and stopped, listening. She heard a yip from up ahead. The sound gave her hope and she made herself move again.

How long would Tanner be out? She should have restrained him, but her strength was gone after choking him. It took everything she had to stay focused. The drugs draped her mind in a fog, making it hard to think.

Just find Juniper, she told herself. Maya came to the end of the aisleway and saw a small covered pen. Excited whines came from inside it.

"There you are, girly," she said, relief flowing through her body. She went over the pen, opened the gate, and out flew Juniper, jumping around, excited to see Maya. Tanner had somehow managed to put a basket muzzle on her. How he'd done that without finding a Malinois attached to his arm, Maya didn't know. Her only guess was that he had drugged Juniper too.

The ground seemed to be moving and the barn was spinning. Her fingers didn't want to work, but Maya was able to undo the muzzle and let it drop to the ground.

"C'mon, girly," she said, hearing her words slur—not a good sign. Her vision narrowed and she thought she might throw up or pass out or both.

Maya checked her pockets for the Narcan she had grabbed. The meds were still down in one of her pants pockets. She was glad Tanner hadn't found them and taken them from her. Grabbing one out, she opened it. It was a nasal spray and she gave herself a dose, hoping that it would kick in so she could get to her vehicle and call for help. With drugs like Gray Death, she might need multiple doses. Juniper seemed okay, so Maya didn't dose her with any, but at first sign of Juniper not feeling right, she would administer Narcan.

She and Juniper found their way back to the stairs. The stairs. She remembered those. They led to the way out. Juniper bounded up ahead, waiting for Maya at the top.

Each step seemed like climbing a mountain, but the Narcan must have been helping because she made it to the top. She went back over to Juniper and thought of Rory. In her drugged-up state, Maya had forgotten about her. She needed to find her. Rory might need Narcan too. Maya was ready to go back down the stairs and see if she was still there when she heard footsteps below coming down the aisle.

"We have to go," Maya said to Juniper.

Hang in there, Rory, I'll figure out a way to come back for you.

The door that she had entered through was still blowing and creaking in the wind. Snow had drifted inside as the storm continued to rage on. The last thing she wanted to do was go outside, especially without her vest and jacket. But if she could make it to her vehicle, maybe she could call for help.

Did she have keys? She felt around. The bastard had taken those too. She had a choice—go outside and face the storm or stay inside and face a monster. Maya heard footsteps at the bottom of the stairs. The wood made a groaning noise as someone climbed them.

She'd face the storm.

She and Juniper sprinted toward the door where the snow continued to blow and swirl inside. After pushing the door all the way open, Maya and Juniper ran outside, straight into an onslaught of wind and blowing snow. Drifts had already started forming and as Maya's clothing became wet, she started shivering again.

Run. Run for your life. Save yourself. Save Juniper. Get to the road.

Her legs tired in the deep snow as she pushed herself to keep going. Juniper didn't seem to mind as much, although judging by the look on her face and the way she squinted, she missed her Doggles and booties. Tanner really must have drugged her to have gotten those off too. Maya needed to get her to a vet and herself to a doctor.

How far was it down the lane to the road? Would anyone be out in this weather?

The barn door made a loud smashing sound. Maya peered back over her shoulder and terror seized her. Tanner had woken up and was outside the barn. She could see him stumbling through the snowdrifts, his arm up to help block the snow and spot her. Why hadn't she restrained him better?

Their eyes locked and Maya started running down the lane. At first, Tanner didn't pursue her, but then she heard an engine firing. *Shit.* He had a snowmobile. Of course he did. He was the one who'd left the evidence for their tracks at Bryce's crime scene.

There was no way Maya and Juniper could outrun a snowmobile. He would capture her again. The sound of the machine made her stop; her breathing was ragged and short from both the cold and the drugs. Juniper stared at Maya and then the snowmobile that was already gaining on them.

Maya studied the mountainside. The trees were thick on this side. It would make it more difficult for a snowmobile. Not impossible, but having to avoid the trees would slow Tanner down. She whistled to Juniper, giving her the signal to stay by her side.

Juniper followed the command and the two started climbing. Maya's legs burned as she sunk into snow. She gulped in breaths. Her body was shaking uncontrollably again and her fingers seemed like they didn't work, but she would never give up.

Keep going, Marine. You've got this.

The mountainside seemed steeper and steeper as Maya tried to remember the map she'd studied when she found this inholding. There had to be a way back around. If Tanner had snowmobiled to the ice-climbing area, then maybe she could make it back there.

With this weather, the crime scene crew had probably left, but there was a visitor's center, and at least Maya could barricade herself inside where it was warm. If she made it there before Tanner caught her. The sound of

the engine from the snowmobile echoed off the hills.
Even with the trees, he was gaining on them.

She had to figure out a way to stop him. As she came
to the top of the steep slope, the wind gusted hard, almost knocking her over. She grabbed on to a tree branch
and held on tight, waiting for the gust to subside. Juniper huddled up against Maya's leg to help shield herself
from the wind.

The gust died down and Maya strained her eyes to
find sight of the trail that would take them to the ice
falls. But instead of a clear path, so much snow had
dumped into an open area that a snow slab had formed.
The slab created a trigger point for an avalanche—
extremely dangerous conditions to try to hike through.

As another gust came up, dizziness washed over her
again. The drugs were still in her system and there was
a good chance the Narcan and adrenaline were wearing off. That coupled with the cold made her realize she
was about at her end. If that was the case, she wouldn't
go down without a fight.

Staring down at Juniper as the sound of the snowmobile continued, warm tears cascaded down Maya's
cheek. She had to at least save her dog. Tanner could
have her, but she would never let him have Juniper.
Just the fact that Tanner was hunting her without Finn
helping him track showed he wasn't a true K-9 handler.

Another round of gusts and snow continued to add to
the snow slab in Maya's path. She could see the snowmobile coming up straight toward the slab. Tanner had
decided to avoid the trees by going at a dangerous angle
in an open area right below the snow slab.

A crazy idea started to form. Maybe Mother Nature
could help them escape.

Chapter Forty-Nine

Josh gripped the wheel and drove as fast as he dared. It would not help if he spun out of control and landed in the roadside ditch. He cursed the storm that continued to dump snow. Clouds had blocked the sun and it was hard to tell how close they were getting to it becoming dark.

He had to find Maya before nightfall due to the temperatures and visibility. Red and blue flashing lights bounced off his rearview mirror and Josh glanced up. It appeared Ben was on his tail along with a black SUV. As he took a curve in the road, he saw there were also a couple county sheriff vehicles too. Good, he had backup.

The turnoff to the property was coming up. Josh didn't know exactly where it was but could estimate based on the map he had found with the inholding area marked on it. Luckily, it was the only private property in the area. Other areas looked like a checkerboard, with the light markings of private property mixed with the dark marking of the national forest.

Slowing down, Josh strained to find the lane. It wasn't easy with the lack of visibility and as he hit his brakes, he felt the ABS working hard to stop him on the slick snow-packed area. The vehicle fishtailed, but eventually straightened enough to turn onto what Josh hoped was an access road. Otherwise, he was just going to be stuck in a snowdrift.

The Jeep bumped along and he made out what seemed like a road. The drifts were deep enough to push his Jeep's clearance. Maya had convinced him earlier that year to make the vehicle better for off-roading by adding bigger tires and lifts for more clearance. At the time, he'd been hesitant, but right now, he was grateful for her talking him into that. The Jeep helped clear a path for the vehicles behind him.

As long as Josh didn't stop, he thought he could continue to make it through the drifts. Hopefully the storm wouldn't get any worse.

Up ahead of him, he saw two vehicles. Both were covered in snow and appeared not to have moved for quite a while. One was marked *Forest Service K-9 Unit*.

Josh swallowed hard. It was Maya's patrol vehicle. He debated going over to see if she was inside, but changed his mind when he saw the driveway leading to a barn and old house. He cranked the wheel hard, turning down the driveway. The vehicles behind him followed. Josh was relieved they had shut off their lights. It's not like they could approach without being noticed, but at least the lack of red and blue strobes helped.

After parking near the barn, he stepped out of his vehicle, his gun in his holster. He still had his heavy winter raid jacket marked *Sheriff* on the back, so he put that on and grabbed his long gun. He was going to be ready for anything.

The door to the barn stood wide open and Josh started that way, not waiting for Ben or whoever else was responding with them. He didn't care about protocol at the moment. He only cared about finding Maya and Juniper.

Please let Maya be okay. I don't know what I'd do without her. And don't let Juniper be injured or dead. I don't know what Maya would do without her either. Everyone has to be okay.

As he approached the barn, Josh heard a muffled sound off in the distance. An engine was straining and he swore it was coming from the mountainside. Staying to the side of the door, he peered into the barn. It seemed empty. He cleared the immediate doorway and was about ready to step inside when he heard barking.

The noise was coming from the mountainside.

Josh left the barn area and started toward the sound. It was hard to pinpoint it exactly in the mountains as it seemed like echoes came off the hills. The snow also muted the barking.

Stopping to listen again, all Josh could hear was the sound of his breathing. He waited and heard the engine noise again.

As he followed the sound, he noticed some areas where the wind had piled less snow. There were footprints. Next to them were paw prints. He was going in the right direction.

Ben and Agent Kessler caught up with him. Josh had only met Kessler a couple times, but he liked the guy and knew that before he went into the FBI he'd had a good career in a city police department. The man knew his stuff.

"I'm hearing engine noise and barking from this direction," Josh said, then pointing at the snow. "I'm following these footprints."

"We'll follow your lead," Kessler said.

Josh nodded and continued forward, trying to keep track of the prints in the snow. The wind had covered up some areas more than others, but he made his way to an area that was probably a watershed. Snow and rain had eroded into a small ravine. In the distance, he could see a snowmobile making its way toward the top of the ridge.

"What type of idiot rides that type of terrain in a snowmobile?" Ben asked.

"The type that enjoys killing people," Josh answered, sarcasm coming into his tone.

He saw movement toward the top of the ridge. From where he stood, it appeared to be a person creeping and shuffling out to the middle of the rim.

Josh put his hand up, trying to block some of the snow blowing in his face. He couldn't tell for sure from this distance, but it appeared the figure was moving slowly and struggling. Even from this distance, he could see the snow slab sticking out. When he had moved to Colorado, he hadn't known anything about avalanches. It wasn't exactly something you worried about in the Midwest.

His first winter with the department, Pops had made him take an avalanche safety course. It had been eye-opening and important since he might be running avalanche rescue ops. He still had a lot to learn, but he knew that slab was a trigger point just waiting to happen and the person up there was walking straight toward it.

Was it Maya?

He hoped not. If so, she was going to force the snow to let go. She would know better, though. She'd grown up in these mountains and knew them like they were her best friends. Maya had taught Josh about the dangers in the mountains. If she was headed in that direction, then it meant she felt like it was her only option.

Josh started up the mountainside, trying to stay where he had a clear shot with the long gun if needed. If that was Maya, then the snowmobile was gaining on her and she was headed straight for a death trap between the snow and the predator chasing her.

Chapter Fifty

The horrible whine of the snowmobile engine contin-ued up the mountainside toward Maya. The incline was steep enough that the machine was already struggling. She hoped that maybe Tanner would somehow trigger his own avalanche, but amazingly the snow held.

The wind continued blowing snow over the edge of the mountain, adding to the slab as it curled over. In its own way the snow slab was beautiful as it curved into a graceful wave shape. Mother Nature creating her own work of art. Right now, as Maya continued edging out toward the spot she thought was most likely to trigger an avalanche, the curl seemed more ominous.

Juniper stood at the edge of the trees and barked. Maya gave the hand signal for her to back up and stay, and could only hope that she was properly estimating where the snow might slide compared to where she had made Juniper wait. Predicting avalanches was not easy.

Pops had once told Maya a story about a film crew on Berthoud Pass who'd thought they were well out of the way of a deliberately triggered avalanche. When the avalanche was set off, it was bigger than expected, cascading all the way down the mountain and across the road, killing two crew members.

Maya had absolutely no idea what kind of slide she would start. She could easily get sucked into it, but in a desperate move, she had taken off her belt. Continuing to inch across the snow ledge, she wrapped the belt around the tree and tested it. Hopefully, if her crazy plan worked, the tree would hold and not be part of the debris going down the mountainside. Although she would rather be buried by an avalanche than give Tanner the satisfaction of killing her. She would never be like Bryce and be found hanging from a rope on display for everyone to see. No way.

After testing the belt and the tree it was attached to, Maya wrapped the strap around her hand and reached with one foot toward the area where she thought the snow slab's weak point might be. Her body was shaking from the cold and wind. How much more exposure could she take before she had frostbite and hypothermia? At least the motion of punching the snow with her foot helped her stay warmer.

She stabbed the snow with her foot over and over, hoping it would break. Something had to give. Everything about this area was perfect for avalanche conditions. It had a steep angle and the way the snow layered on should make it extremely unstable, and yet as she stomped and kicked, it held.

That figures. If I was a backcountry boarder or snowmobiler, this would immediately give way.

Of course, those activities put more strain on the snowpack. The sound of the snowmobile continued toward her. All she could do was to resume kicking. At one point, Maya thought she heard voices from down below.

Now I really am losing my mind. Drugs? Cold? Who

knows. I'll give this a few more tries and then I need to come up with another plan.

Snow pelted her face as she kept stomping and kicking. The snowmobile was now within sight and she could see determination and anger on Tanner's face. Maybe with him coming up the hill and her kicking, this slab would still give way.

Her hand hanging on to her belt was numb, her fingers frozen. Maya's vision narrowed and darkened. She probably needed more Narcan and for sure warm clothes, but there was no way she could administer the drug without letting go of her belt. Of course, the belt was not a guarantee of safety. It wasn't like climbing ropes or something that she knew would for sure hold her if the snow did give way.

Tanner drew closer, and just as Maya was about ready to give up, she felt a shift under her feet. *Could this be working? Please let this happen.* Once the snow let go, it could travel sixty to eighty miles per hour and it would overpower him.

There. There it was again. A shifting feeling, almost like walking on sand. Then with a soft whoosh, Maya's footing dropped out from underneath her. She clung to the belt with both hands, trying to find stable footing so that she wouldn't get sucked down. The giant slide of snow gathered strength and speed as she managed to climb back up onto what she hoped was solid ground.

She watched as the snow picked up speed, crushing anything in its way. Tanner's face registered surprise, shock and horror as he realized what was coming at him. The snow hit Tanner, turning over the snowmobile and covering him up like a concrete blanket. For a

moment, Maya heard his cries for help and then nothing as the snow completely muffled him.

Breathing raggedly, she worked to get her way out of
danger and back over to Juniper. Her body convulsed as
her shivering became violent and out of control. Where
was Juniper? Maya couldn't see her anymore. She was
crawling now on her hands and knees. If she could just
make it to the thick trees, she could rest for a moment,
but she couldn't let herself fall asleep. Maybe she could
find the Narcan and give herself some more. Although
this could easily be hypothermia settling in. The Narcan was worth a try, though.

She continued crawling, her vision narrowing. She
found a solid tree trunk to lean against, and even though
she knew she shouldn't, Maya closed her eyes. It felt so
good to stop for a moment. She promised herself that
she'd start moving again soon. Very soon, since this
storm was still raging.

She could make it to her vehicle, couldn't she? Now
that Tanner was out of the way, she could break a window
or something. Crawl inside. Use the radio. Fight. Survive.
Her hand shook as she tried to open her pocket and find
a Narcan. She thought her fingers were grasping around
what she needed when she heard her name being called.

The snow had stopped. The sun was shining and the
sky was a brilliant blue. She heard her name again and
stared ahead. Nana? Mom? There they were. Standing
together, smiling. Calling to her.

She was dreaming. Nana and her mother weren't
there. Maya tried to slap her own cheek, but her hand
wouldn't work.

Stay awake. Fight. Survive.

Fear coursed through her. Even in Afghanistan she

hadn't had visions like this. She'd held other soldiers as they died. They always seemed afraid until the last moments and then, like her now, it was as if they could see something that no one else could.

Maya tried to lift the Narcan to her nose. As she did, she was back in the storm raging around her. She couldn't quite get her arm to cooperate and lift.

She heard barking. *Juniper.* Thank God. Juniper was okay.

Then she heard another voice encouraging Juniper, telling her to find Maya. Was that really Josh? He wasn't dead, though. Was this a dream? A vision? What the hell was going on?

Not able to fight it anymore, Maya closed her eyes. Her breathing slowed and became shallow.

"Maya. Maya. Maya, wake up."

It was Josh. She managed to force her eyes open for a moment and smiled. There he was. He was taking off a jacket and wrapping it around her.

"Narcan," Maya said, opening her hand. "I think I need Narcan."

"Yeah, okay," Josh said in a worried tone.

"I love you," she said. "Nana and Mom too."

"I love you, Maya," Josh said. "Why are you talking about Nana and your mom?"

"I saw them. They came for me, but I'm not ready to go. They were right there." She tried to lift her arm and point where she had seen them.

"Stay with me," Josh said.

Maya felt him push the Narcan to her nose and dispense it, but her mind was closing off. Going dark.

Then she closed her eyes, peace washing over her, and fell asleep.

Chapter Fifty-One

The dreams continued as Maya drifted in and out of sleep. She was certain Nana and her mother were sitting by her bed. Was she alive? Dead? She wasn't certain until she stirred out of a deep sleep and the pain of a headache nailed her.

She tried to sit up but her stomach churned. She lay back down, feeling tubes and something tight around her body. Shit, Tanner had her again. She had to get out of here. Maya forced her eyes open and started clawing at the tubes.

"Maya. Maya, it's okay." Josh stood over her, a concerned look on his face. He touched her cheek, then tucked a loose piece of hair behind her ear. Taking her hand, he leaned over and kissed her. Pops stood near Josh, concern etched on his face.

"If this is a dream, it's really nice," Maya said.

"It's not a dream. You're in the hospital, it's not a dream."

Her throat seemed scratchy and hurt. Memories of Deputy Glen choking her flooded back. She closed her eyes and took a deep breath.

"You know, I'm really getting tired of hospitals lately. Let's try to stay out of them. How about I get out of here?" Maya flung back the covers and sat up. She immediately felt sick again, and before she could do anything more, Josh gently guided her to lie back down. Hysterical giggles bubbled up and then she felt like crying. What the hell was wrong with her? "How long have I been here?"

"Since last night. Juniper helped me find you and we were able to get you to the Antler Valley hospital."

"Where's Juniper?" Maya asked. "I need to see her. Now."

"She's okay, she's fine. I took her to a vet, and other than snapping at the vet a few times, she's good. I left her there for now just for observation and she'll do better with you coming to get her when we go home."

"Your priority should be to rest," Pops said.

"When can I go home?" Maya asked.

"Maybe as early as this afternoon. The doctors just want to make sure you're stable after the drugs you were given and since you were heading toward hypothermia. They had to dose you with Narcan a couple times. You scared the hell out of me," Josh said.

"Me too," Pops said.

More memories came rushing back to her. Rory. Stabbing and shooting Deputy Glen after he attempted to strangle her. Tanner. Even Finn. Maya wanted a status report on everyone. "What about Rory? Did you find her?"

"Agent Kessler found her in the barn," Josh said. "It looks like Tanner was going to kill her next, but your escaping and distracting him probably saved her life. He came after you and left her alone. She's just down the hall and doing well. Making a good recovery."

"I visited her earlier," Pops said. "She's doing well

and in good spirits. We even discussed her application to my department."

"You have a way with timing, Pops," Maya said with a laugh. "Poor girl. Nothing like her first interview in a hospital after being kidnapped. Hopefully she can get some rest too. And your department? Does that mean the investigation went well?" Pops's brows furrowed and he clenched his jaw. "You're making me nervous. What's wrong?"

"What makes you think something's wrong?" he asked.

"I know you well enough. You have a certain look on your face and it means there's bad news."

Pops and Josh glanced at each other.

"The investigation seemed like it was going well," Pops said. "But turns out we were wrong. There's still going to be a trial, probably in the spring."

Maya took a deep breath and closed her eyes. Not the news they'd wanted. "I'm sorry, Pops. I'll be there for you, though."

"I know you will, Maya. But your job right now is to heal up and get your strength back. Okay?"

She nodded. "You got it. What about Tanner? Did you recover his body?"

"Unfortunately or fortunately, however you want to look at it, Tanner survived that avalanche," Josh said. "Go figure, but Ben was able to dig him out and arrest him. He's sitting in a supermax holding area of a federal prison thanks to Agent Kessler. No visitors. No nothing. The judge agreed that he should have no bail."

"Good," Maya said, closing her eyes as another wave of pain hit her head.

"You okay?"

"I'm fine. Just a stupid headache."

"Yeah, the doctor thought you might have something like that, or feel sick coming off the drugs you were given. You want me to get a nurse? Maybe they can give you something."

"No, I'm good," Maya said. "The pain will subside and I don't need more drugs in my system." She opened her eyes back up. "Josh? Pops?"

"I'm here."

"So am I," Pops said.

"I had to kill Deputy Glen. He was trying to kill me." Maya was hit with a wave of emotion that almost made her start crying, but she pulled herself together. "I should talk to Agent Kessler. My gun is going to come back with matching ballistics."

"Don't worry about it right now," Josh said. "Plus, Ben and Kessler worked through the night and got a search warrant for Deputy Glen's apartment. Apparently, there was all sorts of evidence there that showed he was having homicidal ideations, and they found a burner phone that he was using to text Tanner. You can give your statement, but they're running his DNA and Tanner's to see if it matches what they found on the victims. They're pretty sure it'll be a match based on other things they've found. Agent Kessler also thinks that Deputy Glen kidnapped and helped kill Bryce since he was the officer assigned to watch him when Bryce was released. As all the pieces come together with the investigation, it will help prove that you shooting him was more than justified."

"I actually thought Ben might be the killer or partner," Maya said. "It seemed like he was gone a lot when big things were happening and he's new to this area. Not to mention as Forest Service officers, we travel around a large area."

"I don't know for sure, but when we were in the waiting area while you were being treated, he and I started talking to pass the time. His ex-wife recently moved to Antler Valley and they have a daughter. Ben worked to change jobs so he could be closer to and spend time with his daughter. He was taking time to go visit her while he was working this case."

"He also started acting weird when I told him I am an alcoholic."

Josh nodded. "We discussed that he felt it was important to be a part of his daughter's life because his dad wasn't there for him due to his job and being a heavy drinker."

"I guess we all have our own lives and secrets, don't we?" Maya said. "What about Sheriff Jackson? Has he resigned?"

"Unfortunately, no, he hasn't," Pops said. "However, he was going to run for election again and has agreed not to. There will be continued pressure on him to resign, though."

"Rumor has it that his wife heard about the affairs and left him too."

"Good," Maya said. "I'm sure that's tough for her, though."

"I feel for her," Josh said. "There's another thing I'd like to talk to you about."

"Amber?" Maya asked. "Being intoxicated and having her take you home? Her probably trashing my hotel room?"

"Uh, yeah. There's that too. And I do want to tell you more about that, but before we go there, what do you think about two dogs?"

"Two dogs?"

"Yes. Two dogs. I'm adopting Finn," Josh said.

Maya laughed. "That's fine. Who knows what Juniper will think, but we'll figure it out and manage them."

"Finn is at the vet clinic too and so far, when they briefly met each other, Juniper seems to really like him."

"That's great," Maya said. "Maybe she likes blonds. I thought she didn't like Finn, but it was probably Tanner that Juniper was barking and growling at the whole time. Either that or she just realized that she'll have a partner in crime when it comes to tearing up the house."

Josh laughed. "Pops and I have discussed maybe having a search and rescue dog for the department, or even a bomb dog."

"We think we know a good trainer who might help us out with that," Pops said.

Maya smiled. "Why not make him all of the above? Multipurpose."

"I like that idea," Pops said. "But we'll figure it out later."

"Does that mean Josh still has a job? And what about Amber? Please tell me someone has found her," Maya said.

Pops took her hand and squeezed it. "Josh does still have a job. But you know, I think a lot of this is between you two. I'm going to head out and get back home. That way Josh can fill you in and you two can discuss whatever you need to without me hovering over you both. Love you, Maya Bear."

"Love you, Pops."

She waited for the door to shut and gingerly sat up again. "Let's talk about Amber. Time to fill me in."

Chapter Fifty-Two

Josh sat by Maya's side and took her hand. "I should start with I'm sorry. I'm so sorry for the things I said and kept from you. I never should have done that. I should have told you about Amber a long time ago. I don't know what I was thinking, but I promise it won't happen again. No more secrets. No more holding back. I love you, Maya, and I never want to lose you."

"That's a good place to start," Maya said with a smile. "Has anyone found her yet?"

"Denver PD arrested her last night at the airport. She was getting ready to head home. She'll be brought back to Antler Valley to be charged. I'm sure she'll be released on bail and I'll keep tabs on her location until her trial."

"Fill me in more about Amber. How did you meet her and manage to get engaged to her?"

Josh explained how he and Amber had gone to school together, drifted apart, then started dating. He told Maya everything, including how he broke off the relationship.

"I just knew she wasn't for me," he said. "She wasn't the one, and then I moved here and met you. You've always been different for me, Maya. Always."

Maya smiled. "I didn't even want to give you the time of day. You drove me nuts. I was rude to you."

"I know, and that made you even more intriguing," he said with a laugh.

"I wasn't trying to play hard to get. I really didn't want a relationship with anyone."

"I kind of got that impression," Josh said, smiling and revealing his dimple. "Luckily, I'm persistent."

"What happened the night that you were drugged? Was this type of behavior normal for her? Did she do things like this in the past? I feel like I know pieces of this story. Tell me everything."

Josh filled Maya in more, including about Amber coming to his office and trying to blackmail him over the case going to the appeals court, and when he realized she had stolen his gun. "I never thought about changing the combo because I was living out here and I never imagined I would see her again. I always knew that she was high-maintenance, but I didn't think she'd ever do something like this. I don't know if she has snapped or if there's something more going on that would provide a reasonable explanation. I hope that some of those questions get answered as she's investigated."

"That makes sense. Don't be too hard on yourself. Why do you think she trashed my room?"

"I don't know. Jealousy? Why does anyone do anything? I'm wondering if she's having some sort of mental break, but that's speculation. Otherwise, I really don't know. It's a side to her I haven't seen before."

"What about your gun? Was it on her?" Maya asked.

"No," Josh said, concern crossing his face. "My gun wasn't found and Amber isn't talking. I'm wondering if she stashed it somewhere. Maybe she was going to kidnap you and take you to where she had the gun? I don't know. I think when someone is having a mental health crisis, we can't make sense of some of their actions."

"True," Maya said. "I understand that. We'll get through this. Together. What about your family? Are they still here?"

"No, they headed back home too. Bianca said to give you a hug from her and that she'll be back when you feel better to visit."

"I like her," Maya said with a smile. "Your mother, on the other hand…"

Josh sighed. "I know. My mom can be difficult, but what can I say, she's my mom. That doesn't mean that she gets to treat you with disrespect, though, and I'll make sure she understands that. I told her about what Amber did and my mom apologized for inviting her. Down the road, maybe we can get together and my family can get to know you and how wonderful you are."

"I hope so," Maya said, squeezing Josh's hand. "Because I think what we have going is pretty serious and you're stuck with me."

"That's the best thing I've heard all day. So I'm forgiven?"

"It's a relationship, Josh. We're both going to have our moments, but we'll figure it out."

Josh leaned over and kissed her, making her heart beat a little faster.

"I'm glad to hear that," he said. "On another topic, how are you doing with learning about Eric Torres being your father?"

Maya shrugged. "I guess I know the truth and, with that, I sort of have a family. Eric told me he had two daughters and a son. I'm assuming I'm one of the daughters. He was cryptic that way."

"Do you think you'll try to contact your siblings?"

"I don't know. I mean, I'm the kid that happened because their father had an affair. That's not really the kind of thing most people want to know or the sibling they want to meet."

"I agree, but it's hard telling. Why do you think Abigail let you know that Eric is your father?"

"I don't know that either," Maya said. "But she likes her games. She's smart and manipulative. I don't trust her. She wouldn't have told me this information if there wasn't an endgame in mind."

"We'll figure this out together," Josh said. "Everything. Eric. Abigail. Amber. Everything. As long as we're together, we're good."

"I agree," Maya said as Josh leaned over and kissed her. "Now break me out of here. I'm ready to go home."

Two Days Later

Maya rested in a recliner, flipping through a magazine. Juniper was lying on her bed, but kept sitting up and resting her chin on Maya's lap. She had been clingy since their return home, so Maya had allowed her to stay nearby.

They were off work for a couple more days and then, pending one more doctor's visit, they would be allowed back on patrol. Maya was glad. She was about ready to go stir-crazy and had informed Josh if he told her to keep resting, he'd regret it. She knew he was right, but still, there was only so much sitting around she could take. Juniper at least had been able to get some energy out by going out in the yard and playing in the fresh snow with Finn.

Josh and Finn were sitting on the couch by the fire, napping. Maya had told Josh not to let him get too used to being a house dog if he wanted him to work. Josh had just told her they were bonding. Although in true Lab fashion, Finn had already chewed up a couch cushion and eaten some of the stuffing. Maya was a little concerned about the "bonding" and what else in the house might be eaten during that process.

She set her magazine down and sighed. In so many ways, being here with Josh was what she wanted, but some of her stir-craziness also came from missing the location and quiet of her cabin. She couldn't wait for the rebuilding to start the coming summer.

"What are you sighing about?" Josh asked. His eyes were still shut.

"I thought you were asleep."

"I'm not, just resting. What are you thinking about?"

"Everything. Tanner. Amber. My cabin."

"That's quite the list. What about Tanner? You know he's locked up and he won't be granted bail since his case is federal."

"I know. Right now he's locked up, but what if his defense attorney manages to win in trial? Sheriff Jackson screwed up so many things. It's a defense attorney's dream come true and Tanner's family has money. He's hired the best of the best. What if he gets out and comes after me? Or you? Or anyone we care about, like Pops or Bianca?"

Josh sat up and opened his eyes. "We'll figure it out if he does get released. Until then, try to trust the system and the fact that Agent Kessler has a strong case and is working hard to make sure everything is done right and there's a conviction."

"I'm trying to trust the system, but what about your case? And Pops's? He's going to trial in a couple months."

"I know. I'm sure Pops will be fine. As for my case in Chicago, I don't think there is one. I think Amber was bluffing. I called the prosecutor's office and no one had heard about any case like that coming to the appeals court. I think Amber was having a mental breakdown and at least she's getting the help she needs. Hopefully with therapy she'll stay in Chicago and out of our lives."

"Hopefully," Maya said with some uncertainty. Amber had been evaluated and put on a mental health hold, but that didn't mean that she would leave them alone. Eventually she would be let out of the hospital, and Maya thought there was a good chance she might come after her and Josh again. They had filed a restraining order, but a piece of paper meant nothing if someone was intent on doing harm. "What about here, though? I know Pops reinstated you, but will you be further investigated for being under the influence while on duty?"

"Pops is finishing all that up. It's going to be fine. The bartender at the Black Bear was my best witness and told Pops that I didn't drink the shots, only paid for them, just like I told him. The bloodwork showed roofies and cocaine in my system. I've committed to taking as many UAs as needed to prove that I'm not using again. I've had several clean tests now. We just have some final paperwork to finish and then I'll be cleared to go back to work." Josh gazed at Maya. "Are you doing okay? I mean, after being kidnapped and everything that happened?"

Maya stood and went over to the couch with Josh and Finn. She gave Finn the signal to get off and he sighed, but then slithered off and curled up on his dog bed near Juniper. She was glad the two dogs had become friends and were getting along. Maya snuggled up next to Josh. "I'm struggling again. Nightmares. Unable to sleep. Anxiety. It's like that whole experience triggered my PTSD."

"What does Dr. Meyers think?" Josh asked.

"He thinks that I can work through this. It won't be the last time my job triggers some sort of PTSD so I need to learn to continue to manage it."

Josh kissed her and then pulled away saying, "I wish I could do something to just magically help your PTSD, but I know it takes time. Just let me know what you need."

Maya nodded.

"You mentioned your cabin. What about that?" Josh asked.

"I love your house…"

"But?"

"I miss living out in the forest. The quiet. The wildlife. The solitude. I want to rebuild and move back out there."

"Okay," Josh said. Maya could tell by his expression that he was uncertain if she was trying to use that as an excuse to move out.

"Where I'm going with this is, do you think you could ever live out there with me?"

Josh smiled. "I would love that. I love all the things you mentioned too."

"But what about your house? You've redone the whole thing. It's beautiful. It's you," Maya said.

"I think we could rent it out as an Airbnb. Make some extra money maybe. We can figure it out. We can make the cabin we build out in the woods *our* cabin."

"Really?" Maya said. "You'd be okay with that?"

"Yes. And maybe we build a better run and spot for

the dogs in an area where uniforms and couches can't get chewed up and they have more room to run."

"I like that idea."

"Then it's a plan."

A knock at the door made Juniper and Finn leap up barking. Maya stood, but Josh cut her off. "I got it," he said. "Just rest."

She rolled her eyes, but flopped back down. As much as she was fidgety, she also knew that she wasn't a hundred percent.

Josh came back into the living room with a bouquet of flowers. "These are for you," he said, setting them down on the coffee table. He picked up the card and handed it to her.

"I wonder who sent these," Maya said. "Was it you?"

"No, wasn't me. But I can get you some more if you want."

Maya waved him off. "You know how flowers are for me. I love them, but they die after a few days and it feels like a waste. Plus, Juniper will probably find a way to chew them up and make a mess and then Finn will eat that mess."

Josh laughed. "That's true."

"But if it's not you, I wonder who. They're my favorite—lilies. Not many people know that," she said as she opened the card.

"I didn't even know that," he said. "But now I do."

"Don't you forget it," Maya said with a smile. Her stomach flip-flopped as she read the quick note.

To my lovely daughter. Get better soon. —E

"What is it?" Josh asked.

Maya handed him the card and he read it, raising one eyebrow.

"Do you really think it's from him? Eric?" Josh asked.

"That or Abigail is messing with me. All I know is I need to get better fast so I can figure this out."

"We'll figure it out. Together. I promise."

"I'm holding you to that promise," Maya said. "Speaking of promises, I told Lucas I'd let him know if Eric contacted me. I guess I better call him."

"Yeah, you probably should let him know."

"Sometimes I wish I had a normal family, but maybe there's no such thing," Maya said. Juniper and Finn came over to them. Juniper slapped a paw on Maya's lap and Finn leaned up against Josh. "We have each other and that's all that matters."

"I'm here for you," Josh said. "I love you. I can't imagine spending my life with anyone else."

Maya reached up and pulled Josh down to her, giving him a long kiss. "I can't imagine being with anyone else either."

* * * * *

Acknowledgments

I am so grateful to those who have helped me along the way with my writing journey. When Maya, Juniper, Josh and Pops first came to me, I could never imagine the adventures I would go on with them. To all my readers who have reached out from all over the world, those I've met at book clubs and other events, I can't thank you enough. All of your emails, Facebook posts, reviews and other correspondence sharing your love of these characters, especially Juniper, keeps me inspired. Thank you all so much.

There continue to be so many friends and acquaintances that have provided help and knowledge along the way. I am constantly in awe of your willingness to share stories and real-life experiences to help shape my characters and their adventures. As always, any mistakes or fictional liberties are all on me.

One of those amazing people is U.S. Forest Service Officer Christopher Magallon. I appreciate the time and expertise you've continued to share. Without you, Maya's character would not be as authentic. Thank you! And hopefully your wonderful K-9 partner Ice will continue to live on through Juniper. Thank you both for your service and rest in peace, Ice.

To Cathy Bryarly, thank you so much for sharing the world of human remains detection dogs with me. Your work amazes me and here's to you and your K-9 partner, Sam. Thank you for all you do to find the missing and for your years of service with your other K-9s with Boulder County Sheriff's Office. If you want to help me thank Cathy, check out the website for Friends of Boulder County Sheriff K-9 Association at https://bcsk9.org/.

I'd also love to thank the Larimer County Sheriff's Office and Barbara Bennett for an amazing citizen's police academy. The academy helped me develop all my characters and K-9s—especially K-9 Tyr. Thank you all for sharing your experiences as deputies so that I could better portray the humans behind the badge. I love supporting all the K-9s with Larimer County so make sure to also check out and consider donating to the Larimer Retired K-9 Foundation at https://larimer-retiredk9foundation.com.

A big thank-you to other friends who have served in law enforcement and the military. Your knowledge and expertise continue to help me get the facts right. Many thanks to retired chief of police Dave Lewandowski and his wonderful wife, Jamie Lewandowski. I'm so lucky to call you both friends. And next time, breakfast is on me!

Thank you also to Sergeant Patrick O'Donnell for all your Zoom calls, great podcast episodes, and being willing to talk about any and all law enforcement topics. All writers should check out and join Patrick's great Facebook group, Cops and Writers. Make sure you listen to his podcast and buy him a cup of coffee too.

A big thank-you to MSgt Dr. James A. Burghard, USA/USCG/USAF, Retired, for all your help with everything military. I also have to thank your beautiful wife, Marie, who I get to call my best friend. Thank you, Marie, for always being there for me!

I am lucky to be part of a great group of writers. A big thank-you to Margaret Mizushima, Anne Hunsinger and Kristin Horton for doing such a great beta read on *Killer Secrets*. Your help was invaluable. I'd also like to thank my critique group, Broad Horizons. I treasure your support, encouragement and feedback. Thank you all!

To my wonderful agent, Ella Marie Shupe, and the Belcastro Agency, thank you so much for continuing to believe in this series and in me. I couldn't ask for a better agent as I navigate the world of publishing. I'd also like to thank my editors with Carina Press—Kerri Buckley and Mackenzie Walton. Thank you both for all you've done!

Without the support of my wonderful husband, Jeff, this journey would have been much more difficult. Thank you for always being by my side through the ups and downs. I love you! And to my family, thank you all for your support.

My last thank-you goes to my business partner, Beth Kelly, who helped guide me into the world of K-9s. I couldn't ask for a better friend or business partner. Sherlock Hounds has been a big part of my life, but it wouldn't have been as meaningful without your friendship and love. Here's to all the years we've had together and the many dogs who have come and gone. They are the true heroes. I've been lucky to have so many four-legged partners. Thank you all for the adventures.

About the Author

Award-winning author Kathleen Donnelly has been a handler for Sherlock Hounds Detection Canines—a Colorado-based narcotics K-9 company—since 2005. Enjoying the work and partnership with the dogs, in 2010, Kathleen became part owner of the company. She loves crafting realism into her fictional stories from her dog-handling experience. Along with working dogs, Kathleen trained horses and enjoys spending time with her own mare. Her love of the mountains came from growing up in Colorado. Her debut novel, *Chasing Justice*, won a Best Book Award from the American Book Fest and was a 2023 Silver Falchion finalist in the Suspense category and Readers' Choice Award. She lives near the Colorado foothills with her husband and four-legged coworkers. Visit Kathleen and sign up for her newsletter at www.kathleendonnelly.com, on Facebook at Facebook.com/authorkathleendonnelly, follow her on Twitter @katk9writer or find her on Instagram @authorkathleendonnelly.